Praise for
THE SOLAR SEA

"This story follows the private space industry exploration of the Moon and becomes a kind of *Voyage of the Beagle* as the solar sail ship *Aristarchus* visits Mars, Jupiter, then Saturn and its giant moon Titan … Highly enjoyable read. Highly recommended." T. Jackson King, author of *Battlestar* and *Star Glory*.

"*The Solar Sea* is a high-tech science fiction adventure that spins a new twist on space exploration and alien encounters. Summers's descriptions of technology and scientific theories, along with his alien species, work together to raise the stakes and makes for an entertaining read for teens and adults alike." Erin Durante, author of the Damewood Trilogy.

"In *The Solar Sea*, David Lee Summers creates a page-turning yarn with some of the most dramatic characters I've read in years. You won't want to put it down, and when you're done, you'll only want more." J Alan Erwine, author of *The Opium of the People*.

Other Books by David Lee Summers

The Astronomer's Crypt

The Space Pirates' Legacy Series
Firebrandt's Legacy
The Pirates of Sufiro
Children of the Old Stars
Heirs of the New Earth

The Clockwork Legion Series
Owl Dance
Lightning Wolves
The Brazen Shark
Owl Riders

The Scarlet Order Vampires Series
Dragon's Fall: Rise of the Scarlet Order
Vampires of the Scarlet Order

THE
SOLAR SEA

David Lee Summers

Hadrosaur Productions, Mesilla Park, NM

The Solar Sea
Hadrosaur Productions
Second Edition: March 2018
First date of publication: January 2009

ISBN 1-885093-84-5

Hadrosaur Productions
P.O. Box 2194
Mesilla Park, NM 88047-2194
www.hadrosaur.com

To Myranda and Verity;
may you go where your hearts will take you.

Solar Sail Aristarchus
Sail Array

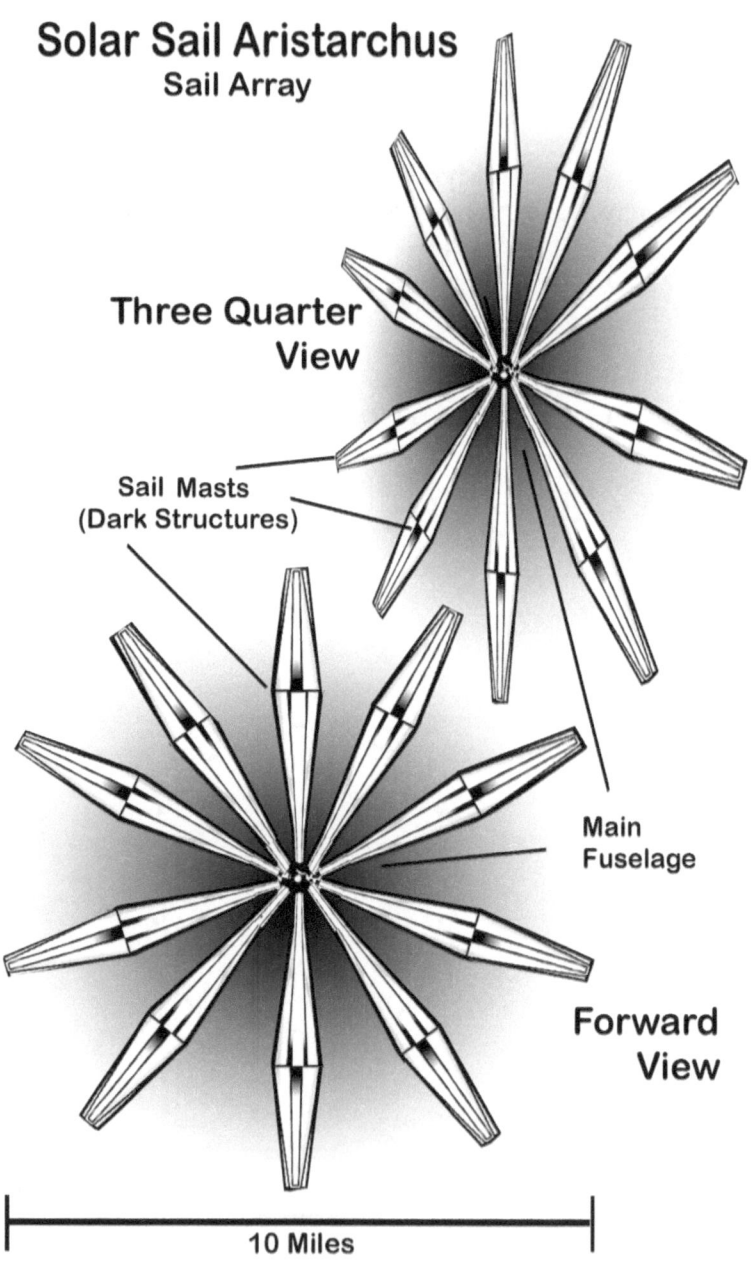

Three Quarter View

Sail Masts
(Dark Structures)

Main
Fuselage

Forward View

10 Miles

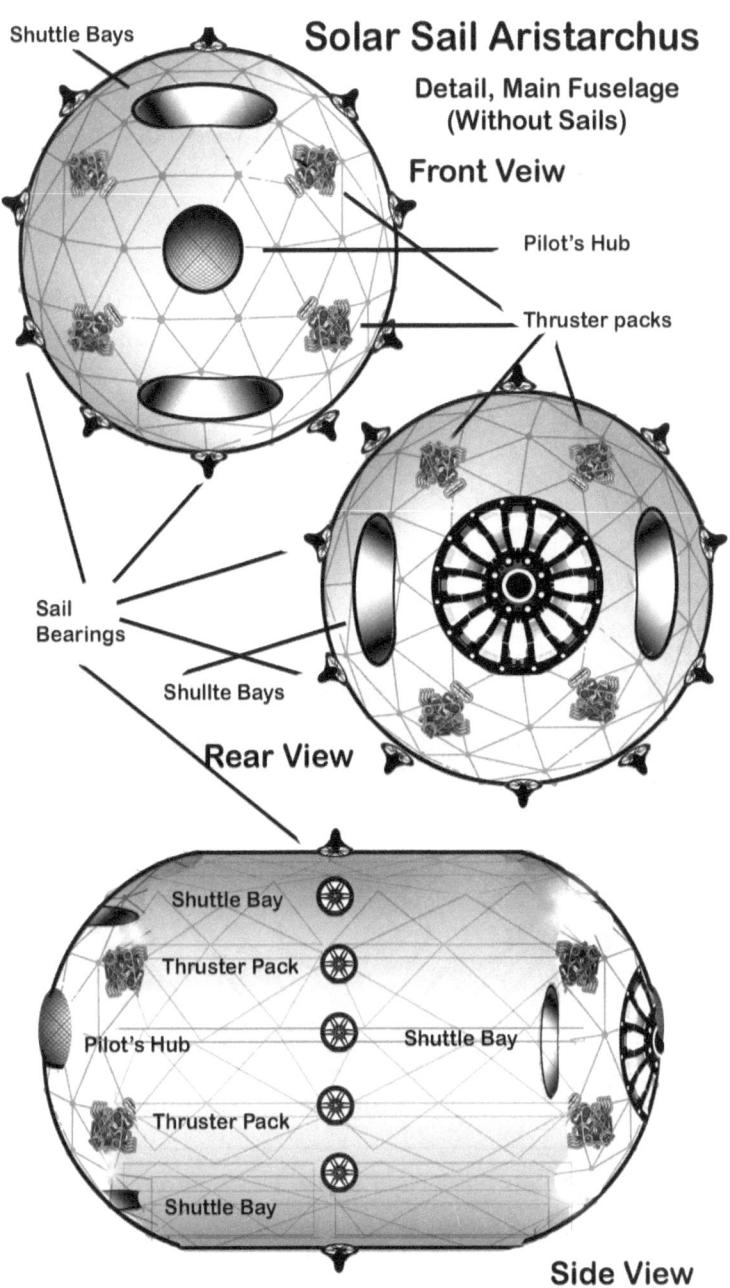

Solar Sail Aristarchus

Detail, Main Fuselage (Without Sails)

Shuttle Bays

Front Veiw

Pilot's Hub

Thruster packs

Sail Bearings

Shullte Bays

Rear View

Shuttle Bay
Thruster Pack
Pilot's Hub — Shuttle Bay
Thruster Pack
Shuttle Bay

Side View

Solar Sail Aristarchus

Detail, Command and Control

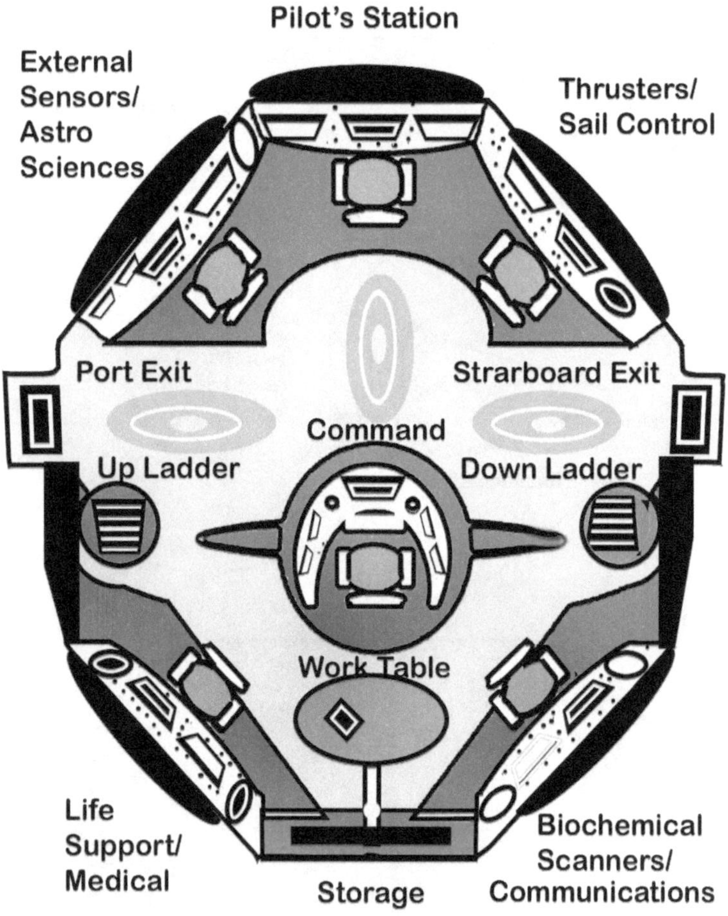

Pilot's Station

External
Sensors/
Astro
Sciences

Thrusters/
Sail Control

Port Exit

Strarboard Exit

Command

Up Ladder

Down Ladder

Work Table

Life
Support/
Medical

Storage

Biochemical
Scanners/
Communications

Safety note: Floor is slightly concave.
3 degree incline from center to walls.
Chairs may be unclamped to roll,
when necessary.

THE
SOLAR SEA

Prologue
Thomas Quinn

Jerome Quinn read the latest report from his son with growing curiosity. He sent a message requesting a videoconference.

The trillionaire technology magnate remembered a day fifteen years before when his son—then a slim, wisp of a boy—approached him in his home office. "It's been over a hundred years since the Apollo missions. Humans still haven't gone farther than Mars. Why not?"

"It's a matter of practicality, son," Jerome Quinn had answered.

"What's practicality mean?" Back then, Thomas preferred lying atop grassy mounds on his father's estate late at night looking up at the stars to playing sports. His father, who lifted weights and boxed to keep fit, was concerned that his son didn't run and play with the other boys at the private school he attended. In that way, he was very different from his younger brother Henry who took a strong interest in the family business and was constantly surrounded by friends.

"Space flight costs a lot of money." Jerome stood. The light streaming in from the tall window behind his great mahogany desk caused the big man to cast a shadow over the little boy. "In this case, practicality means that people want to make more money than they spend. The two Mars missions cost taxpayers too much money. All people ever saw were some red rocks and fossils of long-dead creatures—and they weren't even interesting creatures like dinosaurs." Jerome had laughed at his own comment, but the boy remained serious.

"What if spaceships could be built cheap? Cheaper than the Mars rockets?" he asked.

"That would be a start."

"What if I could find a way for a spaceship to earn money?"

pressed the boy.

Jerome had nodded approval. "Then you might just get me to invest in your dream, son."

Young Thomas Quinn pursed his lips. "I'm gonna do it, dad."

Jerome had dismissed his son. The boy turned, sulking to the door. Before leaving the room, he'd looked over his shoulder as though he were going to say something, but thrust his hands in his pockets and continued on.

Jerome Quinn's thoughts returned to the present as Thomas's face appeared on the monitor. As a young adult, Thomas's features had grown angular. Stubble dotted his cheeks and a mop of hair topped his head. "You read the report?" he asked.

Jerome Quinn turned his attention back to the book-sized tome. "I'm still reading it," he admitted. "Have the people on the Moon really discovered particles that can move through time?"

"Not exactly…." Thomas hesitated. "They've found particles that seem to jump into the fourth dimension. The dimension of time."

The elder Quinn waved his scientist son's words aside as though the details were unimportant. He flipped through the dog-eared copy of the report until he came to the page he wanted. "You say that if you had enough of these particles in one place, you could use them to send bigger objects into the fourth dimension, that it might cause them to move forward or backward through time?"

"Theoretically." Thomas nodded. "Although, I'm not sure how controlled such a journey would be. The objects might just disappear from our reality completely."

Again, Jerome flapped his hand in the air, as though the words had a disagreeable smell. "Do you suppose there are more of those particles at our quinitite manufacturing facility?" He pointed skyward.

"Are you asking whether we should mine the Moon for these particles?" Thomas's eyebrows came together.

Jerome nodded.

Thomas shook his head. "There were only a few of these particles … not enough to indicate that there's any great quantity on the Moon itself. It's like they're being generated from somewhere else in the solar system and we're only seeing the ones that pass by the Moon."

"Where in the solar system?" Jerome leaned in toward his computer monitor.

Again, Thomas shook his head. "I don't know."

"What would you need to find out?"

Thomas typed something on his keyboard. A graph appeared on Quinn's monitor. "The particles produce a very unique spectral signature in the radio band. I'd need to do a survey using a radio telescope like the Very Large Array in New Mexico."

"Is that facility still operating?"

Thomas nodded. "It's old, but it's a work horse. Most of the time's allocated to small colleges these days."

"The VLA has already performed surveys of the solar system, hasn't it?" asked Jerome. "Can't you use archival data? It would save us time and money."

Thomas sighed. "I've looked. There have been some broadband surveys near the spectral region, but nothing that exactly overlaps this—nothing that helps."

"Very well, then. I'll get you some observing time." Jerome reached out to terminate the connection, then paused. "The Quinn name could attract our competitors' attention. You should use an alias as you continue this research."

Thomas considered that, then nodded. "I can do that."

Satisfied, Jerome gave a nod.

"Dad," interjected Thomas before Jerome could terminate the call. "May I ask what you plan to do if we find more of the particles?"

Jerome regarded his son for a moment, then took the report and flipped to the final section. "You're the one who gave me the ideas. Experimenting with time travel is one possibility. It would certainly bring us some good press."

Thomas's face went pale as he looked away. He licked his lips. "A weapon is another ... you could send an enemy into the fourth dimension. They might disappear forever."

Jerome stood and walked to the window, letting his son see only his back. "No matter what the application, if you find those particles, you'll have helped Quinn Corp more than you can imagine. It'll stand you and your brother in good stead. Weapons make a lot of money for the manufacturer."

"I think Quinn Corp would get better press from a time machine and it could bring us still more money," argued Thomas, sounding uncertain. "The particles could even open the door to interstellar travel if they unlock access to other dimensions."

Jerome turned and smiled. "I like the way you think. I always have. No matter what the application, those particles will easily increase Quinn Corp's worth ten-fold. If you find them, how do you propose to get them?"

Thomas stammered as though caught off guard. "We'd need a spaceship...," he said after a moment.

Jerome sat and eyed his son carefully. "Is this like that solar sail you once told me about?"

He remembered a day when his teenaged son brought a set of crudely drawn blueprints to his office and dropped them right on top of a stack of papers in the center of the great mahogany desk.

Jerome had looked up from the computer. "What's this?" Several investors had recently pulled out of Quinn Corp when earnings did not come in as high as expected. In spite of Jerome's hard work to recover his losses he saw the boy was anxious to show off the blueprints.

"Plans for a heliogyro." Thomas had proudly pointed to the top sheet of the plans. The drawing looked a little like a flower constructed of steel beams and aluminum foil.

"What's a heliogyro?" Jerome Quinn inclined his head as he studied the plans, relieved to think about something other than investors.

Fifteen-year-old Thomas Quinn had grown tall, but remained rail-thin. "A heliogyro is a spaceship. You might call it a sailing ship to the planets. The crew quarters are in this ball in the center." He pointed to the picture. Then he pointed to the 'petals' of the flower. "These are giant reflectors made of spun aluminum mounted to a quinitite frame." He referred to the lightweight plastic with a crystalline structure that had revolutionized the computer industry and made Jerome a fortune. "Sunlight could push this ship all the way out to Pluto.

When the crew was ready to return, it would just need to sling-shot around the last planet in its voyage, adjust the sails, and it would be homeward bound. Sunlight also makes the ship spin like a giant pinwheel, so the crew would have simulated gravity."

"Sunlight?" Jerome had rubbed the bridge of his nose. "If it's a sailing ship, wouldn't it be pushed by the solar wind?"

Thomas had rolled his eyes. The mannerism irritated his father then—it still did, for that matter. "The solar wind's just charged particles, it doesn't produce enough energy to move the ship."

Jerome folded his arms across his chest, not appreciating Thomas's tone. Thomas stood his ground, well aware that an employee would have been dismissed by now. "If it's propelled by sunlight, I'm guessing this thing wouldn't go very fast."

"Theoretically, it could get to Mars in about six months … to Jupiter, about a year after that … beyond that, it depends on planetary alignments, but with gravitational assist from Jupiter, the ship could make it to Saturn in as little as six more months…."

Jerome remembered snorting and shaking his head. "I applaud your imagination, son, but it all sounds like science fiction."

"No, it's not. The Planetary Society launched LightSail 3 in 2024, but it had problems because of heat absorption. Carnegie Mellon University built a nanosatellite using an improved design back in 2028, but it was expensive because they used Mylar for the sails. Your quinitite allows us to use fine aluminum fiber which we can produce cheaply in our lunar factory—the quinitite in the frame would help the craft dissipate heat," said Thomas, hopefully.

"How much would it cost?" For a moment, Jerome had been caught up in Thomas's dream.

"I think we could build this ship for about ten billion dollars." Jerome remembered how proud Thomas looked that he'd completed a financial analysis despite his distaste in financial matters.

Jerome Quinn whistled long and low, then shook his head again. "That's hardly cheap, son."

"But it's only a fraction of your fortune, dad," pleaded Thomas.

"What would I get in return?" Jerome Quinn narrowed his gaze at his son. He needed to get him to see the practical side of the equation. "Ten billion dollars is too much just to throw away. You've got to tell me how I'll benefit from this."

In the present day, Jerome looked down at the report about the particles. Particles that could travel through time. Particles that could be used to build new radiation-free weapons. Particles that could unlock interstellar travel.

"The solar sail?" asked Thomas. "Yes, I've improved the design over the years. Just give the word."

Jerome held up his hand. "Start by finding those particles. If they exist, give me a budget for the ship."

Thomas nodded, dumbstruck.

Jerome Quinn reached over and terminated the connection, then smiled, pleased at the prospect of new growth for his company and pleased that his son's dream might become real.

Chapter 1
The Very Large Array

John O'Connell watched an old science fiction show about a starship that traveled to and explored alien worlds. He loved shows like that, but they were harder to find as the years wore on. People just weren't as interested in exploring space as they used to be. As the show finished, he sat back, adjusted his thick glasses and closed the window on the streaming site. It was time to check the status of the Very Large Array telescope antennas.

The VLA—as the telescope was known—was on the plains of San Augustin, about fifty miles away from the control room where John sat. Old antennas painted varying shades of white marred by black graffiti stretched out across the landscape like giant flowers blossoming from the desert. Even though funding for new paint had been cut years ago, the sight was still awe-inspiring. Though John preferred to work at the array site, he was in the Array Operation's Center in Socorro, New Mexico within easy walking distance of his faded adobe house.

The VLA collected data from the planet Saturn. The antennas functioned as expected. John collected the data for an observer he neither knew, nor really cared about. The name Alonzo Thomas meant nothing to him. John was more concerned about his job. In spite of the fact that the VLA was a proven workhorse telescope, Congress threatened to close the doors. The money, they said, could be used better elsewhere. John wasn't sure what he would do with his life if the VLA were shut down.

He looked at his watch and yawned. The observations he took wouldn't be finished for another two hours. Time, he decided, to surf the Internet and see what was happening in the world. He lifted a tattered blue Cassini 2 baseball cap from his head, brushed back an errant strand of sandy blond hair, and replaced the cap while adjusting his position in front of the computer terminal. He went to one of his favorite news sites and read about the state of Middle Eastern relations.

"The U.S.S. *Daniel B. Sherman* under the command of Captain Natalie Freeman has been ordered to the Persian Gulf," began the article that appeared on the screen. "Given Freeman's success handling the Jordanian crisis, hopes are high that she will negotiate a trade settlement and bring more oil to the United States."

The voice of the President of the United States, Oscar Van der Wald, sounded from the computer's speakers: "Iraq has been a valuable ally ever since their liberation earlier this century. We wish to stay on good terms with the new administration while negotiating better oil prices. I can think of no one more qualified for the job than Captain Freeman."

John folded his arms, growing tired of the web. Rarely, if ever, was there any actual news. Rather, all he saw were opinions of people who knew as little as he did. He stood, stretched, then walked over to the coffee maker and retrieved an old white mug. Sipping overdone coffee, he stared out the windows at the small town of Socorro. While the day itself was lovely with fluffy gray-white clouds hanging in a brilliant blue sky, he couldn't help but wonder if he would ever get out of the little town. Beyond the grassy field, just outside the window, stood his small adobe house. He sighed, wondering how he could keep paying rent on an operator's salary. Again, he looked at his watch. With some relief, he realized forty minutes had passed.

He returned to his terminal and brought up a visual display of the radio signal from Saturn. He looked at the image, blinked twice, then tried adjusting the monitor settings.

"Hey, Alan!" he called to the site's programmer working at a nearby console. "Can you take a look at this thing? I'm getting some kind of double image."

Alan Jones looked over and tugged on his long, dark beard. The computer showed a bright red, radio-active planet surrounded by dull, blue, radio-quiet rings. Next to Saturn, in the ring plane, hung a bright yellow ball. "That's not a double image. It looks more like some other object."

John snorted. "What kind of object is it, though?" He looked at the color scale. "That thing's got the radio emission of Jupiter. It's gotta be a glitch—some kind of signal creeping in from somewhere, or old data."

Alan sat back and smirked. "You can't superimpose old data on a real-time display like that."

"Then how do *you* explain it?" demanded John.

"Supernova," said Alan. "Or some previously undiscovered galaxy. Maybe they'll name it after you."

"Get real. And get over here and look at this thing, will ya? I don't want to call the boss in here for some kind of glitch."

"Whatever." Alan took his time finishing the task that John had interrupted, then sulked over and plunked down in the operator's chair. Lithe, pale fingers tapped on the keyboard for some minutes. At last, he looked up at John. "Whatever you're seeing is real. There are no programs running, other than the autocorrelator that's giving you the display. That thing's really in the sky."

John removed his baseball cap and scratched his head. "I better get Jack in here to take a look at this." He referred to his boss, the Supervisor of Observing Support. "We're recording all this data, aren't we?"

"Does President Van der Wald get hair transplants?"

John grimaced, then picked up the phone. A few minutes later, Jack Spear stepped into the control room. "Whatcha' got?"

John pointed at the bright object on the screen. Spear scratched his chin, then walked over to a bookshelf and picked up a copy of *The Astronomical Almanac*. He rifled the pages a few times until he found what he was looking for. "If I didn't know any better, I'd say that hot spot was Titan."

"You mean Saturn's big moon?" John's brow furrowed "So, do you think it's a glitch or a discovery?"

Jack sat down at the console and called up the instrument settings. "Hard to say. This is a really unusual frequency for planetary observation. There's really no archival data to compare it to. Who are you taking these observations for?"

John rifled through notes on a clipboard. "Some guy named Alonzo Thomas. He's with a private company that bought time on the telescope."

"Better grab a few extra minutes on Saturn—my authority," said Spear. "I think I've heard of Alonzo Thomas. He's a real hotshot scientist at Quinn Corp. He'll be ecstatic if this is a discovery, but there'll be hell to pay if it's a glitch and we missed something because we stopped observing." Spear stood up, looked at the screen one last time, then returned to his office. John sat down in the vacated chair, removed his thick glasses, and rubbed the bridge of his nose, thinking he had been working too hard.

*

The next day, Jerome Quinn met with several department managers when an image of Saturn appeared in his computer's message window. Next to Saturn, a bright, ball glowed alongside the word 'Eureka!' Quinn discreetly cleared the image, then brought the meeting to a close. The managers shuffled papers into their briefcases and left the office.

As soon as the door latched, Jerome brought up the message window and called his son. Thomas Quinn beamed happily.

"You found something?" Jerome's eyes narrowed as he studied his son's face.

Thomas vanished from the screen, replaced by Saturn. "The brightly glowing ball next to Saturn is its moon Titan. The moon is literally blanketed in chronotons."

"Chronotons?" Jerome shook his head.

"My name for the time particles," explained Thomas.

Jerome nodded thoughtfully and turned his chair, so he faced the window as his son reappeared on the computer screen. "Have you looked into the idea of constructing a solar sailboat?"

"I've drawn up a complete set of plans and run them by the engineering department for review," reported Thomas. "We can start construction at the factory on the moon as soon as you give the word."

"The word is given." Jerome stood and stepped up to the window. "I should make an announcement to the press—let them know about the ship we're building."

"I thought you wanted to keep this project a secret."

"I want to keep the time particles—the chronotons—a secret," corrected Jerome. "People are going to notice a giant solar sailing ship when it's launched into lunar orbit. Our competitors on the Moon will, at least. We need to let them know what we're doing."

"Aren't you afraid that our competitors will try to race us to Titan?"

Jerome gave a curt nod. "Come up with a cover story, something plausible but not too interesting to our competitors."

Thomas's eyes went wide as though he'd just been presented with a math problem beyond his abilities. "Won't our competitors be suspicious?"

"Of course they will." Jerome returned to the chair. "The idea is simply to get them looking in the wrong direction. You have the plans for the ship and you know what we're looking for. They'll waste time confirming our discovery, then waste more time trying to figure out what we really discovered. By then, you should be well on your way."

Thomas nodded. His glee had dissolved and he now wore a deep frown as though faced with more responsibilities than he'd ever imagined. "I'll need a crew for the ship. It's going to take time to locate the best people and train them."

"You're in charge of that, too." Jerome sat back, folded his arms, and studied his son's face. "I trust you to see this mission through. You've built an alias to conduct the observations. I want you to continue using that alias as you head this project. Can you do that?"

Thomas swallowed hard. "I'll do my best, sir."

*

John O'Connell walked from his house to work, arriving early for his two o'clock shift. He took over from a bleary-eyed woman named Neriah Smith. According to the staff schedule, she'd been on duty since four in the morning. "You look beat," said John.

"So would you after ten hours on duty."

"You should go home and get some sleep."

She sighed, then stood and yawned. She was a little too short and a little too heavy to be what most people called beautiful, but John still found her to be an attractive woman. As she collected her belongings, he sat down at the terminal and logged in, then pulled up the observing roster and noted routine stellar observations were scheduled—calibration data for a new telescope being built somewhere else. He started the prescribed observing routine, then surfed the Internet for the day's news.

Neriah mumbled a goodbye and left. After the door closed, Alan Jones looked up from his computer console. "You know, you should ask her out on a date sometime."

"You should mind your own business," retorted John, not looking up from his console. "Besides, I did ask her out once."

"Turned you down, did she?" asked Alan with a lilt in his voice.

John just shook his head. There wasn't anything of interest on the news site and he nearly moved on when a link flashed. It said something about a new space mission being announced. He selected the link and a live video in progress streamed onto the screen. A man and a teenage boy stood behind a podium at a large house. John guessed it must be in California given the orange trees and the time stamp that said a few minutes after one o'clock—an hour before New Mexico's time. The caption identified the two as Jerome Quinn, owner of Quinn Corp, and his son Henry.

"It is our hope that the *Aristarchus* project will usher in a new era of space exploration," explained the elder Quinn while his son looked on. "Quinn Corp was one of the first companies to build manufacturing facilities on the Moon. Important as our lunar facilities are, we recognize that the Moon's resources are not unlimited. The time has come, therefore, for us to push outward, to see what other resources are available. To do that, we have devised plans for a space vessel that will use sunlight to sail to Jupiter and then on to Saturn—the first manned mission to the outer planets."

John blinked, remembering Quinn Corp's connection to the unusual observation of Titan, two days before. He looked up. Alan Jones stood, peering over his shoulder at the news broadcast.

"Do you think this has anything to do with our Saturn

observations?" asked John.

Alan shrugged. "It would make sense. Spear said we'd never observed Saturn at that particular frequency before."

O'Connell nodded. "They were looking for something."

"And they found it," said Jones.

"O'Connell," called Jack Spear, poking his head through the doors of the control room before Alan could speculate further. "I have a phone call for you in my office."

"Can't you just transfer it here?" John pointed to the phone next to his computer console.

Spear shook his head. "They say it's confidential." The observing supervisor ducked his head back through the doors.

"So, how do you rate confidential phone calls?" asked Alan.

"It's gotta be Neriah," teased John. "She's probably calling to say she's sorry we didn't keep going out and she wants to go to dinner tonight."

"Yeah, right." Alan smirked as he sat down in the operator's chair, taking over while John was away from his post.

Stepping down the corridor to Spear's office, John wondered who really was on the phone. He dreaded a call about his elderly mother in Nebraska who was in poor health. When he arrived at Spear's small office, the supervisor handed him the phone, then ducked out of the room.

"Hello," said John, nervously.

"Hello," came a voice at the other end of the line. "I'm with Quinn Corp's *Aristarchus* project. Have you heard about us?" The voice on the other end of the line had a slight quaver, as though the speaker wasn't used to spending time on the phone.

"Just now. The announcement's just been on the news."

"Good," said the speaker. "I'm the project engineer. I'd like to schedule a meeting with you. I'm looking for some equipment operators and I believe your VLA experience would suit you well for the position I want to fill."

"I like my job here," said John.

"You know as well as I do that the VLA's days are numbered," said the quavering voice.

"Who are you?"

"My name's Alonzo Thomas. I'm Pilot Manager of the *Aristarchus* as well as the project engineer."

*

Thomas Quinn flew home for the weekend. He walked around the grounds of the family home allowing memories to wash over him. Birds chirped in the distance. The hundred acres of grass surrounding the house were trimmed to perfection. Many of the fruit trees were in bloom, causing Thomas's nose to run. Nevertheless, spring signaled a new hope.

His brother Henry never seemed to appreciate nature. He remembered a time when they were both young children. Henry sat in front of a wall-sized video screen, playing a computer game. Henry's warrior lunged and stabbed a monster through the heart, then swung around and sliced another monster in the leg, disabling it.

"Not bad." Thomas had grudgingly admired his little brother's skill.

"Yeah." Henry shrugged. He dropped the keyboard to the floor. "But it's kind of boring. The characters behave the same way each time."

"You know," Thomas's eyebrows came together, "I think we could reprogram the game, so the characters are a little more lifelike."

"Can you really?" Henry's eyes had grown wide.

"Sure." Thomas shrugged. "Quinn Corp owns the company that makes the game. Shouldn't be too hard to find the source code and change the character stats." Thomas had taken the keyboard from his younger brother and searched for the appropriate files. He didn't know then that he would use skills from his youth when building a new persona.

He encountered his father on the path. "We're making good progress. We're almost ready to start manufacturing the quinitite frame for the solar sail. I'll be leaving for the Moon on Monday."

His father quirked a smile. "Seems fitting."

"I've also been designing some bottles to harvest the chronotons—the time particles—for study."

"Chronoton is too generic a name. I think we should refer to these particles as Quinnium."

Thomas turned and looked at his father with genuine confusion. "You want to brand the time particles? I understand quinitite. That's based on a manufacturing process, but as far as we can tell chronotons are natural particles."

Jerome smiled wryly at him, then shuffled down the path a short distance and sat on a concrete bench under a blossoming orange tree. "While I think it's important that we give them a name that ties them to the company, it'll also obscure what they are, assuming any corporate spies see our internal memos or tap into our communications."

Thomas shuffled his feet and sniffed. He was less interested in corporate machinations and more interested in the chronotons—the Quinnium. Since he'd discovered them, he'd devised even more possible applications for the particles. Doing calculations on their energy output, he realized they could be a new power source, possibly better than oil. He told his father.

Jerome squeezed his son's shoulder. "I think you see the need for discretion." They continued down the path together. "Be careful," whispered Jerome.

Chapter 2
Myra Lee

The research vessel *Eleana* gently rocked in the frigid water of Frederick Sound, Alaska. The three-decker boat, once white, was now streaked with the brown of rust. Barnacles lined the hull's dull red bottom. Two poles jutted from the vessel's side and cables extended into the water. The black cables were attached to hydrophones, recording all the sounds of the deep. Standing in the bow of the ship, watching the deepening blue of the twilight sky was *Eleana's* captain, Lance Naftel. He wondered how many hours it would be before he could take his boat home, to Juneau. He looked up at the crescent Moon, high overhead. In the shadowed portion, little pinpricks of light dotted the surface—the lunar factories. When he was a boy, he remembered seeing stars much more clearly during the dark of the Moon.

The vessel was in Frederick Sound to perform a routine count of humpback whales. While there, Dr. Myra Lee recorded the enigmatic, hypnotic music of the giant beasts. Lance Naftel thought there were enough recordings of whale song in the world. However, Dr. Lee had proposed a theory that there might be long-term cycles to the songs. To test her theories, she needed a large, yearly database. The previous night, though, as she analyzed her most recent recordings, something happened that sent her into a flurry of activity.

The captain had been sitting in his tiny cabin, drinking a cup of coffee when someone pounded on his door. Before he could acknowledge the impatient sound, the door burst open. "We have to stay for a couple more days, Skipper," said Myra.

Naftel blinked a couple of times and stated he could only do so with permission from the Oceanographic Institute in Juneau. At that point, Dr. Lee darted from the cabin to make the call. Permission came within the hour. A day later, Captain

Naftel still had no idea what had sent the marine biologist into such a frenzy. As the sky went from indigo to black, the captain decided he needed to find out.

He walked inside the ship and stepped down a narrow ladder. He rapped on a dark wooden door. Just as he was about to knock again, he heard a vaguely distracted voice call, "Come in."

The captain opened the door to find a thin woman sitting at a large wooden table covered in graphs with dates marked at the top. It appeared they were arranged in chronological order. Next to the graphs, headphones were connected to an expensive digital audio system. The system held several compact disks, one of which recorded the sounds coming from the hydrophones. Another disk held an older recording. Myra Lee poured over the graphs.

"Isn't it getting a little late for the whales to be singing?" asked Naftel.

Myra looked up from the charts. "Normally, I'd say yes." She looked toward the silently oscillating pattern of red lights on the audio system's meter. "However, except for breaks to feed and sleep, they've been singing almost constantly since yesterday afternoon."

"What?" The captain tugged at the collar of his beige turtleneck sweater.

"What's more," Myra continued quietly, as though she were speaking in church, "their songs have changed."

The captain stepped up to the table and glanced at the charts of whale songs recorded over several years. "What's unusual about that?" The captain rubbed the stubble on his chin. "I thought humpback whales changed their songs all the time."

"They do." Her brown eyes glimmered in the lamplight. "But this is different. They completely changed their song yesterday, at almost exactly one o'clock in the afternoon." Carefully, she laid the charts she had been looking at on the table. "This graph shows the frequency of one whale's song from three days ago." She traced the undulating pattern of dots with her finger. "If you look, you can see about six distinct phrases in this whale's song."

The captain looked and nodded, again tugging on the neck

of his sweater.

"Each of the whales I've been recording had been singing almost exactly these six phrases since we got out here a week ago."

"Sounds normal," mused the captain.

"Perfectly." Myra reached over and retrieved another graph. "I made this chart from songs recorded yesterday." She drew some lines across the undulating dots with a black pen to help him see the phrases. "Notice that the first three phrases are exactly the same as the beginning of the songs recorded before." The biologist then stabbed her finger on the graph, pointing to the fourth phrase. "Then right at one o'clock, the song changed. It's a completely new pattern."

Captain Naftel studied the charts and saw what she meant. He also noticed another plot that showed a jumble of dots. "What's all that?"

Myra sighed and ran her fingers through long, straight brown hair. "The graph plots the number of whales singing. That's the beginning of the chorus. Every whale in Frederick Sound started singing right then."

"You say they've been singing the new song since yesterday?" The captain moved to the wall and leaned against it. "I take it the song always starts with those same three phrases."

Myra pursed her lips and shook her head. "No, the whales started singing the old song, then changed to a completely new song in the middle. As far as I can tell, they repeated the new song twice. After that, all the whales not singing before, joined in."

"So if you have the new song from the one whale, why are we still recording?" The captain tapped his foot impatiently.

"Confirmation. I want to see if this is an aberration and the whales go back to their old song, or if this is going to continue. I'd at least like to stay until they quiet down a bit."

The captain folded his arms, almost defiantly. "We don't have that much in the way of extra supplies. I'd like to start back tomorrow morning." He inclined his head toward the recorder. "Besides, what if they don't quiet down?"

Myra shuffled her feet on the floor, looking down at the worn, brown tile. "Can't we stay just a little longer?"

The captain removed the black cap he wore and scratched his balding head. "We have enough provisions to stay out here for forty-eight more hours. We'd have to go home then." He replaced the cap and folded his arms. "But it's not just the provisions, there's morale to consider. Dr. Lyons and Dr. Eckhart have all the count data they need. Eckhart's getting anxious because he has classes he needs to prepare."

"Can we at least wait until one o'clock tomorrow? At that point, the whales will have been singing their new song for forty-eight hours." Myra's voice trembled slightly.

Again, the captain tapped his foot. "Tomorrow, one o'clock," he said firmly. With that, he opened the door and stepped out.

∗

Myra turned her attention back to the charts. She picked up the headphones and listened to the haunting rhythms of the new song—the eerie strains, gruntings, and rumbles that could only come from humpback whales. Though mostly familiar, her practiced ear had never heard a song as agitated as this. There was a rare energy, like a wild longing, in this new song. All of the whales in the area seemed to be doing their best to memorize the song and copy it. There were few of the subtle changes that individual whales made to the songs.

The sounds took Myra back to her childhood. She had grown up in the Arizona desert. As a young girl, she thought rivers were mostly mud and quicksand with little trickles of water running through the middle where minnows swam and occasionally great walls of water crashed through the channels during intense rainstorms. When she was ten years old, her father took her to Nantucket Island to be the flower girl in a wedding. While there, her father took her out on a boat. She had never seen so much water in her life. However, she saw something even more amazing—she saw a whale.

Growing up, the biggest fish she had seen in the wild were silvery minnows, little more than an inch long. Several would fit in a coffee can. The whale she had seen was over forty-five feet long. It was a humpback with giant, white paddle-like fins. It rose from the depths and shot a fine spray of water, drenching her, making her laugh. She watched it swim around the boat, never once taking her gaze off the behemoth. When it finally dove back to the depths, it raised its great tail and splashed the ocean, as though waving goodbye.

That night, Myra's father had brought her a compact disk of whale song and the humpback whale sang her to sleep. The next day, she asked her father what the humpback said in the recording.

"I don't know," he said, kindly. "But it's very haunting, isn't it?"

She remembered nodding. "I'm going to find out one day."

Turning her attention to the present, she sat back and considered what the captain said about morale as the whale melodies echoed in her ears. She, too, longed to get back to port and her office. Even so, she was too captivated by the mystery of the whales' new song to be pulled away easily. In a hundred and fifty years of research, no one had ever come across a phenomenon this stunning. Instinct told her this might be the key to unlocking the whales' language.

Chapter 3
Captain and Colonel

President Oscar Van der Wald ordered the aircraft carrier *Daniel B. Sherman* to the Persian Gulf. Over half a century after Iraq's liberation, the country refused to sell more oil to the United States. President Van der Wald expected Captain Natalie Freeman to work a miracle and convince the Iraqis to sell more oil. The problem, as Natalie knew, was that the Iraqis were not being stubborn. They were simply out of oil and the president refused to believe them.

Captain Freeman stepped out on the deck of the aircraft carrier *Daniel B. Sherman*, took off her cap, and felt the warm breeze blow through her hair as she wondered what kind of miracle she could produce.

She remembered growing up in Southern Arkansas. While most of the girls in her neighborhood liked to wear dresses and pretend to be princesses, Natalie liked to dress up in coveralls, make pretend space helmets out of cardboard boxes, and run around shooting the boys with water guns, shouting, "Gotcha with my laser pistol!"

Neither the boys nor the girls in Natalie's neighborhood had particularly understood this behavior. The girls would ask why she didn't want to play house and the boys, soaking wet, declared, "Space is dumb. No one goes there anymore." This was not to say Natalie never played with children her own age. In fact, she did enjoy playing computer games with the girls and sports with the boys.

As she grew older, Natalie had started reading history in addition to science fiction and she introduced both the boys and girls to highly involved games of strategy. Both pursuits suited her well. Her uncle James, a retired admiral from the Second Korean War, sat down with her one day. "Your grades are pretty good, aren't they?" said the old man, firmly.

"I'm top of the class, Uncle James," Natalie told him. "I only got one B last semester."

"That's pretty good." The old man let just a hint of a smile curl his lip. Natalie remembered staring at him. He was a bit fat, but she could see how he had once been powerfully built. Her mother once said he had been a heavyweight boxer. His snow-white hair had been trimmed so short, it made her think of a light frost atop a deep brown mountain. "You know, I have some friends in Congress. I could get you an appointment to Annapolis."

Natalie's heart had skipped a beat. "The Naval Academy?" Back then, she had assumed she would be trapped in the neighborhood she grew up in all her life. She had thought of becoming a teacher to help other kids out of the neighborhood, but Uncle James had just handed her a dream. With Navy experience, she could apply to NASA, maybe even become an astronaut.

"You'll have to work hard," Uncle James had warned her. "Physically and mentally."

Natalie had swallowed hard. "I'll do whatever it takes."

"I'm sure you will." He stood and saluted her. She remembered jumping up and hugging him tight.

As Uncle James had predicted, the Naval Academy proved to be a challenge. Natalie hardly breezed through. Even in the mid-twenty-first century, the male cadets made life difficult for the females and the mostly male teaching faculty wasn't sympathetic to Natalie's plight. Still, she worked hard despite hazings and earned the respect of her fellow classmates. Despite the challenges, her grades were high, bringing her to the attention of a few senior officers at the Pentagon in Washington, D.C.

As a junior officer serving aboard submarines, Natalie kept her eye on the space program and paid particular attention to the *Ares II* mission that went to Mars. Sadly, when *Ares II* returned to Earth, the president announced it was NASA's last mission. Though Natalie's dream of being an astronaut had ended, she ultimately found satisfaction first as executive officer of the Battleship *Oregon,* then as commander of one of the biggest ships in the entire United States Navy, the aircraft carrier U.S.S. *Daniel B. Sherman.*

Even after twenty years in the Navy, Natalie remained the independent thinker she had been as a child. Though she was taught to follow orders—and she did so quite well, when needed—she also knew when and how to question them.

Soon after taking command of the U.S.S. *Sherman*, Captain Natalie Freeman had been ordered to the Mediterranean Sea. Tensions between the United States and Jordan had grown untenable. Natalie was frustrated because she realized the reason for the tensions involved a relatively simple misunderstanding between the Jordanian Prime Minister and the President of the United States, an uncompromising man named Walter Kane.

While Kane and the Jordanian Prime Minister argued, Captain Freeman took several actions that could have resulted in a court-martial. She contacted several high-ranking friends at the Pentagon who put her in touch with members of Congress's armed services committee, including an up-and-coming favorite named Oscar Van der Wald. With their help, she had developed several acceptable solutions to the crisis.

She was disappointed but not surprised when negotiations between President Kane and the Jordanian Prime Minister broke down. The president had ordered her to send an air strike against Amman, the capitol of Jordan. At that point, Natalie took the biggest risk of her career. She did, in fact, order an airplane to fly to Amman. However, she rode in the gunner's seat and the plane landed without firing a shot. She asked to meet with the Jordanian Prime Minister.

After an hour of intense face-to-face discussion, the Prime Minister had agreed to one of the compromises suggested by Natalie's allies in Congress. Together, Natalie and the Prime Minister called President Kane. Senator Van der Wald was in the president's office and a compromise had been reached. Not a single life had been lost. The press declared Natalie Freeman a hero. Embarrassed and humiliated, President Kane had lost the following election to Oscar Van der Wald.

Natalie stared out at the waves rolling by the ship and hoped she could pull off another miracle.

*

In Washington D.C., President Van der Wald sat in the oval

office waiting for a call from Captain Natalie Freeman. In the office with the president was a long-time friend from his days in the Senate named Diana Aguilar. Diana left the Senate when Oscar Van der Wald became president to serve as the Secretary of the Department of Energy.

The president paced through the center of the oval office. His hand gripped a pencil tightly. Diana fidgeted in a high-backed chair. "You know, the real problem is that there just isn't that much oil left in Iraq—or anywhere for that matter."

"They've been saying that for over a hundred years and we're not out of fuel yet," said President Van der Wald.

"It's just a matter of time." Diana shifted, then hastily adjusted her skirt. "It always has been. You know as well as I do that the current administration in Iraq would sell us oil if they had it. The problem is they don't. I don't care how good a miracle worker Natalie Freeman is, she can't put oil back in the ground."

Van der Wald stopped pacing and looked at his friend with sadness. "Two more years. That's all I ask, just two more years of oil, then we'll be up to the next election."

"You've seen the same reports I have." Diana sighed. "They don't even have enough to run their own cars."

The president stepped over to the big window behind his desk. He looked out at the green grass and trees beyond. "What are our options?"

Diana shifted in the seat again. "There just aren't that many. We're getting what we can from Alaska." She fondled a necklace from her home state of New Mexico almost longingly—a small Native American dreamcatcher. "We're even drilling in the Otero Mesa back home."

Oscar Van der Wald turned and looked at his friend. "You used to have family there, didn't you?"

She nodded and looked up. "We have to look for new sources of energy elsewhere."

The president looked back out the window and rubbed his balding head. "Where else can we go? We've drilled everywhere we can in the United States, the Middle East, Russia...."

"There's always space." She stood up. "New Mexico isn't just home to tumbleweeds and oil. We used to have a spaceport there. Two, as a matter of fact."

The president heaved a deep sigh. "We've got to solve our problems right here. The American people have spoken and they don't want us to waste government money in space."

"Quinn Corp doesn't seem to think it's a waste. They're spending a lot of money on their *Aristarchus* project. I think they know something's up there, something that would solve the energy crisis here on Earth."

The president turned, then dropped heavily into his chair behind the desk that once belonged to Abraham Lincoln. "If only President Kane hadn't disbanded NASA...." Van der Wald shook his head. "I'd sure like to know what this *Aristarchus* project is after."

Diana Aguilar smiled. "It occurs to me there may be a way to find out. We might have to reinstate NASA, but I have a cheap way to do it."

The last man to set foot on the planet Mars was Lt. Colonel Jonathan Jefferson. He remembered the voyage vividly. Most people would have thought spending two years in a cramped space capsule with nine other astronauts would have been boring as everyone fell into the routine, or intolerable once everyone got on each other's nerves. However, the time passed surprisingly fast. Each of the team members had been handpicked for the mission and spent many years in careful training and preparation. By the time the rocket launched, Jefferson felt he was among his closest family.

Six of the astronauts, including Jefferson, had made the descent to Mars. On the way down, he and his teammates drew straws to see who would be first to set foot on the planet. Only one other team of humans had been to the red planet before them. Jonathan drew the short straw. All things considered, he was still quite pleased. All that mattered was the opportunity to actually walk around on the Martian surface.

It had been a brisk summer day on Mars, only sixteen degrees below freezing. He remembered looking out the airlock door. A breath of air lifted a small layer of red sand and carried it away. Jonathan descended the Martian Landing Module's ladder and placed his foot on the red sand.

Ten years later, he sat in a cubicle at the headquarters of Earth's largest aerospace technology firm, Martin-Intelsoft. Photographs of his last historic journey to Mars decorated the cubicle's walls. Though he actually had more space in the cubicle than he did aboard the spaceship *Ares II* for two years, it felt much more crowded. Though highly paid as an engineer and consultant for Martin-Intelsoft, he knew he would give it all up in a heartbeat if he could step onto a rocket just one more time.

The phone rang. Grudgingly, Jonathan picked it up. "Sorry, Bill, I forgot about the meeting," he said to his boss. "I'll be down with the plans for the X-3 nanobots in just a few minutes." Hanging up with one hand, he reached out to the computer with the other and printed the plans. Just as he was about to grab the sheets from the printer, the phone rang again. "What is it this time, Bill?"

The voice on the other end of the line chuckled. "Sorry, this isn't Bill Pickett, your boss. My name's Alonzo Thomas and I work for the competition."

"For Quinn Corp?" asked Jonathan, his brow furrowed.

"That's right. You were the last man on Mars. How would you like to be the first man to return?"

"This is a crank call, isn't it?"

"Have you heard of the *Aristarchus* project?"

"I've heard of it." Jonathan hesitated. "The whole thing seems like a long shot to me. It's a very different approach to manned space flight."

"I assure you it will work, but we need help. The ship's design is sound, but we need more mechanical engineers on the project and someone who can fly a shuttle through the atmosphere of a planet."

"I don't know." Jonathan put the papers down and looked at his watch. He might be a famous astronaut, but his boss would kill him for being late to the meeting.

"I want to meet with you soon," said Thomas. "It could be well worth your while. Not only are we going to Mars but onward to Jupiter and Saturn. As shuttle pilot, you'd be the first man to fly through Jupiter's atmosphere and the first man to set foot on Saturn's moon Titan."

"Tell me where to meet you."

Chapter 4
Whale Song

The mystery of the whales' changed songs gnawed at Dr. Myra Lee until she could stand it no longer. She sent a proposal to the director of the Alaskan Oceanographic Institute. A few days later, he called her to his office. The director—a thin man with curly hair—spoke softly, almost as though he were a mystic providing answers to the very mysteries of the universe. "I have a form on my desk requesting permission to take the R/V *Eleana* out again, to make more recordings of whale song." He paused and looked at Myra over the top of his glasses. "You've only been back two weeks."

A knot formed in Myra's stomach. "Yes, sir. I have reason to believe that something very important has happened with the whales. They're all learning a new song."

"Whales change their songs all the time." The director sat back in the cozy leather chair and folded his hands.

"But not all at once." Myra wrung her hands nervously. "It's like they're all trying to learn this particular song as fast as they can and pass it on to as many other whales as possible."

"Why would they do that?"

"I have no idea. That's why I want to go back out. I want to find out if anything has changed, or if the whales have returned to their old routine."

The director reached over and closed the folder on his desk. "I'll call Captain Naftel this afternoon. If he's willing to take the ship out again, you may go."

"Thank you!" She gave a little jump in spite of herself. Feeling the director's gaze on her, she regained her composure. "Thank you," she said again, more calmly. Then she left to go home and pack.

*

Two days later, Myra Lee stood in the bow of the *Eleana* as the wind whipped through her hair and salt stung her face. The air was pleasantly warm for Alaska as spring turned into summer. She enjoyed being out on deck, watching for the spouts that would indicate humpbacks were near. This time, she had *Eleana* all to herself for a week. She felt confident she would be able to discover what the whales had decided to sing about.

She caught herself as the boat listed to the side. Angrily, she looked back toward the windows of the ship's bridge. There, Captain Naftel and the helmsman both pointed out the window. Following their fingers, she saw a spout off in the distance. A broad smile crossed her face in anticipation of seeing the whales.

She made her way to the ship's stern where she found the technician Lisa Henry wearing a sweat suit, lounging on a deck chair. "Up and at 'em!" called Myra, cheerfully. "There be whales off the bow!"

Lisa opened one eye laconically. "The mikes are checked out and wired. I've got the recorders loaded with fresh disks. All I have to do is run out the booms when we reach anchor." Lisa brushed an errant hair from her face and closed her eye.

Myra stepped over to the edge of the boat, leaning on the polished, wooden rail. She wished Lisa would show a little more enthusiasm for the job. However, no one else knew hydrophonic equipment better.

Myra felt a heavy hand on her shoulder and she jumped in spite of herself. Turning, she faced Lance Naftel's weathered features. "Sorry to intrude on your thoughts, but we're about to drop anchor."

"I saw. We're ready to start recording as soon as you give the word." Myra looked up to see the sail crew at work. The boat slowed to a crawl. Shortly after, a squawk came from a radio hanging at the captain's belt.

He thumbed the transmitter. "Naftel. Go ahead."

"Anchor's set, sir," said the voice at the other end.

"Time to start recording." Naftel grinned.

Myra looked up. Lisa was already running out the portside boom. Nodding to herself, Myra made her way into the cabin and checked the equipment.

There was a tap at the door and Lisa poked her head around the corner. "We're all set to go," she said brightly. "I'll be on deck if you need anything." She disappeared with a swish of long blondish-brown hair.

Myra nodded as she turned on the recording equipment. While waiting for sufficient information to come in, she pulled out charts of the whale songs from her last voyage. As she looked at them, she thought she had never seen a whale song that looked quite so agitated. The sequence of rumbles and chirps was far more rapid than anything she had ever seen from a whale. Not only that, the rumbles formed smoother peaks than she had seen before.

Running her fingers over the page, she thought aloud. "Rumble, rumble, squeal, rumble, squeal, rumble, squeal, squeal." She stopped cold and shook her head. "Dot, dot, dash, dot, dash, dot, dash, dash?"

Myra rubbed her chin, trying to tell herself she over-interpreted the data. To clear her head, she stepped out of the cabin and walked back to the tiny galley. There, she absent-mindedly retrieved a mug of coffee and ambled back to the recording equipment. After taking a sip of the strong coffee, she noticed the first recorder had ejected its disk and the second had started recording.

She put the first disk in the playback deck, adjusted the headphones, and listened to the new recording. It was a jumble of whale song. With a sigh, she wondered how she would sort it out. However, as she listened, she caught herself thinking, *Dot, dash, dot, dot.*

Shaking her head again, she removed and labeled the CD. With that, she decided she should clear this crazy notion out of her head once and for all. She took another sip of coffee, then stepped out onto the deck. "Lisa, could you come to the cabin for a second?"

"Anything the matter?" asked the technician, suddenly concerned that some piece of her well-functioning equipment might be in trouble.

"No problems." Myra shook her head, her brow furrowed. "I just want your opinion on something."

Lisa stood, removed her sunglasses, and hooked them over

the collar of the black sweatshirt. She followed Myra into the cabin. The oceanographer put the charts in front of the technician. "What do you make of these?"

Lisa shrugged. "They look like whale song charts."

"Well ... yes, that's what they are, but I'm talking about patterns. Do you see any patterns on these charts?" Myra tried to keep the strain from her voice.

Lisa pursed her lips. "The chirps and clicks are coming a little faster than I've seen them before." She shook her head. "But I thought that was why we were out here."

Myra let out a sigh of relief. However, to be sure she imagined patterns that weren't there, she pushed on. "Do they look like Morse code to you?"

"A little, maybe," said Lisa. Looking closer, she shook her head. "No, there're too many dots and dashes and no pauses." She inclined her head. "But you know, it almost looks like a binary encoded sequence."

"Binary?" Myra sat down. "You mean like computer code?"

"Or old fashioned radio before spread spectrum signals, or any number of other types of electronic communication." Looking at it again, Lisa nodded. "Yeah, it definitely looks like binary code of some kind." Shrugging, Lisa looked back to her boss. "Need anything else?"

"No." Myra sighed. "That's all. Thanks." The oceanographer put on her most confident smile. As Lisa left, Myra tried to pick up her coffee mug but her hand shook so badly, she had to put it down before taking a sip.

*

Aboard the U.S.S. *Sherman,* Captain Natalie Freeman made the best possible speed for the United States. As she expected, she had failed her diplomatic mission to Iraq. Without oil to sell to the United States, she wasn't sure how she could have succeeded. What she didn't expect was the president to order her back home. Instead, she expected to have been ordered to some distant port to await further orders. Standing on the bridge of her beloved ship, she looked out at the miles and miles of ocean. In the distance, she thought she could discern a black shape against the water's blue. She smiled at herself, thinking it must be a whale. She had followed orders. The president had no call to reprimand her. However, he could always transfer her to a new assignment. She sighed, thinking about the water and the whale. *As long as they don't take all this open space from me.*

Chapter 5
The *Aristarchus* Project

Some said privatization was the best thing that ever happened to the American space program. In 2074, even before NASA's *Ares II* mission returned from Mars, Martin-Intelsoft launched its first rocket to the Moon. Within five years, three companies—Martin-Intelsoft, Quinn Corp, and General Nanotech—had operating factories on the Moon. From 1969 to 2074, less than two-dozen humans had set foot on the Moon. By 2078, over two thousand people lived there full time and shuttle flights became routine. Each of the companies sent at least one shuttle per week.

Not everyone appreciated the privatization of space flight. When NASA was disbanded, Martian exploration stopped completely. Environmentalists complained that the factories were destroying the lunar surface. The changes were apparent even from Earth without a telescope. The man on the Moon had developed dark pimples where buildings had been erected and long, thin scars where trenches had been dug. During the dark of the Moon, pinpricks of light stood out on the lunar surface.

Jonathan Jefferson had been to the Moon several times both as a NASA astronaut and aboard Martin-Intelsoft shuttles. Though he knew that corporate loyalty was a thing of the distant past, he felt strangely like a traitor sitting in a Quinn Corp shuttle's cockpit as they approached the Moon. He'd decided to take some annual leave from his job at Martin-Intelsoft to see what the *Aristarchus* project was all about.

As the shuttle swung around to the Moon's dark side, Jefferson caught his breath. On the surface, near the Quinn Corp factory were ten enormous scaffolds. Within each were long, thin, translucent tubes that resembled plastic doweling laid out in the shape of gigantic, narrow kite frames. The material—quinitite—was far lighter and stronger than conventional plastic, grown crystal-like in the moon's light gravity.

"Those quinitite frames," began the colonel, "how big are they? They must be what ... three miles long?" He leaned over the shuttle's command console, peering out the window at the craters and other features on the Moon, trying to get a sense of scale.

The shuttle's pilot grinned. "Try five miles."

"So Jerome Quinn and this ... this Alonzo Thomas ... are really building a solar sail to go to the outer planets?" Jefferson shook his head, amazed. "Where's the main fuselage being built?"

The shuttle pilot pointed to a large building at one end of the factory complex. "It's in there. They're expecting it'll be finished next week."

"Next week?" The colonel's eyes went wide. "They must be devoting a lot of the factory's resources to this project."

"Sir, I'm going to have to ask you to return to your seat in the crew cabin. We're getting ready to land."

Jefferson nodded and then turned, his stomach doing flip-flops. His last trip to the Moon had been over a year before and he was no longer used to the tricks gravity played aboard a spacecraft approaching a moon or planet. They were close enough to the Moon, he felt a small amount of gravity beneath his feet. At the same time, the shuttle decelerated, making it feel like he was being pushed from behind as he fell-stepped-drifted back to his seat in the passenger cabin of the shuttle. He sat down next to John O'Connell, the man who'd met him at Quinn Corp's spaceport. O'Connell's chin had fallen onto his chest and a light snore escaped. Jefferson buckled his harness. Out of habit, he double-checked O'Connell's harness.

O'Connell awoke with a start as the shuttle fired its rockets, preparing to descend. "Are we there?"

"Almost," said Jefferson. "So, tell me, who exactly is this Alonzo Thomas?"

"They say he's a hotshot engineer. He's been working his way through the ranks of the company for about five years." O'Connell stifled a yawn. "The funny part is that no one seems to have met him before the ship started being built." Jefferson lifted an eyebrow and O'Connell continued. "He has Jerome

Quinn's complete confidence and people assume he's been working in the home office but I haven't met anyone who actually worked alongside him."

"Well, Quinn Corp is a big company—lots of divisions." Jefferson narrowed his eyes, suspiciously, belying his offhand tone. "He said something about being the pilot manager?"

"He's going to pilot the ship." O'Connell shrugged as though it were the most natural thing in the world.

Jefferson took a deep breath. "I guess since it's a corporate ship, he wants to avoid giving people ranks like in the military." He shook his head. "Could make discipline aboard ship difficult."

O'Connell pushed his thick glasses up the bridge of his nose. "I don't know…. It's not like there aren't chains of command in the civilian world."

Jefferson pursed his lips, thinking about his civilian bosses. He wondered if someone like Bill Pickett would have actually been promoted above him in the military. "What about Jerome Quinn? Have you met him? Has he been up for an inspection?"

O'Connell shook his head. "From what people say, he rarely leaves his estate in California."

"You'd think he'd take an interest in his highest profile project." Jefferson inclined his head.

"They say the old man has never been to the Moon. Maybe he gets space sick."

"Maybe…." Jefferson looked out the window. "He must trust this Thomas quite a bit."

The shuttle settled onto its landing pad with a gentle thud. The rockets shut off suddenly and the cabin became eerily quiet.

∗

Myra Lee returned to the Oceanographic Institute. Lisa had already read the whale song data into the computer. It was such a jumble that there did not appear to be any way to make sense out of the information. Even so, they hoped the computer's voice recognition software would be able to distinguish each whale's tones and print a plot of the individual songs.

Staring at the plots displayed on the computer screen,

Myra recognized virtually the same pattern over and over again. With just a little relief, she realized some of the individual variations each whale normally added to its songs did appear in the graphs. Still, those changes were not quite as apparent as they should have been and there were phrases in the songs where the whales made no variation at all. Lisa's words about the songs looking like binary encoded messages continued to haunt Myra.

She folded her hands while examining the plots and wondered if the phenomenon she observed was limited to whales in the Frederick Sound area or if it happened worldwide. Opening a new window on her computer, Myra fired off three email messages. One went to her graduate advisor, Dr. Stirling Cristof, who studied humpback whales out of San Francisco. Another went to a cetacean biologist in Hawaii who studied Right Whales. The final message went to a Wood's Hole biologist who worked with Spermaceti Whales.

Within minutes, Stirling Cristof's face appeared in a video chat window on the computer. "Hi, Myra, got a moment?"

With a keystroke, she was in touch with the wiry, sharp-eyed man. "I always have time. Did you get my message?"

"I did. I have to say, I've been thinking about calling or sending a note for some time now."

"Oh? Why so?" Myra leaned toward the computer monitor.

"Having to do with the subject of your email. The whales down here have changed their songs as well, and just as radically. It's downright bizarre. Unfortunately, I wasn't out to sea when it happened, but I just received a disk from one of my students who got in last night." Stirling rubbed the bridge of his hawk-like nose.

Myra twirled the end of her hair in her fingers. "Do you have any idea what it means?"

"None at all. Your guess is as good as mine."

"There's got to be a good explanation," said Myra. "But I can't get over how much the songs look like binary code." She blushed, embarrassed about the observation. "You probably think I'm over-interpreting the data."

Cristof remained silent for a time, as though thinking. "You may be onto something."

Myra snorted a laugh. "Get real, Stir! I called you so I could find an alternative explanation, not have you reinforce my delusions!"

"No, really. What if whales have figured out a way to talk to humans? Binary encoded messages travel through the atmosphere—and through the water—all the time. There are radio signals to submarines, wireless computer communications, all kinds of signals the whales could, in theory, hear or feel in some way."

"Okay, let's say I'm not delusional." Myra sat back and folded her arms. "Why now? Why after all these years? Why speak in code at all? It's not like whales haven't heard English or other languages."

"True, but maybe it's the language that makes sense to them. Or maybe the message isn't meant for humans."

Myra laughed, incredulous. "If it's not meant for humans, who *is* it meant for?"

"Ask the whales," said Cristof with a wry grin.

"Thanks a *lot*."

"Seriously, I have a friend who's a philologist at Oxford University. I'll put you in touch with her. Now that you've identified some definite patterns in the whale song, maybe she can help you interpret what you're hearing."

"If it's binary code, wouldn't I need a computer expert rather than an expert in languages?" Myra inclined her head.

"Binary's a language ... it's just a mathematical one. In many ways, that makes it easier to sort out." Cristof shrugged.

"Stir, this feels like a wild goose chase to me." Myra leaned forward and peered into the screen.

"Are there any other geese to chase?"

Myra sighed and shook her head. "That's the problem. I can't think of any."

"Well, keep thinking," said Stir. "Philologists and language experts have looked at whale songs before and come back with nothing. It'll probably happen again, but I think it's worth asking in light of the new data."

Myra sat back and closed her eyes for a moment. She had sent the email to her former advisor because she trusted him implicitly. "It's worth a shot, I suppose." She sighed and opened her eyes. "Send me the info."

*

John O'Connell led Jonathan Jefferson from the shuttle through a series of corridors. Jefferson couldn't help but be impressed by the decor. Martin-Intelsoft's white corridors connecting large manufacturing chambers and small, utilitarian sleeping quarters leant the facility a sterile quality. Quinn Corp clearly put more effort into making their facility a comfortable living space. Liquid crystals had been set into the walls creating the effect of living, moving murals.

In some places, scenes of forests back on Earth adorned the walls. In other places, the murals were more imaginative, scenes from classic movies or even fantasy scenes with dragons flying high over dramatic mountain ranges. Once again, an uneasy feeling washed over the one-time astronaut. Even though he had caught just a mere glimpse of the *Aristarchus*, he was nearly ready to give up his cubicle on Earth to work for the competition.

O'Connell led Jefferson to a door and sounded the buzzer. "Come in," called a voice from within.

The two entered the small office together. A thin, lanky man sat behind a desk, typing at a computer. He was much younger than Jefferson expected and the astronaut became self-conscious about his own gray hair and stomach that stuck further over his belt than he'd like. The lanky young man looked up with a broad smile. "Ah, Colonel Jefferson, pleased to meet you face to face, at last." He stepped around the desk. "I'm Alonzo Thomas, Pilot Manager of the *Aristarchus*." He shook Jefferson's hand, then indicated a seat.

"Pilot, if you don't need me anymore, I need to continue checking that solar flux data from last week," said O'Connell as Jefferson took a seat in a plastic chair that seemed to mold itself to his frame.

"Go right ahead, Neb," said Alonzo. "Sorry to pull you from that." He looked to Jefferson. "Though this is a big facility, the *Aristarchus* project itself is rather shorthanded. We're trying to fix that as quickly as we can, though."

"Neb?" Jefferson eyed John O'Connell.

"Oh...," he said as though caught off-guard. "It's my old college nickname. I'm from Nebraska. They used to call me Nebraska John..."

"You mean like Kansas Jim in those movies from the '50s?" Jefferson's lip curled upwards. "Those were great! Do you have a fedora?"

"I used to." O'Connell grinned sheepishly. "Anyway, Neb's short for Nebraska." With that, he waved and left Jefferson and the pilot alone to talk.

Jefferson turned to face his host. "They call you Pilot?"

"Sorry, like I said, we're a bit shorthanded on the project. There are only fifteen of us so far. We get familiar with each other rather quickly," explained Thomas. "Pilot's kind of a nickname, but I like it. I've never been all that comfortable with my given name."

"I hope I'm not being rude, but you look awfully young to be in charge of this project." Jefferson leaned forward. "Over at Martin, we know a lot of Quinn engineers, but your name only started appearing regularly with this project. Is there a senior engineer in charge?"

Pilot looked down at the desk for a moment, then looked up with an amused smirk. "I'm older than I look and—if you're worried—those senior engineers have been checking my work. I've even been checking in daily with Old Man Quinn himself."

"Rumor has it that the plans for the ship were originally drawn up by Quinn's son. Some people say this project is being done to indulge the boy."

Thomas's face fell just a bit at the suggestion, then quickly brightened again. "I know the younger Quinn well. He's a talented lad. Does it matter what the motivation for the mission is as long as the design is sound?"

"It matters if I'm putting my life on the line."

"Biochemicals," said Thomas. "Saturn's moon Titan is teeming with organic compounds. Harvesting them will be a gold mine for our pharmaceutical division."

"You'll need a good biology team," said Jefferson. "Anyone I know?"

"We're looking for people with just the right qualifications."

Pilot sat back. "Colonel Jefferson, you came here to learn more about the *Aristarchus*. I think I should give you a tour."

"I'd like that." Jefferson brimmed with questions, but assumed he'd have the opportunity to ask more, later.

Without saying anything further, Pilot stood and led Jefferson back down the corridor. At a junction, they turned left and Pilot stepped into a small glassed-in room that looked out over a vast enclosed space. "I present the heart of the *Aristarchus*." Pilot held his hand out toward the window and beamed like a proud parent.

A great silver spheroid sat on the floor, surrounded by scaffoldings. It reminded Jefferson of photos he'd seen of the very first machine humans had launched into Earth's orbit— the Sputnik. This spheroid was much bigger than the old Soviet satellite and somewhat elongated—similar to a pill. Where Sputnik had been the size of a basketball, the silver spheroid that served as *Aristarchus's* fuselage seemed to be about the diameter of a football field, about ten times the size of the craft he'd traveled to Mars aboard. "Would you like to see inside?" asked Pilot.

"I would love to," said Jefferson.

Pilot stepped back into the corridor and around to a gangplank that led into the silver spheroid.

Captain Natalie Freeman was led into the oval office. Her one-time ally Oscar Van der Wald sat behind the desk, looking stern. Sitting in one of the high-backed chairs flanking the desk was a Latina woman the captain did not recognize. "Captain Freeman, reporting as ordered, sir." She snapped a salute as the doors closed behind her.

The president waved at a chair. "There's no need for that," he said dismissively. "Have a seat." He gestured to the other woman in the room. "Captain Freeman, I'd like you to meet Secretary Aguilar, Department of Energy."

Natalie reached over and shook Diana's hand, then took a seat in the other high-backed chair. Seeing Diana Aguilar's discomfort in the chair, Natalie was glad women's dress uniforms had been changed so they included pants rather than skirts. Her only real challenge was sitting such that the hilt of her dress-uniform sword didn't tear the expensive fabric of the chair.

"Captain Freeman," began the president, "we have a proposition for you. Have you heard of the *Aristarchus* project?"

Natalie nodded slowly.

"We're concerned about the mission proceeding without an observer from NASA aboard." Aguilar leaned forward.

"NASA was disbanded eight years ago," said Natalie, warily.

"It's just been reinstated," said the president. He pointed to a paper on his desk. "The film crews just left."

Diana Aguilar stood and offered Natalie Freeman her hand. "Congratulations, Captain Freeman, we've decided to appoint you as first administrator of the new NASA."

Natalie's mouth dropped open as she stood and first took Diana's hand followed by the president's. "So what exactly does this entail?" asked Natalie, still afraid she was being punished for failing in her negotiations with the Iraqi Prime Minister.

Chapter 6
A New Age

Pilot led Jonathan Jefferson down a sloping gangway into the great spheroid—the fuselage of the *Aristarchus*. They entered through an open airlock door near the middle of the craft. Even though gravity on the Moon was only one-sixth that of the Earth, the ship's floor seemed to slope away at a dangerous angle both up and away from the airlock and down toward the ground. Pilot indicated a set of handholds.

"Of course, the ship will be rotating in flight, so down will be toward the outer walls once we're underway," explained Pilot. "The ship is designed with that in mind."

"What if gravity fails?" asked Jefferson.

"That's like asking 'what if the sun turns off?'" Pilot gave a self-satisfied smile. "Even so, our engineers have built in safety contingencies." He tugged on the handhold for emphasis, then made his way downslope to the next room.

Passing through the door, they found a motor that stood about as tall as Pilot, clamped to a set of rails on the floor. Tool kits were mounted to the room's walls. "This is one of the steerage rooms," explained Pilot. "There are ten of these rooms. The motors will adjust the trim of the sails giving us the ability to maximize speed and adjust course."

"What happens if one of the motors breaks down?" Jefferson looked for a way to bring in a backup motor.

Pilot pointed to the rails. "The motor can be unclamped and rolled away, allowing the crew to turn the sail by hand." He knelt down next to the motor and pointed out marks on the floor. "We can measure the angle of the sails with these marks. As such, the *Aristarchus* may be the first space vessel in human history that does not require computers for in-flight operations."

"A spaceship that can be flown manually?" Jefferson's eyes

went wide. "That's almost completely unheard of." He knelt down next to Pilot and looked at the floor. The markings were inscribed in brass rings like one might find on an old-fashioned sailing ship.

"The humans aboard this ship will have more control than even the Mercury astronauts who'd asked for joysticks, so they could fly their ship like an airplane."

"That motor looks heavy." Jefferson stood, then carefully grabbed handholds and fell-stepped around the unit. "How many people would it take to disconnect and move it in the event of an emergency?"

"One." Pilot grinned as Jefferson narrowed his eyes, trying to figure out how one person could move the motor. "In flight with full gravity, the motor will weigh about 500 pounds. However, it's so carefully balanced that one person can unclamp the motor and move it back. The sails will also have weight because of the rotation, but there's a gearing system that allows one person to unlock the sail and move it by hand."

"I presume that's a worst case scenario." Jefferson tried to imagine coordinating ten people turning sails by hand.

"Indeed it is." Pilot stood and moved over to the wall and grabbed a capped pipe. He dropped the hinged lid and blew in. "But we even have an old-fashioned comm system in the event that electronic communications break down." With that, he moved downslope and grabbed onto a ladder mounted on the wall and climbed toward the center of the sphere. Opening a hatch in the ceiling of the steerage room, he disappeared. Jefferson grabbed onto the ladder and followed him up through a tube.

Jefferson emerged from the tube at one end of a brightly lit, octagonal room. Plastic consoles faced five of the eight walls. A supply cabinet took up the back wall. In front of it stood a small worktable. There were doors in the other two walls as well as two ladders, one leading up and the other down. At the center of the room was a semi-circular console with a chair in the middle.

"This is the command and control room or C-and-C for short." Pilot pointed to the chair in the center. "That's where the captain sits. He can monitor all ship's operations from there."

"In other words, that's your station," said Jefferson, knowingly.

"Hardly." Pilot seemed taken aback. He pointed to one of the five consoles lining the walls of the room. "When I'm here, I'll sit there, at the pilot's station." He pointed out each of the other stations in turn. "Communications and biosciences, life support, external sensors, and astrosciences—that's Neb O'Connell's station—and sail and thruster control."

"When you're here?" The colonel inclined his head. "This would seem to be the nerve center of the ship. Wouldn't you be on duty here most of the time?"

"The central hub of the ship—the null gravity core—has windows that look out each side. There are telescopes, sextants, and other navigational aides installed in the hub. If the navigational computer goes down, we'll still be able to steer the ship from there."

"If I didn't know better, I'd say you were a Luddite, Mr. Thomas," declared Jefferson. "It sounds like you don't trust computers at all."

Pilot grinned. "I think most technicians and engineers are Luddites at heart. Computers are just tools and like all tools, they can fail. Even so, there is one computer that's all-but vital." He pointed to the station he'd called 'life support.' "We have numerous backup systems to power the lights, the food service units, and air supply, but if we lost the life support computer, we'd have to abandon the mission and return to Earth as fast as we could. Well as this ship is designed, we frail humans just couldn't sit out in space in a round metal can and keep ourselves alive for an extended time without the computer."

The colonel looked around at the command and control room, impressed. "Okay, if you're not going to occupy the command chair, who will?"

"You, of course," said Pilot. "You're one of the planet's most experienced astronauts. I want you to make sure we make it to Saturn in one piece and get back home."

Jefferson caught his breath. "Why me? Why not one of the other astronauts that was aboard *Ares II*?" Even as he asked the question, he approached the command console in the center of the room and gave it the once over, already getting acquainted with it as though he knew for a fact he would be sitting there for the next few years.

"You're the youngest," said Alonzo. "Also, your personality profile matches what we want for this mission more than many of your fellow astronauts."

The colonel scowled. "That brings up another point. I trained for years to go to Mars, got to know my fellow astronauts like they were family. How soon will we be launching this ship?"

"If we're able to stay on schedule, I hope to assemble the ship next week. With training for new personnel, we should be ready to launch inside a month."

"One month," said Jefferson slowly. "How can you expect a crew that has been together for less than a month to form a cohesive team that will make this mission a success? I read up on heliogyro theory and checked the alignment of Jupiter and Saturn before coming to this meeting, Mr. Thomas. I know we'll make it to Saturn in about the time it took me to get to Mars, but it'll still take a well-trained team to accomplish the task."

"This is a new age, Colonel Jefferson." Pilot stepped over to the external sensor station and brushed his fingers over its surface. "If spaceflight is going to be a reality for mankind, we've got to move away from the mentality that long years of preparation are necessary for a short voyage. After all, Columbus put his crew together for the voyage to America in about a month. If he could do it and succeed, why can't we?"

The colonel took a deep breath and frowned. "Columbus had his share of problems."

Pilot rolled his eyes and moved past Jefferson to the door at the far end of C-and-C. "Let me show you the crew cabins."

The one-time astronaut followed Pilot through the far door, past a galley that seemed more like a country kitchen than a sterile shipboard mess hall and into a nicely appointed bedroom. With a touch of a button, one wall of the cabin came to life, showing a scene of a mountain stream. Deer stood a ways off, munching grass. Clouds drifted lazily through the sky. Jefferson almost thought he could reach out and touch the pine tree nearest to him. Instead, since they were now in a part of the sphere parallel to the ground, Jefferson sat down on the bed and admired the scenery.

"You can download movies, television, Internet, even scenes from home right to the wall of your cabin. You won't even need to miss the latest movies that are playing back home while we're on the mission." Pilot looked Jefferson in the eye. "Off hand, I'd say it's a far cry from anything NASA was ever able to provide on the *Ares II*."

"Creating a luxury liner in space may help stave off morale problems, but it won't prevent them."

"That's why Mr. Quinn and I want you in command." Pilot sat down in one of the chairs at the table. "I want someone who can help keep the crew in line, keep them working as a unit. Also, your recent work in nanotechnology overlaps several key specialties."

Jefferson took a deep breath and let it out slowly. "You said you don't have a full crew, how's all this been built?"

"We've been utilizing as much of the factory labor as Old Man Quinn will allow. However, most of them will be staying behind. I'd like to get ten more crewmembers—that would bring us up to a compliment of twenty-five. Among other things, I still need a top-notch communication's specialist and a biochemist or biologist. If I can find one or two people whose specialties specialties overlap, it would be perfect."

"Why's that?" asked Jefferson.

"The biological scanners are slaved into the communications gear. Sensors for organic compounds are tied into the low gain sending and receiving equipment. Also, by having the bio scanners and communications tied together, it allows for easy recording of the data."

Jefferson rubbed his chin and considered the explanation. It seemed to make sense—mostly. "What about a high gain antenna? I didn't see one on the fuselage."

Pilot smiled disarmingly. "The whole ship's a high gain antenna." When Jefferson raised his eyebrows, Pilot gestured all around. "Aluminum sails are great radio frequency receivers."

Jefferson nodded, understanding. His thoughts turned to other things Pilot said. "Twenty-five people," he mused slowly. He looked up at the mountain scene on the wall, felt the comfortable bed beneath him, then thought of setting foot on

Mars again and exploring the atmospheres of Jupiter and Saturn. It was almost enough to make him willing to risk the voyage. "There's one more thing I'd like to see. You mentioned the shuttle-lander."

"Right this way." Pilot shut off the view screen.

*

The phone rang while Myra Lee showered. Grumbling to herself, she shut off the water, wrapped a warm, fuzzy towel around her middle and started drying her hair with another. After a minute, she found her cell and answered.

"This is Joyce Harmer at Oxford," said a very precise voice on the other end of the line. "We believe we are close to translating a portion of the whale song for you."

Myra's knees went watery and she fought not to drop the phone.

"Dr. Lee, are you there?" asked Harmer, vaguely distressed.

"Yes, I'm here. It's just that no one has ever come up with a translation script for whales before. This is epic. It's history in the making."

"I know. Can we set up an Internet chat and I'll show you what I've got?"

"Absolutely, I'll just sit down at the computer." Myra's towel slipped an inch. "Actually, better give me a couple minutes to get dressed. You caught me in the shower."

"Certainly. I'll wait for your ping."

Myra let the towel drop as she stepped through the house, thinking about the implications of the first words from whales. She found a T-shirt and some slacks and dressed as quickly as she could—which wasn't very fast since her mind kept turning around in circles. Finally, she started toward her computer, just remembering to grab a brush, so she could comb out her hair as she talked.

She logged into the computer and pinged the Oxford philologist. Harmer's face appeared in a window on the computer. Her short, gray-blond hair was a mess, not matching her precise speech at all. Dark bags under her eyes indicated she'd been up all night working on the complex problem. Suddenly, Myra didn't feel so bad about combing her hair in front of her own camera.

Harmer sent some charts over to Myra, who recognized them as being very similar to her own charts of recorded whale song. "You were right," said Joyce. "This new song is very like binary code."

"You said you have a translation?" Myra forgot her hair and leaned forward.

"Not exactly, but we do have a sense for what they're trying to say." Joyce closed her eyes for a moment, then opened them and continued. "It's as though they're sending a message. The context makes it sound like a warning. If we've got it right, it's something like, 'The land dwellers are on their way.'"

Myra sat back and stared at the Oxford linguist. "That doesn't make any sense. Who are they warning?"

"That's difficult to say." Joyce's brow furrowed. "It's like they've been reading too much Tolkien. They're warning someone they call 'the keepers of the rings.'" She paused and sent some more information across. "I know it sounds utterly fantastic, but I'm sending along all of the notes and programs I used to come to my conclusions."

"Any idea who 'the keepers of the rings' are?" Visions of dolphins jumping through hoops at Marineland in California came unbidden to Myra's mind.

"You said the whales started their song at one o'clock in the afternoon of April 17?"

Myra nodded, remembering the event clearly. It was difficult to believe that almost two months had passed since then.

Joyce hesitated before answering, "That was the exact time Quinn Corp executives announced a mission to Saturn."

"The ringed planet," mused Myra. "Are you trying to suggest that these 'keepers of the rings' are little green men from Saturn?"

Joyce shrugged and sighed. "I almost hesitated to mention it."

Myra nodded. "Thanks. Can the programs you've devised tell us anything about what the whales say in any of their other songs?"

"I haven't had time to do much with the other songs." Joyce appeared relieved by the change of subject. "All we can really pick up are sequences that repeat with subtle changes more than any specific words. It's as though the whales are reciting poetry or repeating a litany."

Myra nodded to herself. "That's what I would have expected to find given their behavior."

"Us too."

Myra thanked the linguist, then shut down the computer connection. She brushed tangles out of her hair while visions of whales floating in the clouds of Saturn came to her mind.

*

Pilot smiled when Jefferson's jaw dropped as they entered a launch bay, near the spheroid's central core. The craft before them was like nothing the colonel had ever seen. The lunar transportation shuttles were large, chunky ships with cylindrical bodies mounted on broad delta wings. Aside from their size and the power of their engines, they were reminiscent of late twentieth century space shuttles. Even the Martian Lander was a large bug-like craft, built more for functionality than for grace and speed. The shuttle aboard the *Aristarchus* was trim, with graceful, curving lines. On one hand, the sloping delta wings made the craft look a little like the fighter jets that Jefferson had once flown for the Air Force. On the other hand, the gently sloping top and sleek lines gave him the impression of a sports car.

"It'll hold a crew of six," explained Pilot. "This one is optimized to handle the high winds of Jupiter and Saturn's upper atmospheres and stay there for an extended time."

"This one?"

"There are four extravehicular craft in all." Pilot stepped over and ran his hand along the shining, silver wing. "This one is for the Jovian planets. We also have one for the thin, Martian atmosphere, one for the thicker atmosphere we're going to encounter on Titan and one for deep space exploration and towing—another redundancy in the ship's control system. Though they are optimized for certain environments, each ship can operate in all of the environments we're likely to encounter."

"So, we have a way to rescue someone who's stranded, for instance," said Jefferson.

"Precisely. Or if one shuttle malfunctions for some reason, we don't have to abort the entire landing mission." Pilot looked lovingly up at the little silver ship.

Jefferson walked over and touched the wing, intrigued despite his skepticism. After a moment, he scowled. "Have any of these ships been tested?"

Pilot looked up at Jefferson, as though he'd been slapped. "Of course. Each of these has been flight tested between the Earth and the Moon." His gaze fell to the floor for a moment and he turned his back to the one-time astronaut. "Admittedly, we may encounter … unexpected variables along the way that might give us problems."

"That's the nature of exploring the unknown."

Pilot turned and looked at him. "All of our data, all of our information for how to design these craft came from NASA missions—either yours to Mars or unmanned missions to the outer planets."

Jefferson rubbed his chin and smiled darkly. "In other words, you're working with the best you've got. I understand that. I hope *you* understand that sometimes the best you got just isn't good enough. Sometimes, every backup system in the world fails and that's the end of the mission and the end of us. We learned that with *Challenger* and *Columbia*. Each and every one of us will have to face that possibility out there and I'm afraid you don't know what you're getting us into. I worry about people like O'Connell who've never had to risk their lives before."

Pilot nodded and frowned. "I suppose you think I'm an over-excited schoolboy who can't wait for the next field trip."

Jefferson snorted and turned away. "Not exactly…." He stepped over to the hatchway. "More like an over-excited Boy Scout. You're prepared. I'll give you that. I'm just used to having more training time, getting to know my crew better. I also don't think you're being one hundred percent honest with me, Mr. Thomas." Jefferson descended the ladder.

Alonzo kangaroo-hopped to the ladder and looked down at the top of Jefferson's head. "I take it that means you've decided to turn down my offer."

Jefferson looked back up. "No, it means I need to sleep

on it. Show me to my quarters and I'll talk to you more in the morning."

Pilot smiled and descended behind Jefferson when the cell-phone in his pocket buzzed. He hit the button, putting it on speaker while hanging from the ladder. "Hello."

"Sir," came the station operator's voice. "The president's secretary is on the line and she says he would like to speak with you."

"The president? He has my number. Why is he going through the switchboard?" asked Pilot, indignantly.

"Not the president of Quinn Corp, sir. The President of the United States."

"I'll take the call in my office." Pilot turned off the phone.

Chapter 7
Communications

Distracted by her own thoughts, Myra Lee ran a red light on her way to the Oceanographic Institute and nearly hit another car. She waved an apology to the other driver, who already sped away, flashing a rude gesture at her. Myra pulled off to the side of the road and took several deep breaths.

Her mind raced through numerous possibilities now that an Oxford University linguist had confirmed her wild theory that the new whale songs were, in fact, a binary encoded message. She wanted to apply that knowledge to other recorded whale songs as soon as possible. Joyce Harmer's algorithms and programs now resided on her laptop computer on the car's passenger's side floor. She hoped she could make a little more sense of the data once she got into the office and had Lisa Henry's help. She also thought about placing a call to Stirling Cristof in San Francisco to get his take on the findings.

Feeling a little more collected, Myra pulled back out onto the street and continued into the office. When she arrived, Lisa Henry hadn't yet reported to work. She fired off an email to Stirling Cristof, not certain whether he'd be in his office yet, or not. He tended to be a late riser. To her surprise, he responded almost instantly, then initiated a video call.

"Your friend the Oxford philologist says the whales are sending some kind of warning," explained Myra.

"Are you serious?" Cristof's eyebrows rose. "Who are they warning?"

"Little green dolphins on Saturn—or maybe a jeweler in Santa Monica—if we believe your friend." Myra laughed nervously, then gave a more reasoned explanation. "She says it's someone called 'the keepers of the rings.' It just so happens that the whales changed their song at the same time as Jerome Quinn announced the Saturn mission he's organizing. Because of that, she's speculating that the 'keepers' are connected to Saturn in some way."

Cristof chewed his lip and thought about what Myra told him. "It's not unreasonable," he said after a moment. "I take it you don't agree with her assessment."

"I don't know what to think." Myra ran her fingers through her hair. "It just seems so incredible and there's always the chance she's got it wrong." Myra sat back and looked at her bookshelf while she weighed different possibilities. Finally, she turned back to Stirling. "She seemed pretty convinced about the warning part and I buy her explanation about how she came to that conclusion. It's the 'keeper of the rings' part that really bothers me."

"Let's table that for the time being," said Stir. "Rest assured, she'll be checking her preliminary conclusions with her colleagues. Did she say anything about how the whales are delivering their warning?"

"Professor Harmer says that the language is a binary-type sequence, as we suggested." She shrugged, as though apologizing for guessing correctly.

"That's not what I mean." Cristof shook his head. "How are they transmitting? It's not like the whales are using radios."

"I didn't think about that." Myra sat back stunned. She thought for a moment and frowned. "That must mean the people from Saturn—or whoever the whales are warning—are listening in."

Cristof nodded slowly. "It also means that the whales know they have an audience. They expect to be heard. If it is someone from Saturn, they're watching us."

*

Pilot kangaroo-hopped through the Moon base's corridors telling Jefferson about the president's phone call and asking him to follow. "If you're still willing to consider commanding this mission, this call could affect you as much as me."

Pilot frowned and slowed his pace when he heard Jefferson's labored breathing. Once they arrived at the office, Pilot waved a huffing, puffing Colonel Jefferson to a chair while he picked up the office phone and asked the person on the other end to put him through to the president.

"Hello, Mr. Thomas," came Oscar Van der Wald's voice. "I've been following the progress of the *Aristarchus* and I'm calling to congratulate you on your initiative."

"Thank you, sir," said Pilot, genuinely flattered. He sat down behind the desk. "However, I must say that I'm caught off guard. I certainly wasn't expecting a phone call today."

"My call isn't entirely social." The president's words took on a dark timber. "I have concerns about your venture."

"I can assure you, Mr. President, that we're taking every safety precaution…" Pilot's mind raced, trying to anticipate what the president would say next.

"I'm sure you are." Van der Wald impatiently cut him off. "We're more concerned about what you might find and how it may affect the interests of the United States."

Pilot widened his eyes and sat back in the chair while he found his voice. "Mr. President, this is purely a scientific endeavor."

"Scientific endeavors routinely generate more … how shall we say … tangible results." Van der Wald paused, letting that sink in. "We are naturally concerned about what your mission means for national security."

"In what way, sir?" Pilot's eyes narrowed. "We've been exploring the solar system for the past century, both with manned spacecraft and unmanned probes. There's never been any evidence for intelligent life outside of the Earth."

"I'm more concerned with intelligent life that started on Earth." The president's tone—already dark—turned menacing. "Specifically, I'm concerned about a private corporation establishing a foothold on another world that's not U.S. territory."

"Are you suggesting that we might try to break away from the United States, sir?" Pilot stood up, his mouth hanging open for a moment while he tried to find suitable words. "Sir, Quinn Corp along with two of our competitors have bases on the Moon. We've never shown any sign of trying to form our own government up here. It's not in our best interest."

"That may be true, but the Moon was established as United States territory during the lunar landings of the '40s. We have some claim on Mars since we're the only country to have sent a mission there. After that, you're moving on to completely undeclared territory. You're certain to make many discoveries, Mr. Thomas. Who will those discoveries belong to, the United States or Quinn Corp?"

Pilot started sweating. His knees weakened and he had to sit down again. "What are you suggesting?"

"I would like a representative of the United States military to join your crew'" The president's tone turned gentle and reasonable. "Captain Natalie Freeman of the Navy."

"Absolutely not." Pilot didn't care for a moment who he was talking to. "We've already selected a mission commander. I won't have his authority undermined."

Jefferson made a cutting motion across his throat. Pilot uttered a hasty apology and covered the phone's receiver. "Who does he want to send?" asked the one-time astronaut.

"Some Navy captain named Natalie Freeman."

"Natalie Freeman?" asked Jefferson.

Pilot nodded, eyes narrowed.

"Take her." The colonel's tone was like an order.

Pilot nearly dropped the receiver. "You can't be serious!"

"First off, she's about the best officer the Navy has. I've followed her career for years. You need hands and she's one of the best you could possibly find," said Jefferson. "Second, I haven't said 'yes' to this mission yet. She would be a great mission commander."

"I don't want her to be mission commander." Pilot huffed. "I want you. If I can't have you, I have other choices already lined up."

"I'd be her second-in-command any day," said Jefferson. Then, he pointed to the phone. "That's the President of the United States you're tying up there."

"Oh." Pilot hastily returned to the line. "I'm sorry to keep you waiting, Mr. President."

"That's quite all right," said Van der Wald. "I wasn't so much thinking about having Captain Freeman aboard as the mission commander. Rather, I'd be willing to have her aboard in an advisory capacity. If that's all right with you and Jerome Quinn."

Pilot took a deep breath and glared at Jefferson. "Very well.

It would seem Captain Freeman comes highly recommended. We'll bring her up to the Moon on Monday. Is that fine with you, sir?"

The president agreed and hung up. Pilot held the receiver for a few moments before setting it back in the cradle. Jefferson nodded approvingly. "With her aboard, you've just increased the odds I'll say 'yes' to this mission," he said.

"I hope so," said Pilot. "Let me show you to the dining hall and we'll grab some dinner, then I'll show you to your quarters."

Just as they stood, John O'Connell appeared in the office doorway. "I just came across some chatter on the Internet. I think you'd better see it. Something about whales talking to Saturn."

When Lisa Henry arrived at work, Myra asked her to examine Joyce Harmer's translation programs. Lisa sat down in front of the computer and spent much of the morning looking over the programs while Myra paced back and forth behind her. She wanted to interrupt but knew she should stay out of the way as much as possible. She wracked her brain trying to decide if the phrase about the 'keeper of the rings' could mean anything other than someone who lived on or near Saturn.

"Well, the binary translation algorithm looks good to me," said Lisa. "The Oxford people really are seeing sensible patterns in the whale song and they've identified several words in the new message. Their translation looks good, given the limited vocabulary."

"So, can we use this program to translate other whale songs?" Myra stepped over to her desk and picked up a bristly piece of whale baleen.

Lisa shook her head, then leaned back in the chair, propping her feet on the desk. "I don't think so. First off, we only have five words. Secondly, if this new song is a warning, wouldn't it make sense if it was in the language of the people the whales were trying to warn?"

Myra looked at the baleen as though she would find the answer there. "It does and it ties in with Stirling Cristof's ideas about the songs." She placed the baleen back on the desk. "The problem is, if that's true, none of this actually helps us translate the older songs."

"Maybe, maybe not," said Lisa. "The Oxford people can tell that they're hearing a litany in the older songs, but can't necessarily make out the words. Maybe the people the whales are talking to can help us understand the whales' native vocabulary. After all, someone had to teach the whales the new song."

Just then, the phone rang. Lisa reached over and picked it up. A moment later, she handed the receiver to Myra. "It's some guy who calls himself Pilot."

✳

Two days later, Myra Lee and Lisa Henry boarded a shuttle bound for the Moon. Though all three companies that had factories on the Moon offered tour packages, they were quite expensive—well beyond the budget of a scientist or a technician employed by an under-funded oceanographic institute. As such, neither Myra nor Lisa had made the trip before.

On the way to the Moon, Myra virtually demanded to sit in a window seat so she could see everything along the way. She looked forward to a distraction from the problem of the whale songs. The more Harmer and her colleagues examined the message, the more convinced they were it was intended for 'ring keepers' or 'ring watchers' of some kind.

Lisa lay the aisle seat back and fell into a light doze. When the flight attendant came by, Myra was delighted to try the gooey 'astronaut food' that had been the fare of shuttle crews for most of a century. She regretted it, though, when her stomach started doing flip-flops after a few bites. Though used to ships rocking on waves, she wasn't used to null gravity. Lisa woke up long enough to eat her meal, then fell asleep again.

When the shuttle finally landed on the Moon, Myra gratefully unbuckled her seatbelt and pushed herself upright only to crash into the luggage rack above her head. Lisa held onto Myra's arm and helped her navigate the corridors to Pilot's office. He welcomed them and asked them to sit. "I gather you're on the verge of quite an extraordinary breakthrough," he said.

"Possibly," said Myra. "We have a crude translation of a

whale song, but that translation doesn't seem to help us translate any other whale songs. Either we've got it wrong or the whales are bilingual. If the latter's true, our findings will be extraordinary, but perhaps little more than a curiosity."

"On the contrary." Pilot stepped over to a coffee pot and offered some to them. Lisa accepted while Myra politely declined. "I believe you've discovered the whales are speaking to someone called the 'keepers of the rings.'"

Myra leaned forward. "How do you know that?"

Pilot poured two cups of coffee and handed one to Lisa. With the other cup, he gestured toward the computer on his desk. "You and your colleague, Dr. Cristof, have insecure Internet connections."

"You mean you were spying on our conversation?" Myra asked, incensed. "What gives you the right?"

Pilot shrugged. "Quinitite's used in almost all computers these days. When the Oceanographic Institute bought your computer, they signed a user agreement granting us license to any information transmitted or received from that computer." He took a sip of coffee. "It's allowed under the Gates Act from the beginning of the century."

"I thought the act only governed information regarding commerce," said Lisa, more curious, than angry.

Pilot nodded and perched on the edge of the desk. "This *is* a matter of commerce." Sitting the coffee cup down, he retrieved a bound report from the bookshelf at his elbow. He opened it to a chart and handed it to Myra. "The conditions on Saturn's moon Titan are almost identical to those of the early Earth. We know the atmosphere is full of biocarbons. It's not impossible that some form of life has evolved there. Understanding life on Titan could help us understand life on Earth better."

"Pushing biological and medical science forward hundreds of years," affirmed Myra. "But..."

Pilot held up his hand, cutting her off. "I'm looking for a team that can run our biological scanners and communication gear. I've read through both of your resumes." He nodded toward Lisa. "You're an audio and computer technician par excellence. Not only can you assist Dr. Lee with the scientific analysis, you're well qualified to operate the communication's equipment."

Lisa frowned. "If you think I'm going to be like that woman in the old television show that wears a red mini skirt and says, 'Hailing frequencies open, Captain,' every five minutes, you've got another thing coming."

Pilot rolled his eyes both at the comment and Myra's laughter. He sipped his coffee.

Myra put her hands on her knees and leaned forward. "I'm still waiting to hear how I can help you. I'm a cetacean biologist…"

"Who minored in organic chemistry," finished Pilot. "You have the knowledge we need to find the biological compounds we're looking for, and perhaps more importantly, the two of you have demonstrated that you make an excellent team."

"Plus we've been studying whales that are talking to 'the keepers of the rings,'" said Myra with more than a little sarcasm.

"Exactly," said Pilot, unfazed.

"Well, I hate to burst your bubble…" Myra stood quickly and gasped as her stomach rumbled. She sat down again, looking deflated. "Fact is, we don't know if our translation is right. Even if it is, it's only speculation that the message is meant for someone at Saturn. It could easily be coincidence that the whales altered their song at the same time as Quinn's announcement. Other things were happening around the world at the same time."

"I know that." Pilot's eyes narrowed and he sat the coffee cup down. His voice turned icy. "Don't lecture me like a child until you hear me out." He hopped off the desk, then sat in the chair and folded his hands. "I propose that your colleagues—Dr. Cristof and Dr. Harmer—come to work for Quinn Corp. They'll have access to a ship and all the computers, equipment, and other resources they need to continue the research you started. Your team will have better funding and facilities than they do now." He rubbed the bridge of his nose. "You see, I'm betting they're right and if these ring keepers are from Titan—or anywhere else in the Saturn system—you will hold the key to communicating with that life."

"What if they're wrong?" asked Myra, quietly.

"Then I still have an excellent biosciences and communication team and Quinn Corp still benefits from Harmer and Cristof's research."

Myra sat back and closed her eyes. If the whales really were talking to someone on Saturn, she wanted more than anything to know who that was and why. "There's one other problem." Sorely tempted as she was, reality battled with curiosity. "What makes you think I'm cut out to be an astronaut?"

"You should have seen her on the flight up here." Lisa nudged her boss's arm.

Pilot shook his head and sighed. "I want the people in charge of biosciences and communications to be experts. I want you to be able to talk to whom or whatever we find. I think you two are the best qualified to do that."

"So why not bring Cristof and Harmer up here and leave us behind on Earth?" asked Myra.

"Neither of them are audio technicians and neither of them have a background in biochemistry. Even if there is no one at Saturn for you to talk to, I still need people who can help me achieve the primary mission goals." Pilot grinned wryly. "Besides, Harmer's a landlubber and I gather Cristof prefers his office to a boat. The two of you are used to spending time at sea and we're going on a voyage through the biggest sea of them all. If you think you're having trouble with null gravity, think how it would be for them."

"I'll have to think about it." Myra chewed on her lip for a moment. "I think I could use that coffee now ... or better yet, something a little stronger."

Chapter 8
Assembly

Jonathan Jefferson sent his resignation to Martin-Intelsoft the morning after he met with Alonzo Thomas. Pilot said he could go back to Earth to retrieve anything he needed from his house. "I have my toothbrush and some spare underwear," he replied. "Will you provide me with a uniform?"

"You'll have everything you need," said Pilot. "We'll allow the crew to wear civilian clothes off-duty, but we have coveralls, coats, boots, and so forth that we recommend for on-duty wear."

"Is there a weight allowance?"

Pilot quoted a figure. "Still, we can be quite flexible. A few kilos one way or the other isn't going to affect our velocity much given the ship's design."

Jefferson returned to Earth for a day, retrieved some belongings and made arrangements for the care of his house. Two days later, he found himself back on the Moon and outfitted in a space suit, walking out on the lunar surface. The sand crunched like snow under his feet and he turned and looked back at his footprints. He shook his head when he saw a work crew drive over his tracks, eroding them away almost as fast as they were created. A few miles away, a fence surrounded another set of footprints, those belonging to Neil Armstrong and Buzz Aldrin. Those footprints would be there for centuries, until micrometeorites erased them.

A Quinn Corp technician named Vanda Berko led Jefferson to a scaffold. The two climbed a ladder and Jefferson found himself standing above one of the quinitite sail frames. From that vantage, he watched as a device mounted on rails rolled over the frame, unfurling a fine sheet of aluminum. Robotic arms on mobile platforms followed and attached the aluminum fabric to the frame.

"It looks like foil," explained Berko, "but it's actually tightly compressed aluminum fiber. The earliest solar sails used flat sheets of aluminum pressed as thin as possible, but it was still thicker than ideal. It needed to be compressed into nanosatellites, folded and unfolded. In the Moon's low gravity, we can extrude the aluminum thread directly onto the sail frames and not worry about it rupturing or tearing as its deployed."

"Impressive." Jefferson watched the giant machine continued along the track, weaving sail as it went. "How long will this take?"

"We're hoping to deploy the sails later this week," said Berko.

*

Natalie Freeman arrived on the Moon in her full dress uniform, carrying a duffel bag. Neb O'Connell showed her to her quarters and gave her directions to the dining room. "Is there anything else I can show you?" he asked, breathless.

She smiled. "It seems like you're in a hurry to get out of here. Is something the matter?"

O'Connell shook his head. "Nothing at all, ma'am. It's just that they're getting ready to lift the *Aristarchus's* fuselage into lunar orbit and I don't want to miss it."

"Well, why didn't you say so?" chided Freeman. "That sounds like something I don't want to miss, either."

"I thought you might want to get comfortable." O'Connell shifted uncomfortably from one foot to the other. "Freshen up or something."

Freeman shook her head. "I've been in the Navy a long time, Mr. O'Connell. I care a lot more about the ship that's gonna carry me across the water than taking a few minutes to 'pretty up.'" She batted her eyelashes at him.

O'Connell made an indiscernible noise—something halfway between a moan and a gurgle—then quickly recovered. "This way, then." He led her toward the vehicle assembly building's observation deck.

Numerous other members of the *Aristarchus* crew had already gathered. Natalie Freeman took in their faces. Two women stood together. One was young with long, blondish hair. She leaned languorously on a railing, but her blue eyes watched absolutely everything happening outside the windows of the observation deck. Natalie surmised that must be Lisa Henry. The other woman—Dr. Myra Lee—was slightly taller with a sun-darkened face and dark brown hair—a few strands streaked white. While Lisa remained still, Myra kept adjusting her position, as though trying to find the best possible vantage.

A lanky, young man, with a mop of wiry hair and blue coveralls, watched the action happening outside with intense interest and carried on a fervent conversation via handheld radio. From the sound of his voice, Natalie could tell he was Alonzo Thomas, the pilot. Yet another man was unmistakable to Natalie even with white hair. He was tall, handsome, and wore the same coveralls as Pilot—Jonathan Jefferson, the last astronaut to walk on Mars. Jefferson turned around and caught sight of Natalie, then stepped between two other people, extending his hand.

"Captain Freeman, I presume."

Natalie took Jefferson's hand. "The pleasure is all mine, Colonel." She looked around. "I take it I've arrived just in time for a big show."

"Indeed," said Jefferson. "They're getting ready to lift the fuselage of the *Aristarchus*." He led her back to the spot he'd occupied near the window.

Looking out, she saw the large, silver spheroid that was the hull of the *Aristarchus*. Scaffoldings were pulled back against the walls of the vehicle assembly building. The two halves of the roof over the giant ball crept apart. Even with the reflections in the observing gallery's glass, she could see bright stars clearly through the opening. Alonzo Thomas—finished with his radio conversation for a time—stepped over and introduced himself while the roof opened. "I believe you've already met Captain Jefferson," he said. The captain and colonel nodded. Pilot waved over a short man, with a neat, pencil-thin mustache. "Dr. Kurata Nagamine is our chief planetary scientist."

Natalie shook Dr. Nagamine's hand. "Pleased to meet you."

"John O'Connell, whom I believe you've met, will be serving as Dr. Nagamine's assistant as well as taking charge of the ship's astronomy sensors." A radio call interrupted Pilot.

Together, Natalie and Dr. Nagamine moved up to the window again. The roof overhead was wide open.

Four shuttles drifted down through the open roof. The sun shining off their metallic hulls made them resemble delicate snowflakes. Jefferson turned to Natalie and explained these ships were similar to the *Aristarchus's* landing craft, except each of these was equipped with a pair of grappling arms on the front and a booster assembly in the rear. The arms grabbed hold of bars mounted to the spheroid.

"Steady ... easy," Pilot said into the radio.

Once each of the four shuttles reached position, they hovered in place for a few minutes. Radio chatter indicated the shuttle pilots were coordinating clocks and synchronizing their onboard computers. When they all indicated readiness, Pilot called the order to lift.

Tongues of flame flared out from each of the four shuttles' booster assemblies. Natalie wondered whether the shuttles were going to be able to lift the great spheroid. At that moment, Myra Lee leaned over to get a better look and lifted herself off the ground, reminding Natalie of the Moon's lower gravity. The fuselage began to rise, seemingly an inch at a time. As the shuttles gained momentum, the sphere rose faster and faster until it cleared the roof. Natalie found herself cheering with the other people gathered.

Pilot breathed a relieved sigh, then turned to face the assembled group. "I want the day tech crew to assemble their gear. We'll move to the *Aristarchus* first thing in the morning." At that, the group began to break up and move out into the corridor. Pilot stepped up to Natalie. "Captain Freeman, have you had lunch yet?"

"No," said Natalie.

"Would you join me, please? There's a lot we need to discuss." Pilot led the way out to the corridor with Natalie close behind.

*

Jonathan Jefferson approached Myra Lee and Lisa Henry who loitered in the observation area as the others left. Myra still stared upward through the rooftop. The silver fuselage had grown tiny, barely distinguishable from the stars visible through the roof.

"What do you think, Myra?" asked Lisa. "Are you ready to join this crew?"

"I don't know what to think." Myra shook her head, still looking upward.

"It'll be quite an adventure," said Lisa.

"And there will be times when it'll be very boring," Jefferson interrupted.

Myra finally tore her gaze from the sky and looked into Jefferson's blue eyes. "So, what do you think of having a cetacean biologist aboard your ship as 'Biosciences Manager,' or whatever Pilot calls it?"

"Well, if the whales really are talking to some kind of life near Saturn, I can't think of anyone more qualified to talk to it." The colonel flashed a disarmingly boyish smile. "I have no doubt that either one of you can handle the radio and sensory equipment on that ship. I've looked it over. I think even I can operate it." They all laughed, lightly.

"What kind of life do you think we're going to find on Saturn, Captain?" asked Lisa.

Jefferson hesitated for a moment. He hadn't been called 'Captain' in a long time. He had to remind himself in most navies, the rank of captain was actually equivalent to his rank of lieutenant colonel. "Whatever it is, it has to be something that's never been seen by the space probes we've sent out that way. If it's on Saturn, it would have to be something that floats in the atmosphere the way whales drift through the water."

Myra smiled at the image. "I'd like to see creatures like that," she said. "What about something that might live on Titan?"

"Well," said Jefferson. "It would have to be something that was invisible to the Huygens probe that landed on the surface earlier this century. I can't imagine anything living on Titan would be big enough to send signals to the whales."

The halves of the vehicle assembly building's roof moved toward each other and Lisa led the way out of the observing deck. Myra and Jonathan followed. "So, does this mean that you've decided to join us on this expedition?" asked Jonathan.

Myra smiled. "Well, we're part of Pilot's technical crew. Let me spend some time up in that ball tomorrow and I'll let you know."

*

Neb O'Connell packed his last pair of socks into the suitcase, then closed the lid. He moved over to the computer console and sat down with a sigh. He pinged his mother's computer. Her face appeared on the console a few minutes later. "Hello, John." She put on a brave smile, which disintegrated into a coughing fit.

"Hi, mom," he said, unable to hide his concern.

She looked back into the camera. "Don't you look so worried, I'm fine. I just need my inhaler." She reached out of the camera's range and Neb heard the puff of the inhaler. When she returned, she looked a little better. "How are you doing? I've been following the *Aristarchus* project on the news. They say they launched the fuselage today."

"Just a little while ago." Neb nodded. "I've just been packing up to go aboard."

"I'm so proud of you, John."

"Mom," said Neb, "I'm worried."

"You'll do fine," she said confidently, her face breaking into a proud smile.

Neb shook his head and sniffed. "Not about me." His voice cracked. "I'm worried about you."

His mom frowned, then coughed again. She held a tissue to her lips and spit out some phlegm. "Your brother is here with me." She leaned in close to her camera and Neb felt the intensity of her gaze across the miles. "I will be here, John. I will be here to welcome you with open arms when you get back home. I wouldn't miss the parade they'll throw for you for all the world." She sat back. "Now you go do your job and don't you worry about me."

"Okay, Mom." Neb suppressed a sniffle.

"Don't forget to send messages," she said. "I don't want to hear about you only through the news."

"I love you, mom."

"I love you, too. Now make me proud."

Neb was too tear-choked to continue. He reached over and

terminated the connection with one hand while the fingers of the other hand rested on the image of his mother on the computer screen.

*

Pilot sat with Natalie Freeman in the Quinn Corp cafeteria. Untouched trays of food sat in front of them. "Captain Freeman," Pilot poked at a pork chop with his fork, "you pose a difficult problem for me."

"You didn't invite me on this mission, and frankly, you don't know what to do with me." Natalie smiled cautiously.

"That's it, in a nutshell," said Pilot.

Natalie sat back and removed her hat. Pilot's mouth fell open as though taken aback by her crew cut. "If it's any help, my first tour of duty was aboard submarines. Though I was an officer, my first captain insisted that the juniors work a number of the jobs. I have experience as a mechanic and an electrician."

"Those are very useful skills." Pilot finally grabbed a knife, cut off a piece of the pork chop, and lifted it to his mouth. "But does the captain of the U.S.S. *Sherman* easily step down to pick up her tool kit again?"

Natalie shrugged, then looked down at her plate. "I'm used to following orders."

As Pilot chewed, Jefferson entered the cafeteria. Pilot swallowed and took a drink. "It's Captain Jefferson's orders I'm concerned about you following."

"What is your rank structure aboard the ship?" asked Natalie.

"The captain has final authority over the ship. Under him are six managers—the pilot manager, communications and biosciences manager, sail master, sensory systems manager, technical systems manager, and ship's doctor. The rest of the people are crew and scientific staff."

Jefferson made it through the line and arrived at the table as Pilot finished his explanation. "What the ship does not have is an executive officer," he said as he sat down.

"The ship only has a crew of twenty-five," said Pilot, impatiently.

"Still, it would be good to have an exec who could be in

charge of C-and-C when I'm off duty or away from the ship,"
said Jefferson.

"As Pilot Manager, that's my job," said Pilot a little more
sharply than he intended.

"With all due respect," interjected Natalie. "The job of a
pilot—in the old shipboard sense—was that of navigator and
helmsman. That's difficult to do and watch over all the other
jobs as well."

"Okay." Pilot tensed. "You'll be the executive officer. But
what do we do about your rank? We can't go around calling
both of you captain."

Natalie and Jonathan looked at each other, then back at
Pilot. "Why not?" both asked in unison.

"Won't there be confusion about who's in charge?"

"You're clearly a civilian, Mr. Alonzo." Natalie smiled
broadly. Pilot sat back and huffed, as though insulted. "Colonel
Jefferson is my senior. He's clearly in charge of the ship."

"Hey," said Jefferson, pretending insult. "I only *look* older
than you. I'm prematurely gray!"

"Sir, I was watching your Moon landings when I was in
kindergarten." Natalie remembered the first time she dressed
in coveralls and wore a cardboard 'space helmet.'

"Ouch!" Jefferson held his hands over his chest as though
mortally wounded.

Pilot shook his head. "Okay, I wasn't planning on having
an executive officer, but have it your way. It sounds like the
two of you will work well together." He ate the rest of his meal,
then excused himself, saying he had work to finish before going to the ship the next day.

Once he left, Natalie turned to Jefferson. "So, what exactly
is this Mr. Thomas hiding?"

The next day, Myra Lee and Lisa Henry floated above the communications and biosciences station on the *Aristarchus's* command and control deck. With no sails attached to the ship, it
wasn't rotating and there was no gravity. They ran through
several simulations, making sure they understood how the
equipment operated. Lisa was impressed with the console's

simple labels and straightforward operation. It only took her about an hour to learn how to work the communications equipment itself, which allowed her time to work with Myra, learning about the ship's biosensors and computer network.

"This is Quinn Shuttle Seven calling *Aristarchus*," said a voice from the console's speaker.

"Hey, that's not a simulation, is it?" asked Myra.

"Nope, better answer it." Lisa scanned the console quickly, then found the correct button. "This is *Aristarchus*, go ahead Quinn Shuttle Seven."

"We're ready to attach the first sail," came the voice of the shuttle's pilot.

Lisa looked toward the pilot's console and beckoned Alonzo. He drifted over and touched a button. "We're ready on this end," said Pilot. Then he nodded to Lisa who touched another button.

"Steerage crew one, Quinn Shuttle Seven is ready to attach," she said.

"Acknowledged," came Vanda Berko's response from the steerage room.

Lisa hit the button again. "Hailing frequencies closed, sir." She smirked at Thomas, who just shook his head.

The room pitched and rolled as the sail was attached. The motion was only slight, but enough that Myra lost all sense of up and down, left and right. Her stomach heaved and she vomited up globules that floated in the air, then blushed bright red.

Neb O'Connell belched loudly in response. Apparently his stomach threatened to follow suit as he covered his mouth. He turned away quickly and pushed off from his console to the storage locker. Using a porta-vac, he cleaned up the mess.

"Thanks," said Myra, sheepishly. Pilot brought her a bottle of water with a lid and straw. She sucked the contents down.

"Don't mention it," said O'Connell, holding the vacuum well away from himself, so he wouldn't have to smell the contents.

Myra looked toward Pilot. "Still want me for the crew?"

Pilot nodded, though his grimace betrayed some misgivings. "Fortunately, we'll have gravity for most of the journey."

*

Throughout the day, teams of three shuttles lifted sails from the lunar surface. Two grabbed on to the strut near the sail's base, while a third steadied the top—the part that would be farthest away from the ship. Two astronauts wearing magnetic boots stood on the ship's outer hull, and as the sail approached, installed the outer vacuum gasket and guided the sail's mast into the bearing assembly.

Within *Aristarchus*, space-suited teams working in the sealed steerage rooms waited for the mast to appear through the bearing and then they carefully placed the inner vacuum gaskets around the mast, and guided it into the motor assembly where they locked it down. If the sails had been made of mylar and the masts made of aluminum as originally proposed in the twentieth century, the sails would have been much too massive to have been held in place by such a flimsy structure. However, the quinitite masts and spun aluminum sails were held quite securely.

Just before shuttles hoisted the final sail from the lunar surface, Pilot located a bottle of champagne. He showed it around to the crew in C-and-C. It was an expensive vintage, bottled in France about ten years before. "This is a very special bottle, for a very special occasion." He left C-and-C, suited up, and went into the final steerage room.

Using a set of hex wrenches, he disconnected the mast bearing to enlarge the hole. With a carefully planned push, he shoved the bottle through the hole, then replaced the bearing. He looked through the bearing and watched the bottle of champagne drift slowly away, in lunar orbit like the *Aristarchus* itself. He signaled the shuttles on the Moon. "We're ready to attach the final sail."

Chapter 9
Launching the Aristarchus

Captain Jonathan Jefferson sat behind the controls of *Aristarchus's* last shuttle still on the Moon. Behind him were the last five crewmembers to board the new ship. The astronomer—Dr. Nagamine—sat next to him. Jefferson pulled the joystick back and the shuttle rumbled forward, then lifted off the runway. A wide grin formed as he held the joystick again. To actually fly a spaceship after ten years of sitting behind a desk, working at a computer and designing nanobots made him breathless.

He pushed the joystick ever so slightly forward and rolled the shuttle to starboard, taking a long, low path around the Moon. The shuttle had big, wrap-around windows that allowed an excellent view for all of the passengers. He pulled the joystick back again, causing the shuttle to rise slightly, presenting the full Earth to the passengers. He smiled when he heard a collective gasp from behind and next to him.

Dr. Nagamine heaved a deep sigh. "We astronomers spend so much time trying to get away from the Earth and its atmosphere, that we don't always appreciate its beauty. I'm going to miss it." He looked over at Jefferson. "What about you?"

"I will … eventually," he said.

"Earth is our home, Captain." Nagamine narrowed his eyes. "Surely you above all know how precious it is."

"It is precious," said Jefferson, "but I don't see it as the only place we humans can consider home. In recent years, I've been feeling a kind of homesickness for Mars. I'll be glad to see it again. I'm looking forward to seeing the other planets we're going to encounter." He moved the joystick again, causing the shuttle to roll back toward the Moon. "There's an old song about being born under a wandering star, about never being able to settle down. I think something of that is part of every person."

"Perhaps..." The astronomer nodded to himself as the Earth moved away and behind the shuttle.

Jefferson took the shuttle low over the Moon again, as close as he could to the Martin-Intelsoft factory without violating their space. As he brought the shuttle into a higher orbit, the passengers gasped in unison.

"I think you have found your wandering star," said Dr. Nagamine.

As he'd planned, the *Aristarchus* rose over the Moon's horizon in all of its glory. Spinning slowly, the ship could be described any number of ways. The ship's doctor who grew up on the eastern plains of Colorado described a gleaming windmill. Next to him sat a mechanic, whose children had just finished college, and who was starting her dream retirement in space. "It reminds me of the pinwheels my kids used to play with." Jonathan Jefferson imagined a giant metal sunflower, carefully sculpted by a master craftsman.

Jefferson pushed the joystick over to the side, easing the shuttle into a gentle spin. For a moment, the *Aristarchus* appeared to stop, then spin backward. "What's going on?" asked the mechanic.

"Just getting used to flying this thing," said Jefferson. He adjusted the controls and the *Aristarchus* seemed to stop spinning again. He applied a slight bit of reverse thrust, so that the shuttle held position relative to the mother ship.

Looking around, Dr. Nagamine noticed the Moon now appeared to be spinning around the shuttle and the *Aristarchus*. "What's happened? Aren't we going aboard the ship?"

Without answering, the captain turned on the intercom so they could hear Pilot's words from the *Aristarchus's* central core.

"Since childhood, most of us have been taught that Copernicus discovered the sun was the center of our solar system," said Pilot. "However, long before Copernicus was born—in 280 BC—a Greek astronomer called Aristarchus of Samos made long, careful observations of planetary motions. By watching the Earth's shadow on the Moon during a lunar eclipse, he deduced that the sun must be much larger than the Earth and much farther away. He reasoned that it was ridiculous for so large a body as the Sun to orbit such a small body as the Earth, so he put the Sun at the center of the solar system. History largely forgot Aristarchus of Samos because most of his writings were burned with the great library at Alexandria in Egypt. We do not forget. It's for that reason..."

Just then, a small, green object drifted past the shuttle and smashed into the front of the *Aristarchus* sending up thousands of bright green stars and golden champagne globules. It was the bottle that Pilot had ejected through the sail bearing, sent on several orbits around the Moon to wind up in the ship's path.

*

"We christen thee *Aristarchus*," finished Pilot. The champagne bottle's impact was little more than a light thud, but the crystalline shards reflecting the sunlight provided a dazzling show. He floated in the central core of the ship, looking through the great window of the pilot's berth. Six others floated in the core with him, admiring the view from the great window. All applauded at the end of his speech. Others aboard the ship watched the champagne bottle strike from other forward windows. Leaning forward, Pilot saw the final shuttle, appearing motionless in front of the ship. He thought he could make out the forms of Jonathan Jefferson and Kurata Nagamine in the front seats. He gave them a thumbs up and thought he saw one in return from the captain.

"Permission to dock?" came Jefferson's voice from Pilot's tablet computer.

"Permission granted," said Pilot. "Welcome to your new home." He looked behind, to the crewmembers with him. "Look sharp, the captain's coming aboard. To your duty stations."

The men and women behind him pushed forward and shook the pilot's hand, then caught the doors rotating around them which provided access to the decks "below" and the welcome tug of simulated gravity. With some regret, Pilot followed them from the hub.

*

Captain Jefferson climbed down the ladder into *Aristarchus's* command and control center and surveyed the deck. Lisa Henry sat at the communications station. Nebraska John

O'Connell watched the external sensors from his post. Dr. Garcia, the ship's physician came in behind the captain and took his post at the ship's life support station. He'd been aboard before, but upon inspecting the ship's supplies, realized they required a few essentials before leaving Earth.

At C-and-C's central console Natalie Freeman reviewed the ship's status. She looked up and caught Jefferson's eye. "Captain on deck," she said from long habit. Even though she knew that most of the people aboard the ship were not military personnel, she was still a bit disconcerted when no one stood at attention.

"As you were," said Jefferson, out of similar habit.

Pilot climbed down the ladder and moved to his station at the front of the deck. He brought up a plot of the Earth/Moon system on the large display above his console. He displayed the *Aristarchus's* position over the plot. "I'd say a short burst from thrusters to give us some impulse in the right direction and we'll be on our way."

Jefferson stepped past Natalie Freeman and looked up at Pilot's display. Quietly, he asked a couple of questions, then looked over to the astrosciences station. "Mr. O'Connell, what's the status of lunar traffic?"

O'Connell turned around and checked the displays. "One shuttle has just departed the General Nanotech plant. Based on Pilot's orbital projection, it's well clear of our course."

"Ms. Henry," called the captain. "Send a general notice to the lunar facilities with our projected course."

"Will do," she said.

Jefferson smiled at Pilot. "You may fire your thrusters."

Pilot typed in a short command sequence on his computer console, then pushed one final button. There was a gentle nudge, nothing too auspicious. "We are on a hyperbolic orbit that will take us out of the Earth/Moon system in about two days. Then it's sit back and enjoy the six-month cruise to Mars."

Applause and cheers broke out. Neb stood and gave Pilot a high five while Jefferson, still getting used to the sloped deck, stepped to the command center and shook Natalie Freeman's hand. The captains heard more cheers echoing from the corridors as word spread through the ship.

"Very good, Pilot," said Jefferson. He turned around and looked at the command crew. "Well done, everyone." Several murmured acknowledgments continued as everyone settled back into their seats. Dr. Garcia chewed his lip, looking worried that he'd forgotten something. Lisa Henry faced the pilot's console, watching the slow-moving image of the *Aristarchus* as it moved along the projected course. Neb O'Connell was tense, waiting for something to happen. After a few moments, he turned back to his console to check the sensory data.

Natalie Freeman stood up from the command seat. She held her hand toward the chair. "You have the bridge," she said.

"And you?" asked Jefferson, genuinely curious.

"I just want to check on a couple crewmembers."

✳

Natalie Freeman left C-and-C and made her way toward the crew cabins. She came to Myra Lee's door and knocked. Just as she was about to knock again, she heard a muffled, "Come in," from the other side of the door.

Inside, Natalie found Myra curled up on her bed. Her skin had a vaguely greenish tinge. Most of her baggage was scattered around the room, still packed.

"How are you doing, Myra?" Natalie pulled up a chair and sat by the biologist's side.

"If I didn't know any better, I'd say I was seasick."

"You probably are motion sick." Natalie unbuttoned one of the pockets on her coveralls and removed a pill. "Here. This will help."

Myra took the pill and swallowed it down without water.

"It's not easy to get used to this simulated gravity," said Natalie. "I've spent my whole adult life on ships. Even in the worst storms, it's easier to tell which way is 'down' than it is in this can."

"That's true." Myra sat up tentatively on the bed. "I feel like I'm in a giant fast-moving Ferris wheel."

"Well, that's more or less what you *are* on," said Natalie with a motherly smile. "Are you sorry you came along on this trip? I'm afraid there's no turning back now."

"Bad time to ask." Myra quickly covered her mouth as she burped. "But I am beginning to wonder what I'm going to do for six months. It seemed like an exciting adventure just a few days ago. All of a sudden, I realize just how long it'll be before we get to Mars. After that, it's another year to Jupiter."

"In some ways, you've got it easy," said Natalie. "You've got the whale song translation project to keep you occupied en route."

Myra looked around the room. "Yeah, and I've got some unpacking to do. What about you?"

Natalie stood and stepped over to an empty bookshelf. She ran her finger along the top, then looked at it. "I have work that will keep me occupied. After all, I'm a Navy captain on assignment for the president. There's a lot of paperwork that goes with that."

"What kind of paperwork?"

"Progress reports, crew status, things like that." She returned to the chair by the bedside. "Of course the president is concerned about security interests…."

Myra sat up straighter. "You mean the president's taking this business of intelligent life at Saturn seriously?"

Natalie inclined her head, neither confirming nor denying Myra's statement, just noting it. "Aren't you taking it seriously?"

"Well, yes…," said Myra, reclining again, "but I can take something seriously and still be skeptical."

Natalie raised an eyebrow. "If you're skeptical, why did you agree to come along on this mission?"

Myra laughed lightly and shook her head. "You of all people should ask! Did you seriously consider turning away from this mission when you were asked to join?"

"I have to admit, I was concerned when I saw how young Pilot was." Natalie shot a furtive glance toward the door. She remembered seeing his picture for the first time while sitting in the president's office and wondering how he could be old enough to have invented a spaceship. It was like seeing a reflection of her childhood fantasies. Her uncle had offered her an appointment to Annapolis. What if he'd given her the facilities to build her own spaceship? "I really thought he'd be older," she whispered conspiratorially.

"His age gave me pause, too," admitted Myra. "I also hated to leave the whales behind, but you know what? I really hope Joyce Harmer is right and the whales are indeed talking to someone at Saturn."

"Why's that?"

"If all the speculation is true—and I'm not saying it is—then it doesn't take much of a leap to say the people at Saturn know the whales' normal language."

Natalie sat back, considered that, and finally nodded, not certain she agreed, but accepting the scientist's belief. "Keep me posted on what you learn."

"Of course," said Myra.

With that, Natalie stood, patted the biologist on the shoulder, and told her to get some rest.

Chapter 10
Underway

The first two days of the *Aristarchus* mission were busy for the entire crew. A near-constant barrage of radio chatter arrived from people wishing the ship well on its voyage. Lisa Henry spent her first few hours doing little more than fielding messages. Myra Lee began to feel better and came to C-and-C after Lisa had been on watch for about eight hours and took over. Though she wasn't completely happy about it, she tolerated the communications responsibilities in exchange for the time she'd spend doing science later.

Small shuttles flew out from the lunar factories just to spend a few minutes alongside the ship that looked like a giant pinwheel. This kept John O'Connell and Kurata Nagamine busy, simply monitoring to make sure none of the ships came too close to the delicate sails. Likewise, Dr. Garcia spent several hours making certain life support systems functioned well. Once satisfied, he left C-and-C to organize the infirmary and make one last check that he had all he needed.

Pilot trimmed the sails, optimizing their angle, helping the ship achieve escape velocity from Earth's orbit. His technical crew monitored data streams from the sails themselves and from different parts of the ship's hull, making sure everything behaved as predicted.

Just as the ship was about to break free of Earth's gravitational well, Myra looked over her shoulder at Natalie Freeman who sat at the command console. "Ma'am," she said. "The president is calling."

Natalie straightened up in her chair and made sure the top button of her coveralls was done up. "Put him on speakers."

"Crew of the *Aristarchus*. This is your president, Oscar Van der Wald. I just wanted to call and wish you bon voyage."

"Thank you, Mr. President," said Natalie.

"Captain Freeman, I trust all is operating smoothly."

"All operations are proceeding on schedule, Mr. President," reported Natalie. From the corner of her eye, she noticed Pilot evaluating her carefully.

"Very good," said Van der Wald. "Best of luck to you all. Success to you, Captain Freeman and success to Quinn Corp." With that, the president signed off.

Pilot approached the central console. "The president does realize that Captain Jefferson is in operational command of this vessel, doesn't he?"

"He knows who's in operational command." She looked up into Pilot's eyes.

*

Later that day, Pilot watched his display intently. The red dot marking *Aristarchus's* position slowly approached a green line. Jonathan Jefferson entered C-and-C and walked over to the central console. Natalie watched Pilot's display. "I'd like to have a word, please." Jefferson's voice had a razor-sharp edge.

"With all due respect, sir," said Natalie, "We're approaching a milestone. I think we should both be here for this."

Jefferson clasped his hands behind his back and faced Pilot's display.

The red dot crossed the green line. "We have reached escape velocity," announced Pilot. "We are out of Earth's gravity well." He tapped a few controls on his console. "I'm adjusting the sail trim to put us on course for Mars."

Natalie looked over her shoulder to the thruster control console. The Technical Systems Manager, Daryl LaRue, ran computations. Several numbers flashed on his screen. He looked back toward Freeman and Jefferson. "Confirmed. We have reached escape velocity."

"I could use a slight course adjustment," said Pilot. "One degree to starboard if you please, Mr. LaRue."

LaRue looked toward the two captains who nodded in unison, then turned back to his station and fired the thrusters. "One degree to starboard, aye."

Jefferson looked at Freeman again. "Now?"

She nodded, then stood up and followed Jefferson to the

down-ladder. Just before they left, she turned to Pilot. "You have command."

Freeman followed Jefferson down one deck. He led the way to a small lounge area set along the sphere's outer wall. A semi-circular couch surrounded a porthole in the floor. The Moon, visible through the porthole, cast a cold, wan light through the room.

Jefferson held his hand toward the couch as he sat on the opposite side. "I understand the President of the United States called earlier this afternoon."

"He did," said Freeman. "It caught me by surprise."

"I wasn't expecting the call, either," said Jefferson. "However, it's traditional on space voyages for the ship's commander to speak to the president. I should have been called to command and control."

"Ah…" Freeman took a deep breath, then continued. "Captain, sir, I had no intention of undermining your authority. However, may I respectfully point out, that you're an employee of Quinn Corp while I'm the active duty officer and a NASA official. The president is my commander-in-chief, not yours."

Jefferson folded his hands and looked down through the porthole in the floor. "That doesn't excuse your breach of protocol, Ms. Freeman. You're the executive officer, not the captain of the ship. We explained that very carefully to Pilot. We can't create an atmosphere of confusion among the crew."

"You're right, of course, sir," said Freeman. "I apologize. It won't happen again."

Jefferson nodded, then looked up into Freeman's dark eyes. "There's only one other thing that bothers me." He paused for a moment. "Why are you here?"

"I'm here to observe the mission." Freeman's answer was very precise and practiced.

"I think there's more you're not telling me." Jefferson sat forward slightly.

Freeman sat back and studied the curved walls for a moment, more to avoid Jefferson's gaze than through any curiosity about the ship's construction. Finally, she looked back at him. "Why are we really going to Saturn?"

Jefferson smiled. "We're looking for organic compounds

and possibly life at Saturn." Jefferson echoed the tone of Freeman's precise, practiced answer from before. "The biomedical implications would be astounding."

"They would be, but how profitable would any of it be for Quinn Corp? Most of the answers Thomas says we're seeking can be found on Earth, in the laboratory. The possibility of finding intelligent life is a big deal, of course, but that came up only after the project began. Quinn Corp is investing a lot of money in this mission. I'd like to know why."

Jefferson chewed on his lower lip. "I'm aboard this ship to make sure she gets safely to Saturn and returns home. Just make sure you don't interfere with the ship's operation as you 'observe the mission.'"

"I understand, sir," said Freeman. "One more thing—does Pilot seem a bit young to you?"

"At first." Jefferson nodded. "Then I remembered something I'd read at the Air Force Academy—that most scientists make their greatest discoveries before they turn thirty."

"Thomas is brilliant, I'll give you that, but is he experienced?"

Jefferson ran fingers through his white hair, then smiled disarmingly. "That's why I'm here and why I'm glad you're here, too."

*

After the *Aristarchus* left Earth's gravity well, space traffic died off completely, giving Neb O'Connell much less to worry about. Out of lunar orbit, there were no more spaceships transporting goods to and from the Earth. There were no more shuttles to buzz by the *Aristarchus*, serving as collision hazards. Seeing that Neb was less occupied with ship's business, Dr. Nagamine ordered him to start a series of observations, using the ship's telescopic cameras to take pictures of Mars, Jupiter, and Saturn. In that way, Neb's job aboard ship became very much like his job back on Earth.

The first week of observations interested Neb O'Connell greatly. He had new equipment to learn and his other duties kept the routine from getting dull. He monitored the ship itself to assure its good operating condition and monitored the area immediately ahead of the ship to make sure nothing dangerous crossed their path. Also, though there was a radio-frequency antenna aboard *Aristarchus*, most of Neb's photos were in the optical band. For the first time in his professional career, he photographed the planets as they appeared to the human eye.

By the voyage's second week, O'Connell had the new routine down pat. It required very little concentration on his part. Though he was still delighted to be aboard a spaceship heading toward the outer planets, he grew bored.

*

Over the course of the voyage's first month, phone calls and radio communication with the *Aristarchus* tapered off. During the first weeks, Lisa Henry and Myra Lee felt far too much like telephone operators as family and friends called crewmembers to wish them well on their journey. Members of the press called repeatedly to interview Captain Jefferson or Captain Freeman. Alonzo Thomas refused interviews, saying the cameras made him nervous. Once *Aristarchus* left Earth's gravity well, the limit imposed by the speed of light took its toll on phone conversations. The delay between the time someone aboard ship spoke and it could be heard on the Earth increased rapidly. As phone calls between Earth and the ship died down, email traffic picked up, but that required much less attention from Myra and Lisa.

The cetacean biologist's stomach settled as she grew more accustomed to the ship's strange gravity. She and Lisa used the *Aristarchus's* communications computer to examine whale song with Joyce Harmer's translation programs.

During the first week of the flight's second month, a phone call from Earth surprised Myra. Responding, she found it was Joyce Harmer, calling from her new office at Quinn Corp. "We think we have a more-or-less exact translation of the whale's message," she said. Without waiting for a response, she continued on. "It says, 'The cycle continues. The tool builders prepare to cross the great void. For them, the art is the death. The keepers of the rings are advised, many hunters and bards have been lost to them. The cycle resumes.' The reference to crossing a great void or emptiness convinces me more that the whales are speaking to someone in space, if not Saturn itself."

A shiver traveled down Myra's spine as she considered the translation. "What does that bit about 'the cycle' mean?"

There was a brief pause as Myra's signal traveled to Earth and Joyce's answer returned. "We're not exactly sure. We think it might be something like 'begin transmission' or 'end transmission.' Of course, we could have details wrong. If they're speaking in idiom, the meaning may have little to do with the actual words."

"It's not a lot of words to build a translation on," said Myra, frowning.

A moment later, Joyce's response came. "Twenty-eight words," she said. "It's not a bad start and there are some good ones, like the verb 'to be.' You can input the words into the program I gave you. If you meet anyone who speaks this language, it'll be a good start to understanding them."

Myra pushed the transmit button. "I certainly hope so. Thank you, Dr. Harmer."

∗

There was only one cook aboard *Aristarchus*, a man named Angus MacDonald. The kitchen was well equipped with a number of automated appliances, so MacDonald actually could cook meals all on his own. However, during the flight's sixth week, several crewmembers, including Captain Freeman, Dr. Garcia, Lisa Henry, and Vanda Berko decided during a card game to volunteer their services in the kitchen. Not only did it provide MacDonald some relief, it also provided the crew with some relief from his cooking. It wasn't that MacDonald's fare was poor. Most crewmembers rather liked his cooking, but his repertoire was a bit limited.

One day soon after, the aroma of onions, garlic, and chilies greeted Neb O'Connell as he entered the galley. "It smells good," he said.

Dr. Garcia looked up from behind the counter. "Thanks. It's an old recipe of my mother's—chilaquiles." He handed Neb a plate covered with tortilla chips smothered in a red chile sauce topped with chicken, onions, and sour cream.

"I thought you'd make us eat healthier food than this," chided Neb, taking the plate.

"It's not that bad." The doctor shrugged.

"Don't listen to him," said Lisa Henry from a table in the corner. "The doc's the least healthy cook of the lot. I'd take the soup if I were you. That tortilla pie thing about seared my tonsils."

"You don't have any tonsils, my dear," said the doctor. "I know. I've looked down your throat myself."

Lisa rolled her eyes. Neb took the plate and stepped over to her table. "May I join you?"

"Sure." She shrugged but wore a cautious smile.

Neb sat down and took a tentative bite of the chilaquiles. After the first, he took several more. "That's really good."

Lisa looked at him, wide eyed. "How can you stand that stuff?"

"He obviously has good taste," said the doctor.

"I've been living in New Mexico for the last few years. Red and green chilies are a staple of the diet. You get addicted," said Neb, by way of explanation. "This is actually a little mild for my taste, but I didn't even think we had any chile aboard the ship."

"That's 'cause MacDonald's scared to use it," said Dr. Garcia.

Lisa inclined her head. "Hey, maybe you should volunteer for the kitchen crew, then you and the doctor can take turns torturing the rest of us."

"It *would* be torture," said Neb. "I've been known to burn soup from a can." He took several more bites of the chilaquiles, then washed it down with some iced tea. "But the thing is, I would like to find something to do in my off hours."

Lisa smiled openly. "You could help me pick a movie to watch tonight."

Neb sputtered for a moment, then came to his senses. "I'd like that."

"No popcorn, though," said the doctor. "You've used up your allotment of carbohydrates eating the chilaquiles."

✳

Captain Jefferson carefully observed the crew. He noticed how Neb O'Connell and Lisa Henry would steal glances at one another. More than once, she made a point of asking for advice or help. He would unclamp his chair from its restraints and roll it across to her station. Once there, their conversation would drift from the original topic into movies, books, or even food. The camaraderie between them felt natural and relaxed. They were two technicians who had been working behind the scenes and as they grew to know each other better, it was apparent they had other things in common, as well.

Unfortunately, not everyone got along as well as Neb and Lisa. One day, Jefferson went to the kitchen for lunch. As he sat down to eat, Angus MacDonald asked Daryl LaRue about his day.

"Just great," growled LaRue. "I had to track down a dodgy relay that was causing the port aft thruster to act up and you know somethin', I had to do it all myself. Unlike some of the crew who have people lining up to help them out."

On Earth, at Martin-Intelsoft, Jefferson would have dismissed the incident entirely, assuming LaRue was just having a bad day.

Jefferson abandoned his tray and sat next to LaRue. "Is everything okay?"

"I've had better days," said the Tech System's Manager, a little irritably.

"We're a long way from home," said Jefferson.

"And getting further every minute."

"Any reason to take it out on Mr. MacDonald?"

LaRue waved dismissively. "He's been working in the Quinn Corp cafeteria on the Moon for years. I'm sure he's used to people griping and complaining."

"Maybe..." Jefferson ran his fingers through his hair. "Maybe in a factory complex with hundreds of people and lots of space, it's easier to turn a deaf ear to complaints. We're stuck together in this little can for the next four years or so. Who knows? Maybe getting a card game together every now and then would help break the ice. Maybe MacDonald would volunteer to help you once and a while?"

"The cook help with a technical problem?" He snorted.

Jefferson glared at him and he held up his hands in mock surrender as he stood and returned to his meal. As he finished eating, Jefferson thought back to the *Ares* mission. There had been disagreements and even arguments, but rarely did people resort to sarcasm and they all saw each other as equals.

Jefferson's worries about morale were slight compared to his concerns about training and experience. One day as he, Pilot, and Natalie gathered around the worktable on the bridge discussing the ship's trajectory, she pointed to the chart. "How bad will the passage through the asteroid belt be?"

Pilot scratched the wiry hair on his head. "I don't understand."

Again, Jefferson noted something just a little pedantic and condescending in Pilot's tone, but he filed it away as he listened to Freeman elaborate.

"The ship's over ten miles wide," she said. "It's been a long time since I studied astronomy. Just how close together are the asteroids? I'm picturing us trying to steer this ship through a field of rocks."

"Ah," said Pilot, comprehension dawning. "You've been watching too many bad science fiction films. Our solar system's asteroid belt is pretty sparsely populated, only about one large rock every two million miles or so. I think a ten-mile-wide spaceship might just squeak through."

Natalie scowled at him.

"Of course, we will want to keep extra careful watch on the sensors," said Pilot. "The large rocks are well-plotted, even from Earth. It's some of the smaller debris we'll have to watch out for. Still, we've been sending unmanned probes this way for years. We shouldn't have any problem."

Jefferson nodded. He realized Pilot was correct in his assessment and Natalie was right to bring up a concern. However, he couldn't help but think that in his astronaut days, this point would have been raised while they were in training, months before leaving Earth, not weeks into the mission.

Two months into the voyage, Natalie Freeman sat at the command console. She discovered that shipboard computers had access to Quinn Corp's internal network. Even though transmission time made the network sluggish, a brief search led Natalie to some general information files about Alonzo Thomas.

She found nothing confidential, nor anything she didn't already know. The files mentioned he was twenty-four years old, he'd interned with Quinn Corp for two years before graduation from MIT. Upon graduation, he went to work for Quinn Corp full time. There was a brief notation he was taking graduate classes. That had led President Van der Wald to speculate that Alonzo may be working on a thesis. There was even a recent photo. Also in the files was a listing of the Quinn facilities where Thomas had worked. Again, she had seen all this information. However, these listings contained links to those facilities' sites. She clicked the link to Alonzo's last work site: Quinn Corp's San Antonio facility.

Once there, she followed a link to a personnel listing. There was a chance Thomas would already be deleted from the list. The list had not been updated, though, and she quickly found another link that sent her to the facility's file for Alonzo Thomas. When she clicked that, she gasped. There was a photo, but it was not what she expected.

She sent an email to the personnel office in San Antonio.

Chapter 11
Alonzo Thomas

Pilot spent more and more of his duty shifts in the ship's hub. He enjoyed floating in null gravity and watching the stars through the big windows on either side of the ship. Mars looked like a bright red spot dead ahead. To Pilot, it was like a homing beacon.

Pilot could control all piloting functions from his tablet computer. As he'd explained to Captain Jefferson, there was actually little need for him to spend time in the ship's nerve center. Pilot even spent many nights asleep in the null gravity hub, just floating in the middle of the room illuminated by the soft glow of a thousand stars and one planet.

Even so, Pilot was required to stand watch in command and control to relieve Captain Freeman and Captain Jefferson from constant duty. However, both captains had grown so accustomed to their military regimens, that they simply traded out watches, eight hours on duty, eight hours off, for several days in a row without complaint.

Jefferson arrived at C-and-C to relieve Freeman the day she had perused the Quinn Corp files. "I've discovered something about Alonzo Thomas," she said. "It's something I think you need to know."

Jefferson looked around the deck. "I think it would be better if we find a time when we're both off duty to discuss this."

"When?"

"Next time Pilot comes down, whichever of us is on duty will have him take over for a while. We could use the break."

Natalie frowned.

"Is it an emergency?" The captain's brow furrowed as her silence concerned him.

Natalie thought some more and then shook her head. "No, just a puzzle."

Four hours after Natalie's next duty shift began, Daryl LaRue asked Pilot to come down to check an anomaly on his console. "I'm having some problems with a couple of indicators," explained the Technical System's Manager. "It's probably something stupid and simple, but I can't quite figure it out. I'd like you to take a look and see what you think."

Reluctantly, Pilot agreed and about ten minutes later, he crawled down the ladder from the ship's core and approached the thruster control station. Pilot looked it over, retrieved a pair of tweezers from his coveralls and removed a couple of buttons from the console, then replaced the miniature light bulbs behind them and returned the buttons to their place. Just as Pilot was about to ascend the ladder again, Freeman called him over.

"Would you mind taking over for about half an hour while I go get a cup of coffee and stretch my legs?" she asked.

He looked down at the deck, as though trying to find an excuse for not staying. After a moment, he looked up, blushing. "I guess I have been spending a lot of time off deck. Take as long as you need."

Freeman stood, patted Pilot on the shoulder, then went to Jefferson's quarters and knocked on the door. "Come in," he said.

Inside, she found him sitting in a chair, his feet propped up, watching a movie. He slid a bowl of popcorn across the table toward her. "What can I do for you?" he asked.

She took the wireless keyboard and set it on her lap. "I wanted to show you what I learned about Alonzo Thomas. It'll only take a moment." She paused the movie, then accessed her files on the ship's computer. She pulled up a copy of the photo she'd found a few hours earlier. It showed a man who looked nothing like Pilot. Underneath was the caption "Alonzo Thomas."

Jefferson pursed his lips while reaching out for a handful of popcorn. "That's not our Pilot," he said at last.

"No, it's not. What do you think it means?"

He shrugged. "Maybe the San Antonio facility posted the wrong photo. That kind of mistake does happen."

Freeman shook her head. "I thought of that. I wrote to the personnel office in San Antonio. The manager there was a recent transfer and didn't remember Thomas, but she confirmed that the electronic file matched their hard copy. If it's a mistake, it propagated through the system."

"Well, if it's not the wrong photo, how do you explain it?"

Freeman stood up and paced. "One explanation is that our Alonzo Thomas is not the same man who worked at Quinn Corp for the past five years. Somehow he's been substituted for the real Thomas."

Jefferson shook his head and folded his arms. "I don't buy that. 'Our' Thomas knows too much about this craft. He's brash and arrogant, inexperienced at some things, but he's not stupid. Why would there be a substitution anyway?"

She stopped pacing and shook her head. "I keep wanting to say 'corporate spy' or 'saboteur.' That's why I came to you with this even though I know both of those sound completely whacky. I know the ship's safety is your first priority and this is just something that doesn't add up." She dropped back into the chair, defeated.

"I'll keep my eyes open." Jefferson looked over at Freeman. "I'm guessing it's just a mistake, though. San Antonio got the wrong photo and propagated it through their system. I've poked through the Quinn Corp files, too. I've seen photos that are clearly our Pilot."

She ran her tongue over her teeth and studied the photo on the screen for a moment. "You're probably right."

Jefferson looked at his watch. "I suspect your break's about over. You should get back to C-and-C."

She nodded and took another handful of popcorn before she left.

*

Neb O'Connell sat in his quarters, keyboard in his lap, staring at a schematic of a spaceship. A knock at the door broke his concentration. "Come in," he said.

Lisa Henry peered around the corner. "Whatcha' doin'?"

"Playing 'Starship Creator.' Wanna give it a try?"

"Sure." She sat on the edge of the bed while Neb cleared the display. He handed her the keyboard and then explained the rules.

"Basically, the objective of the game is to create a ship that will make it to Alpha Centauri and back," he said.

"And this is what you do in your off time?" She winked at him. Neb shrugged and she turned her attention to the game. She chose a deck layout, attached the most powerful engine she could, and chose an aluminum skin for the ship—same as the shell of the Apollo capsules. "Okay, I think I'm ready to try the ship," she said.

Neb smirked. "Are you absolutely sure?"

She narrowed her eyes suspiciously. "What? Don't you think my ship will do the trick? It's lightweight, and it's got a big engine. It should make the round trip in about twenty years."

"Let's give it a try." Neb took the keyboard back and typed in some commands. On the screen, they watched as Lisa's ship moved toward Alpha Centauri. Everything went well until the ship was five years from Earth. At that point, Lisa's crew started dropping dead from cancer.

"That doesn't make sense." Lisa studied the stats on the screen, trying to understand what happened.

"You didn't provide any cosmic ray shielding," explained Neb. "In five years, your crew got the equivalent of eighty chest X-rays worth of radiation."

Lisa looked around at the walls of the ship. "Isn't *Aristarchus* made of aluminum?" She poked her finger into Neb's chest. "There's something you're not telling me."

Neb held up his hands in surrender. "The game's got it right, honest!" He brought up Lisa's ship design. "Look what happens if we line the ship's hull with polyethylene and restart the simulation."

"Isn't polyethylene the plastic they make garbage bags out of?" she asked as her simulated ship made its way to Alpha Centauri.

Neb nodded. "I used blocks a couple of inches thick, but yeah, it's the same stuff." This time, the crew survived for fifteen years. "They would have been fine," he said. "The problem now is the increased radiation from Alpha Centauri's sun. The plastic didn't quite absorb enough of the radiation."

"You mean all I needed to do to keep my crew alive was line

the ship with garbage bags?" Lisa inclined her head. "Would a thicker layer do the trick?"

"That's about the size of it." Neb beamed at her. "That's how they kept Captain Jefferson alive on the trip to Mars—only it was polyethylene blocks, not heaps of garbage bags."

Lisa's gaze roved to the walls again. "What about us?"

Neb stood and patted the wall. "Quinitite," he said. "The same stuff that the sails struts are made from. It actually deflects cosmic rays, just like it disperses electric charge."

"You really should get out more." Lisa cracked a grin.

"And go where?"

*

On Earth, Henry Quinn entered his father's office. "Dad, something strange is going on."

Without looking up from his computer, Jerome grunted acknowledgement and motioned for Henry to take a seat. Henry sat down and picked up a paperweight. It was a plastic cube with four coins embedded inside. After a moment, Jerome looked up. "Well?"

"Ever since Tom's last visit, I've been emailing him—keeping in touch, asking him for help with my homework, that sort of thing." He returned the paperweight to the desk. "I think we may be closer now than when he lived here."

Jerome nodded at his son and prompted him to continue.

"It's just that his emails have become erratic. It's like he's really preoccupied. I know you have him busy supporting the Aristarchus project, so I wasn't all that concerned until today. I wanted to talk to him about Massachusetts since I'm thinking about applying to Babson. I realized he never sent me his new phone number, so I called the Boston office where he's been working." Henry licked his lips. His mouth was suddenly dry. "Dad, they say he left four months ago. He's not there anymore."

"I know," said Jerome. "He's perfectly safe and he is working on the Aristarchus project, but he has to be careful about outside communication."

Henry frowned but accepted the explanation. He never fully understood the relationship between his father and brother.

He remembered the day Thomas ran into his bedroom, waving a sheaf of papers. "I got accepted into MIT!"

Without looking up from the video game he had been playing, Henry shook his head. "Dad's gonna go ballistic. He wants you to go to Harvard, so you can get degrees in both business and science."

"Harvard's good and all." Thomas had shrugged. "But I don't want a business degree."

"Suit yourself. Dad already told us the deal—no business degree, no seat on the board."

"I don't care about the board of directors." Thomas had said it with an air of conviction.

Henry looked up into his father's unwavering gaze and realized for the first time how much his father probably respected his brother's convictions

As Henry stood and left the office, he remembered the taunt he'd fired at his brother. "You'll be lucky if you even get a back corner office somewhere. Dad may have a degree in materials engineering, but he's always said science is nothing without marketing."

"I don't care." Thomas had waved his hand through the air as though brushing the words aside. "All those stupid meetings and all that publicity, it just distracts people from doing anything real—anything productive."

Henry turned around and sighed as the warrior character he'd been playing died a horrible death on the screen. "That just means I'll get the lion's share of the inheritance."

"You can have the money." He remembered Thomas looking over at the screen as though seeing it for the first time. "You're still playing that game I hacked for you?"

"Yeah, it's great. The characters are so much like real people, I never get bored," Henry honestly admired his brother's skill with computers. "You know, you should show dad some of the computer stuff you do. He'd probably take a lot more interest in that than all the space stuff you show him."

"Computers are just tools." At that point, Thomas had strolled to the window and looked outside. "When you know them as well as I do, you know you can only trust them so far. The real adventure's out there."

"In the yard?" asked Henry.

Thomas had rubbed the bridge of his nose. Henry smiled. Even then, the gesture reminded him of their father. "I'm talking about the sky," said Thomas, irritably. "I'm talking about space."

"What is it with you and space, anyway? It's just a bunch of nothing that can get you killed real fast."

"It's not the nothing. It's the something—the places we haven't been to—six whole planets in our solar system humans haven't seen with their own eyes—more dwarf planets and moons than I can even name…"

"And if anyone could name them, it would be you," quipped Henry.

"I'll find a way."

In the present, Henry's memory faded as he strolled down the hall. He entered his room and looked out the window at the rolling grass and trees outside. He thought of Thomas standing there, and realized his brother must have found a way to explore the solar system after all.

Chapter 12
Halfway to Mars

Three months into the voyage, Angus MacDonald, Daryl LaRue, Vanda Berko, and a mechanic named Randal Hoffman gathered in the ship's galley for a card game. Angus retrieved a hidden bottle of Scotch Whiskey for the occasion. He lifted a toast to the others. "Halfway to Mars." The others lifted their glasses with the cook.

As the evening wore on, the four crewmembers drank more and more of the scotch as they played cards. Daryl LaRue won far more often than he lost and somewhere around midnight, ship's time, he pulled a large stack of coins toward himself. "Gentlemen," he said, then noticed Vanda Berko glaring at him, "and lady. I think it's time for me to call it a night. I'm expected at my post early in the morning."

Angus MacDonald scowled at LaRue. "I think you owe me a chance to win back some of my money."

"You know, it is getting awfully late," said Hoffman, looking at his watch. "I think it's time to call it a night."

Vanda Berko folded her arms across her stomach, waiting to see what would happen.

"I'm sorry, Angus," said LaRue. "The way you've been playing tonight, you'd just lose more money to me. You're just a cook and not too good with figures, and your poker face ain't so good when you've been drinking."

MacDonald reached up, touched his face, then dropped his hand and sneered at the tech manager. "Some men may be lucky, but no one's as lucky as you were tonight." The cook leaned forward, across the table.

"Are you accusing me of cheating?" said LaRue dangerously. MacDonald nodded and the tech manager's face turned beet red. He tried to shove the table aside, but couldn't because it was bolted to the floor. When that didn't work, he just leapt across the table at the cook.

*

John O'Connell and Lisa Henry strolled through the corridor hand-in-hand after watching a movie. They decided a trip to the galley for some tea or hot cocoa would be the perfect way to end the evening. When they opened the door, they found Angus MacDonald on the floor with Daryl LaRue sitting atop him, fist poised to strike. Vanda Berko had LaRue's arm and Randal Hoffman held Daryl around the chest. When he saw John and Lisa step in, he called, "Get some help!"

Lisa ran to the nearest comm port, and called command and control. "Get the captain down here, fast."

*

A few minutes later, Captain Jefferson appeared, running down the corridor from C-and-C. He took in the situation and with the help of those on hand, subdued both LaRue and MacDonald.

"All right, what happened?" demanded Jefferson.

Several voices spoke at once.

"One at a time," growled the captain.

Hoffman spoke up and told about the card game and how MacDonald had accused LaRue of cheating. Lisa Henry looked at the table, retrieved a bottle, and took it to the captain.

Jefferson grabbed the mostly-empty bottle and looked at it, then shook his head. "Alcohol is prohibited aboard this ship, gentlemen," he said. "So is fighting." He set the bottle down on a nearby table and clasped his hands behind his back and paced. "Mr. LaRue, Mr. MacDonald, you're both confined to your quarters for a week. All computer and video access will be denied. Perhaps some quiet time on your own will help you both cool off."

While Jefferson spoke, Pilot appeared in the doorway. "Captain," he said, almost frantic, "you can't do that. We need both of these men on duty. We can't confine crewmembers."

"Why not?" Jefferson's voice rose. "We have the volunteer cooks to take MacDonald's place. You and several of the other techs can run the thrusters in LaRue's place. If we don't set an example, there could be more trouble."

As they continued to argue, Neb O'Connell looked at Lisa. "Maybe you should get Captain Freeman down here." Lisa nodded agreement and quietly stepped out of the galley. A few minutes later, she returned with Natalie Freeman. Lace poked up over rumpled coveralls as though she had hastily thrown the uniform on over a nightgown.

"Sir ... Mr. Alonzo," she said, her arms folded. "What's going on?"

Jefferson took a deep breath and explained his side of the story.

"But we have just enough crewmembers to handle the ship as it is," countered Pilot. "We can't afford to confine them to quarters for a week."

Captain Freeman looked at MacDonald and LaRue, who were both looking at the floor, partly out of shame for what they'd done and partly to avoid the iciness of Freeman's gaze. MacDonald's right eye was turning purple and swelling shut.

Freeman turned on her heel and looked at Pilot. "Jonathan Jefferson is the captain of this vessel," she said coldly. "If you have a disagreement with him, you take it out of the crew's view. Do I make myself clear?"

Pilot sputtered for a moment, but then finally took a deep breath. "You're absolutely right." He turned to Jefferson, who stood very straight, looking self-satisfied and offered his hand. Jefferson took it and the two men shook.

With that, Freeman led both men out into the corridor. In a whisper that was even harsher than her reprimand of Pilot, she said to Jefferson, "Pilot's right, Captain. We can't take these men off duty. Did you consider that?"

Jefferson's self-satisfied grin vanished. "No, I hadn't."

"Perhaps a few shifts of watch-on-watch would be a more appropriate punishment under the circumstances," said Freeman.

Pilot started to interrupt, but stopped when she glared at him. She let Jefferson go into the galley to announce the compromise.

*

In the weeks after the fight, the crew's mood grew somber.

Arguments occasionally flared up, but they died down just as quickly. No one wanted to do sixteen hours on shift, followed by eight hours for sleep, then do it all over again for a week.

A week after the fight, Jefferson ascended the ladder into the ship's hub. He found Pilot staring out the window. The captain drifted over, joining him. Mars had grown bright, casting shadows through the ship's central section, even though the lack of gravity in the ship's hub was disconcerting it was nothing compared to the sensation of the walls rotating around them while they floated stationary in the center. A few consoles lined the walls where the rotation created microgravity, but Pilot mostly worked from his tablet.

"I'm sorry I didn't listen when you told me we needed to keep LaRue and MacDonald on duty," said the captain, quietly. He looked at the door and watched it rotate around him.

"You were right, too," said Pilot, breaking Jefferson's reverie. "You were right at the beginning. We should have trained longer before starting."

Jefferson nodded. "Maybe … but we've had far fewer troubles than I would have expected. You did a good job putting this crew together."

"Thanks." Pilot looked up at Jefferson. "Although, I didn't put a lot of thought into compatibility. I just wanted the best people for the jobs."

"You got them," admitted Jefferson.

Pilot smiled a little at that, then looked forward, out the window. "I've been double checking calculations. Given our approach and escape vectors, we're only going to get four orbits of Mars, about twenty-four hours, then we'll reach escape velocity and be on our way to Jupiter."

"I know, I've been checking, too," said Jefferson. He'd been disappointed on the Moon when he first heard they'd only have a day at Mars. He and Pilot had agreed to revisit the calculations to see if they could buy even a few more hours.

"Have you chosen a landing site?" asked Pilot. "Better make it a good one."

Jefferson had been reading up on the specs of *Aristarchus's* landers. There were surprisingly few limits to their abilities. "If I had to pick one place to go on Mars, I know just where it would be." Jefferson looked toward the red planet.

*

Aboard the *Aristarchus*, it was easy to forget about the passage of time back on Earth. The lights in the corridors were always on and the seasons did not change outside the windows. For that reason, Angus MacDonald maintained a calendar in the galley. Near the beginning of December, Vanda Berko brought out a small menorah and set it up to mark the days of Hanukah. "Surrounded by darkness as we are, it's important to remember the miracle of light," she said.

Around that time, Jonathan Jefferson and Pilot met to decide who should go down to Mars. Kurata Nagamine, the planetary astronomer, was an obvious choice. After some discussion, they decided that Myra Lee should also go to the planet. As a biologist, she was the most likely aboard to notice any fossils or other evidence of life.

"Daryl, Vanda, and I are the most qualified mechanics to repair the shuttle should problems occur," said Pilot. "I should probably sit this trip out."

Jefferson blinked back surprise. He'd expected Pilot to come along on all the planetary missions. "As senior Quinn Corp official aboard, wouldn't it be fitting for you to accompany us?"

"Believe me, when we get to Jupiter and Saturn, I'll be there." Pilot grinned. "However, given the short time we have at Mars, I should stay aboard to make sure we execute the slingshot out of orbit correctly. If we don't, we'll still make it to Jupiter, but it could add a year to the trip. Maybe I'll go down when we return."

"Okay," said Jefferson. "If you stay with the ship and I'm piloting the shuttle, that means Daryl LaRue is the only other qualified pilot. He should stay behind in case we need a rescue."

"Agreed," said Pilot. "That leaves Vanda to accompany you as mechanic."

That left two seats on the shuttle. After some consideration, they decided that Neb O'Connell and Lisa Henry should go along. Though both were technicians, each had logged more hours with cameras and recording equipment than either Nag-amine or Lee. That made the astronomy and biology teams complete.

Training for the trip to the Martian surface helped break the monotony of shipboard routine, not only for the six sched-uled to go to Mars, but the rest of the crew as well. Six others were picked to be a rescue team in the event of a planetside problem. They included Pilot, Dr. Garcia, and Daryl LaRue. The remaining thirteen crewmembers worked on mission support and prepared for the very worst-case scenario—two lost shut-tles and no pilot, which would mean a short-handed return to Earth.

During one of the landing crew meetings around the con-ference table in C-and-C, Jefferson looked at the assembled group. "I'm impressed with how well this team is coming to-gether. I have no reservations about this mission. That said, I need to know if any of you have questions or issues you need to raise."

Myra shot a glance at Lisa, then raised her hand. "I'm a little concerned about our landing site—Olympus Mons," she said. "Both Lisa and I have done search and rescue training at the Oceanographic Institute and helped with rescues at sea and in the mountains. Isn't landing atop the solar system's tallest mountain going to be a tricky proposition?"

"It won't be as bad as you might think," said Jefferson. "Olympus Mons isn't really built like the tallest mountains of Earth. Even though it's over twice the height of Mt. Everest, it's much wider—bigger around than Texas. There's only about a ten-degree grade near the summit. Conditions are more like Bolivia's alto plano than Alaska's mountain peaks."

"Will it even seem like we're on a mountain?" asked Neb

Jefferson shrugged. "It certainly won't be the same dramat-ic view as on an Earth mountain. The base of Olympus Mons is over the horizon line from the summit." He folded his hands on the tabletop. "I won't kid you, the landing will be challeng-ing, but it won't be anything like trying to land a helicopter on Denali Peak."

"I'm almost tempted to ask why go there," said Myra, "but I know the only answer is the one Sir Edmund Hillary gave

when asked about climbing Mt. Everest." With no other questions or concerns, Jefferson adjourned the meeting.

As the month progressed, Angus produced a tiny artificial
tree and set it up on one of the tables in the galley, decorating
it with bits of tin foil. On Christmas morning, several members
of the crew gathered around the tree and sang carols. When
the ship's clock marked noon, Angus, dressed in his finest kilt,
brought out a roast turkey with all the trimmings. Natalie Freeman, sipping a cup of hot cocoa, noticed Daryl LaRue was at
the party, though he took care to sit at the opposite side of the
room from Angus.

Chapter 13
Mount Olympus

As *Aristarchus* approached Mars, members of the crew went up to the hub to look out at the sight through the great forward window. Lisa Henry and Neb O'Connell went up together and spent over an hour staring at the rust-colored planet as it grew slowly larger.

"I thought seeing Earth from space was the greatest thing," said Lisa, her voice little more than a whisper. "But I think this is even better."

Neb gave a reverent nod. "I've seen the planet through telescopes, but seeing it in person isn't quite like I'd imagined. Somehow, it seems more real, like I can reach out and touch it, especially from here, where you can really see the polar ice caps and clouds drifting over the surface, just like Earth."

"You know what it makes me think of?" mused Lisa. "My grandmother used to show me these old black and white photographs that were kind of reddish-yellow with age. She called it sepia. The people in the photos were all relatives—long gone. Mars kind of looks like what Earth would if it were in one of those old sepia-colored photos. It's almost like Mars is some long lost ancestor of the Earth, waiting for us to come and visit."

Neb smiled at the idea. Just then, he caught sight of a potato-shaped rock, with one deep crater that took up almost a third of the surface. "Hey, it's Phobos," he said, "one of Mars's two moons."

"It looks more like an asteroid than a moon."

"They think it was an asteroid, at one time. It got too close and Mars captured it." As he spoke, Lisa leaned in close. Surrendering to fate, he kissed her by the light of the silvery moon.

The night before the landing, Myra found it virtually impossible to sleep. She tossed and turned until about two in the morning. She woke up, frantic, afraid she'd overslept only to discover it was just a little before three. With a deep breath, she lay down and tried not to count the minutes until her six o'clock wake-up time. Somewhere before morning, she finally did drift off to sleep.

When her alarm rang, Myra was surprised how rested she felt given that she'd had so little sleep. She threw back the blankets, padded to the shower, got dressed, and went to the galley to meet the rest of the landing party.

She found Dr. Nagamine already in the kitchen, drinking coffee and making notes in a journal. She filled a cup and joined him. Soon after, the others arrived. Jefferson's veneer of professional calm barely concealed sheer joy. Neb O'Connell and Lisa Henry looked like star-struck teenagers about to embark on the greatest adventures of their lives. Vanda Berko plodded into the kitchen, looked around and said, "Where the hell is MacDonald with our chow?"

Angus MacDonald showed up a few minutes later and assembled a large breakfast of eggs, potatoes, sausage, fruit, toast, and juice.

"I don't know if I could eat all that," said Myra, aghast at the size of the breakfast.

"I want us to have a large breakfast," said Jefferson. "It's going to be a busy day."

"Won't do me any good if I lose it on the way down," complained Myra.

"I have some motion sickness pills." Lisa patted a pocket on the arm of her coveralls.

After eating, the team of six made their way to the Mars lander's launch bay. Painted metallic red, the sleek craft had the name *Ares III* stenciled on the side. After suiting up in their survival gear, Jefferson opened the hatch and the crew boarded the shuttle. Once again, the captain found himself sitting next to Dr. Nagamine.

"Jefferson to command and control," called the captain. "Requesting permission to launch this bird."

"Stand by," came Natalie Freeman's voice. "We're opening the bay doors and Pilot is calculating counterthrust maneuvers."

The shuttle bay door opened, revealing the red planet ahead. Once the door was fully open, Freeman's voice came over the intercom again. *"Ares III,* you're clear to launch."

Captain Jefferson pulled the joystick back and applied thrust, taking the small shuttle-lander out of the bay. He maneuvered slowly away from the ship, both getting the feel of the controls after six months away from them and making sure they didn't collide with the ship. Once fully clear, he called C-and-C. "We're heading down."

"See you in eighteen hours," said Freeman.

Dr. Nagamine shook his head. "It's so different from the Earth, so lifeless."

"I think it's like coming home." Jefferson grinned broadly. He pushed the joystick forward and began the descent to the surface. Crossing the terminator to the planet's night side, he eased the shuttle into the atmosphere. Even so, the tiny ship rocked and bounced violently and the stars outside the window vanished, replaced by a raging inferno. Myra nearly did get sick, but a pill from Lisa helped calm her stomach.

Jefferson took the lander down over Utopia Planitia, a great plain in the Northern Martian hemisphere. Traveling eastward, the shuttle crossed from night to day and the sky turned brown around them. Below, they could see miles and miles of rust-red sand. There were few mountains, and individual rocks were still too far away to be distinguished. Lisa caught sight of the sun looking far too small on the horizon.

"That's where the Viking 2 Lander touched down one hundred years ago," explained Dr. Nagamine pointing toward the ground.

As the sky brightened from brown to butterscotch, Jefferson continued to lower the shuttle's altitude as they crossed over the Amazonis Planitia. They were able to make out more surface details.

"Except for the color, it almost looks like White Sands National Monument, back in New Mexico," said Neb O'Connell.

Myra grinned. "If there were some cactus, it might even look like Arizona."

"Like I said." Nagamine snorted. "Lifeless." Then he turned in his chair and faced the others, a broad grin forming. "But that's the mystery, isn't it? Why does Earth have life but this planet is barren?" He reached into the equipment rack, pulled out a camera, and took snapshots of the surface below.

The land rose beneath the shuttle as though it were coming up to meet them. "Are we landing?" asked Berko.

Neb nudged her elbow and pointed to Jefferson, who pulled back on the stick, causing the shuttle to lift slightly. At the same time, he slowed the thrusters. Low over the ground by this time, they came to a place where the land just dropped away. Below, a few gauzy white clouds barely concealed land that looked like great waves frozen in time. As they continued on, Neb noticed the waves of rock formed concentric circles that were miles in diameter. It was as though someone had thrown a rock into the middle of a still pond and it had frozen instantly, preserving the ripples for eternity.

At last, the shuttle came to another wall of rock. Flying beyond it, Jefferson sought a place to land. He found a smooth area and set the shuttle down. As soon as he killed the engines, he turned around and smiled. "Welcome to Mars, my friends, make sure your suit heaters are on. It's brisk out there even for Mars, only forty below zero." With that, he unbuckled his harness, retrieved his helmet, latched it, and made sure the oxygen and heating units functioned properly. He watched as the others did the same.

Once certain they were ready, Jefferson opened the hatch and stepped down the stairs. He stopped on the last step, his right foot hovering a few inches from the Martian soil. "I feel like I should say something momentous." He thought for a moment, then looked at the others. "Because it's there." With that, Jonathan Jefferson stepped down onto the Martian surface.

The others followed him down the stairs.

"Because it's where?" asked Myra. "I know we talked about Sir Edmund Hillary and how different Olympus Mons would be from Everest, but I still thought it would be more ... well ... dramatic."

Dr. Nagamine took Myra's gauntleted hand and helped her balance as she stepped onto the soft red soil. She looked into his helmet and saw he was beaming. "I've dreamed of coming here since I was a boy. I even designed a space probe to come here, but could never get it funded. They said the landing system was too complicated."

Myra looked out over the terrain that gently sloped upward toward the cliff they had flown over. Turning around to face the other side of the shuttle, she saw the land gently sloped away. "Why? I see now how gentle the slope is. It doesn't seem like it would be difficult to land a probe here. The captain made it look easy."

"The landing is much easier for a human pilot who can adjust for variables than it would be for a robotic probe." Nagamine pointed downhill. "Slight as the incline is if a probe tumbled on landing, it could keep going for some distance, causing much damage." He led Myra uphill, toward the top of the cliff. "And there are other hazards...." Together they looked over the cliff and saw the great concentric circles of jagged rock below them. "Landing down there would be a problem."

"Welcome to Mount Olympus," said Jefferson as he joined them.

Myra looked first one direction, then the other, following the cliff with her gaze as far as she could. It curved around gently, as though it might form a great circle. She looked across the way and tried to see the first cliff they passed, but it was too distant. "Is this really a caldera? I've never seen anything like it!"

"Yes," said Nagamine. "All of that down there used to be molten lava." He pointed to the giant pond ripple frozen in time.

"We're at 69,844 feet above the surface of Mars," said Jefferson. "What I wouldn't give to actually have time to climb this mountain."

Myra turned and walked a short distance back toward the shuttle. She looked at the gentle downslope beyond. "Well, it doesn't look like it would be a very rigorous climb. Just a long walk."

"A long walk, indeed." Dr. Nagamine followed her gaze. "From here to the base of the mountain would be like walking from Dallas, Texas to New Orleans, Louisiana."

*

Neb O'Connell and Lisa Henry walked along the caldera's edge. Both of them took photographs and measured the atmosphere. Sunlight glinted off something small, embedded in the ground. Neb stopped short. His eyes narrowed and he stepped over to it. "Give me a hand."

Lisa held out her hand, helping Neb bend low. He dug something out of the sand and stood up, showing it to Lisa. It was a polished, silver disk, about the size of a half-dollar.

"Is that writing?" asked Lisa.

Neb held the disk up and examined it carefully. "I believe it may be, but it's not any language I recognize." He toggled his suit radio, so he broadcast to the entire landing party. "I think we found something."

The two walked back toward the landing site. Dr. Nagamine had collected rock samples to take back for examination. Vanda helped Myra set up a small telescope to take photos down in the caldera. Jefferson walked along the caldera's rim, in the opposite direction of Neb and Lisa, but started back as soon as he heard the broadcast message.

The entire group had converged around Neb and his find by the time Jefferson returned. Myra looked up at him. "Did either of the *Ares* missions ever come up here to Olympus Mons?"

"No, we landed in the south," explained Jefferson, "near the lowest point on Mars, in Hellas Planitia. *Ares I* landed over in Chryse Planitia, between the Viking I and Mars Pathfinder sites. They actually found the remains of Viking."

Myra passed the metal disk to Jefferson. "Any idea what this could be? We've certainly been sending enough junk up here to Mars. Do you suppose this came from a probe?"

Jefferson took the disk and flipped it over a couple of times. "It looks like a token or a coin, nothing really practical to be on a probe. Certainly nothing I recognize from an American probe." He handed the disk to Vanda Berko. "Does this look Russian or Soviet to you?"

Vanda—who had grown up and went to university in Russia before immigrating to the United States to work for Quinn Corp—took a closer look at the disk. She shook her head. "The writing's not Cyrillic or any other Eastern alphabet that I know.

Doesn't even look like any runes I've seen." She passed the disk back to Myra.

"What do you think?" Jefferson turned to Myra. "Was that created by intelligent life?"

"I think so," she said. "The bigger question is whether the intelligent life that made this came from Earth or someplace else." She looked at Lisa. "Where did you find this?"

Lisa and Neb led the landing party to the place where they'd found the disk. Myra took a photograph of the area, then knelt down and examined it. After a moment, she carefully dug into the rust-colored soil. Finally, she shook her head. "I don't think there are any others."

Vanda Berko looked around. "I don't see any signs that a craft has been here," she said. "At least not in the recent past."

"Well, the weather up here can be rough at times," said Jefferson.

"I think it may get rough here sooner than we'd like." Dr. Nagamine pointed across the caldera.

Dark storm clouds had built up in the northwest. Ahead of the clouds, red dust billowed from the ground, kicked up by high winds. A lightning bolt crackled.

Jefferson looked at the watch mounted in his gauntlet. "We need to get moving soon, anyway. I think we'll have to solve the mystery of that coin when we get back to the *Aristarchus*. Let's gather up the gear and get aboard the shuttle. If we lift within fifteen minutes, we'll still have time for a little more sightseeing."

Myra stashed the coin in one of her suit pockets, then followed the others back to the shuttle. As they gathered their gear, the wind blew, lifting the fine red dust from the ground, making it difficult to see. Once everything was aboard, Jefferson ascended the steps. He nearly toppled over as a wind gust lifted one side of the shuttle off the ground.

The storm was moving dangerously fast. Inside the shuttle, he fell into his chair. Without removing his helmet, he started the launch sequence and buckled his harness. With just a quick check to make sure the others were ready, he fired the thrusters and lifted the shuttle, fighting the joystick to keep the ship steady in the turbulent air ahead of the storm. The crew of the shuttle was jostled violently from side to side. Neb cried out when his head struck the window. Vanda checked he was uninjured, then checked the window.

Jefferson turned the shuttle, and flew southeast, away from the storm. After a few minutes, the air settled down and flight smoothed out. The ground below the shuttle fell away as they left Olympus Mons behind. Continuing on their course, two mountains, almost as impressive as the one they just left, rose on either side. "That would be Pavonis to the south," said Dr. Nagamine. "And that would be Ascraeus to the north."

The shuttle continued over the plains for a few minutes more. Jefferson lowered the shuttle's altitude so it skimmed a thousand feet above the ground, then slowed the shuttle. Without warning, the ground fell away. Jefferson turned the shuttle to follow the cliff they just passed over. Without thinking, Myra unbuckled her harness and stood up, peering out of the shuttle's window. "I think I see another cliff, way over there." She pointed. Then she looked down as best she could. "Where are we? I think I may see a bottom down there."

"Valles Marineris," said Nagamine. "The Valley of the Mariners. The Grand Canyon of Earth would fit into one of these canyon's tributaries."

"I'll say." Myra whistled long and low. She turned and looked out the other side where the canyon wall was more visible. "Look at the rock layers over there! That must be billions of years of geological history."

"She's got a point," said Nagamine. "We should turn on the wing cameras and get some video."

"Be my guest," said Jefferson. "Dr. Lee. Please sit down and put on your harness. I'm going to take us a little lower into the canyon."

As Myra sat down in her seat, Jefferson pushed the joystick forward and plunged the shuttle downward. Enormous buttes jutted up from the canyon floor. The canyon wall, like that of Earth's Grand Canyon, was painted in many different shades, from the red of the surface to light yellow to black.

"Is that green rock over there or some kind of vegetation?" asked Dr. Nagamine, pointing.

"Fog bank," said Jefferson, but not in response to the

astronomer's question. Ahead of the shuttle, fog filled the canyon from wall to wall. Jefferson pulled back on the joystick and rose above the fog, flying over the lip of the canyon. Below them, the white water vapor billowed and made shapes like fairy castles.

"It's like the palace of Deja Thoris from the Mars books of Edgar Rice Burroughs," said Neb O'Connell.

"Indeed it is," mused the captain. With a look at the control panel's clock, he sighed. "I'm afraid the party's over. We need to get back to *Aristarchus* if we don't want to be stranded here."

"Like being marooned on a desert island." Lisa sighed. "Sounds kind of romantic."

"It would be at that," said Jefferson. "At least until tomorrow when the emergency rations ran out." With that, the captain pulled the joystick back, taking the shuttle skyward.

Chapter 14
Making Discoveries

Back aboard the *Aristarchus*, Myra Lee's lack of sleep the night before caught up with her. Exhausted, she pulled off the space suit and hung it in its locker, then pulled on her uniform coveralls. She started to walk toward her quarters when she remembered the strange coin she'd brought back from Mars. She retrieved it from the spacesuit and put it in the pocket of her coveralls. She left the women's locker room and met Jonathan Jefferson and Dr. Nagamine, looking both too happy and too awake for her current state.

"Congratulations, Dr. Lee," said Nagamine. "I think that was quite a successful landing, even if it was too brief."

Myra yawned and shook both the captain's hand and Nagamine's.

"Care for some dinner, Dr. Lee?" Jefferson moved from one foot to the other, even though the dark circles forming under his eyes betrayed his own exhaustion.

Myra shook her head. "Not right now." She rubbed her eyes. "I'm afraid I need to go get some sleep."

"Yes, do," said the captain. "What are your plans for that coin Neb and Lisa found?"

"First thing we need to figure out is where it came from." She yawned again and then muttered an apology.

Jefferson waved the apology aside. "I'd like to show it to Pilot and Captain Freeman—Daryl LaRue for that matter. Between them, they have some experience with different coins and different spaceship components. Maybe one of them might recognize it."

"Be my guest." Myra handed Jefferson the coin, then trudged off to her quarters.

*

In command and control, Pilot checked and rechecked calculations. He looked up at Natalie Freeman and smiled. "Everything looks good. We're on course for Jupiter. I think we even gained a little more speed than I'd originally estimated. At this point, we should reach the asteroid belt in about a month and a half, and Jupiter in just over a year."

Natalie Freeman looked over to the unoccupied astrosciences station. "Let's set up extra watches on the external sensors. I want to make sure someone's on duty there twenty-four hours a day until we get through the asteroids."

"We have automated alarms," protested Pilot.

"Automated alarms are no substitute for someone watching the sensors who can take immediate action if we run into something unexpected." Freeman wore a worried frown. As she stepped back to the central console, Captain Jefferson strode onto the deck. "Well, well, well, don't we look proud of ourselves," she teased.

Pilot reached out and shook Jefferson's hand. "Well done, Captain! I'm looking forward to seeing the video from your foray. It sounds like quite a success."

"Indeed." Jefferson clapped his hands together. "We even found a bit of a mystery." He reached into his pocket and retrieved the coin and handed it to Pilot. "What do you make of this?"

Pilot narrowed his eyes and looked at the coin. "I've never seen anything like it. The writing isn't at all familiar." Then he held it up to the light. Rainbow patterns appeared along the surface of the coin. "If I didn't know better, I'd say it looks like an optical data disk of some kind."

"You mean like a CD or a DVD?" Freeman inclined her head and stepped up for a closer look.

Pilot handed her the coin. "Exactly."

She held it up and looked at it. "What about this writing? It looks like it's on both sides. Wouldn't a data disk only have writing on the top?"

Pilot shrugged. "Not necessarily. It would depend on a lot of things, like the type of reader and whether the writing is actually transparent at the light frequencies that are needed to read the data."

"That assumes this is a data disk at all," said Jefferson.

"Where did you find it?" asked Pilot.

Jefferson told them how Neb had found the disk buried in the sand on Olympus Mons.

"No Earth spacecraft that I know have ever tried a landing up there," said Pilot. "At least until your landing this morning."

Freeman took another look at the disk and the writing on its surface. A little shiver ran up her spine at the mere possibility the disk came from anywhere but Earth. She handed it back to Pilot. "Well, if it is a data disk, maybe the thing to do is try to read it. Maybe it'll have some answers about where it came from."

"If it's from Earth, that should be pretty easy. If not…." Pilot's voice caught in his throat. He held the disk up in the light again. "Reading this may be easier said than done."

"Nothing ventured, nothing gained," said Jefferson with a wink.

*

Two days after returning from Mars, Lisa entered her quarters and logged into her email. Most of the mail was junk, but she smiled when she saw a video from her little sister, Mika. Lisa tapped the control on her keyboard and Mika appeared life-size and smiling on the wall of her room. The image was so realistic that Lisa almost believed she could walk right into her sister's bedroom and pick up a stuffed animal.

"Hey, big sister," said Mika, "we just saw some of the pictures you guys sent back from Mars. Wow!" She paused and shook her head. "Imagine that! My big sister on Mars. I am *so* jealous!"

Lisa smiled to herself. Indeed it seemed strange to think about. Mika was always the one who climbed over things and dug in the dirt while Lisa played quietly with dolls or read. Of course, Lisa often pretended her dolls were pirates on the high seas or explorers of some kind. She returned her attention to the message.

"So, what's this that Mom tells me? She says you have a boyfriend!" Lisa's cheeks warmed. "When you send a message back, you have to tell me all about him … or better yet, send a picture.

"Also, I wanted to let you know, I got accepted to State. I am so excited. I can't wait to start packing." Lisa looked up at her sister again as though it were the first time. She pulled up the calendar program and shook her head, having a hard time believing so much time had passed.

Mika fell silent for a moment and shuffled her feet. "I hate to admit this, sis, but I really miss you. You be careful out there. I want you home in one piece. Send me a message soon, okay?"

With that, Mika's image vanished from the wall. Lisa smiled as she thought about home. She went to the refrigerator and retrieved a glass of tea, then sat on the edge of the bed and thought of the message she would send back to her sister.

Pilot first tried to read the Martian disk using the data readers on *Aristarchus's* computers. The disk wasn't a standard size and there was no spindle hole, so he instructed Daryl LaRue to manufacture an adapter. Even with an adapter, none of the software recognized it as a data disk. He downloaded a data decryption tool from Quinn Corp that was supposed to read disks manufactured anywhere in the world. He had no luck with that, either.

Over the course of the following month, Pilot assembled a makeshift optical bench in the *Ares* lander bay. He borrowed two spare communications lasers from ship's stores along with a scanning target. He asked Daryl to machine some clamps and a tabletop to hold it all. Then he began the painstaking process of shooting the laser and sensing the reflections to see if he detected any indications of data on the disk.

At one point, he looked at the coin-shaped disk and thought about the family business. His father would only see value in the project if there were potential profit. Pilot was too caught up in solving the mystery to care about much else. He wondered if his father had ever been so intrigued by something to feel that way.

As Pilot worked, speculation about the disk ran rampant through the crew. Vanda Berko and Angus MacDonald were convinced the disk was an alien artifact and even hung a star chart in the galley and started a pool, taking guesses of which star the aliens were from. The more skeptical people, such as Dr. Nagamine, thought it was simply a glass-like volcanic rock, polished to a high shine by the fierce Martian winds and the 'writing' was merely a series of scratches.

Dr. Nagamine, who shared Pilot's joy of learning in spite of his skepticism, started cataloging the photos and recordings they made on the Martian surface, leaving Neb O'Connell to spend somewhat longer shifts in C-and-C. In spite of Pilot's assurances that they would have no problem traversing the asteroid belt, O'Connell scanned for rocks or debris that might be in their path well before the ship actually entered the belt. Over time, he became aware that Lisa also spent more time on duty, even though her job didn't require it. He appreciated the company. She often brought coffee or cookies from the kitchen to share.

Though pleased with the trip to the Martian surface, Captain Jefferson already looked forward to the trip into the Jovian atmosphere. He was well aware that there would be no surface to land on, but just the idea of being one of the first humans to fly through Jupiter's atmosphere excited him. He spent what off-watch time he could afford aboard the *Zeus I* shuttle-lander, running simulations. He'd felt a little sluggish handling the *Ares* in Martian orbit and in the atmosphere. He knew in some regions of Jupiter, the winds were far more violent than those they faced in the small Martian storm.

Myra Lee heard no more from her colleagues on Earth and began to despair they had run into a dead end on the whale communication project. She sent an email burst to Earth asking Cristof and Harmer if they'd learned anything new. In their return message, she learned they suspected the phrases, "the cycle continues" and "the cycle resumes" were a regular part of the whale songs. Working on that assumption, they thought they could pick up other instances of those words in the extended songs. However, it wasn't enough yet to attempt a complete translation.

Knowing Pilot was engaged in a project that kept him away from both the central hub and his quarters—where he rarely spent time anyway—Natalie Freeman decided to continue her investigation into his background and his reasons for traveling to Saturn. She started her investigation in his quarters. Looking in the closet, she found several pairs of coveralls and boots. There were also some nice items of clothing—fine shirts and tailored slacks that she suspected were beyond the means of most Quinn Corp engineers. She wondered if Alonzo Thomas came from a wealthy family. If so, perhaps that implied a corporate alliance between the Quinns and Thomas's family, which might provide a clue.

She moved on to Pilot's desk. Inside one of the drawers, she found a report binder. Opening the first page, she read the title "*Lunar Chronotons: An Important New Resource by Alonzo Thomas*." As she thumbed through the report, she heard footsteps approaching from the corridor. Quickly, she put the report back in the drawer and ducked into the closet just as the door opened. Pilot crossed the room and stepped into the bathroom, closing the door part way. Quietly, Freeman slipped out of the closet and sneaked to the door.

Once out, she went to her own quarters and dropped into her chair. That had been closer than she'd liked. Taking a few deep breaths, she went to her own bathroom, got a glass of water, then went back to the chair, bringing up a computer information screen. She did a search on the word 'chronoton.' The computer came back with no results, but it did ask if she'd made a spelling error and meant something else. It presented her with a list of options, including chronos, chronograph, and chronology. She chose 'chronos.' The computer informed her it was the Greek word for time. Unless she was reaching too far, Natalie Freeman realized Alonzo Thomas had discovered something about the nature of time while on the Moon. However, she wasn't quite sure what that had to do with Saturn.

Later that afternoon, Freeman took her shift at the command console and surfed the web, hoping to find a connection between the time particles, Quinn Corp, and Alonzo Thomas. The web was sluggish because of the transmission time to Earth. She would send a command, then peruse shipboard status reports while waiting for data to upload to the ship's computer.

She found a website that talked about the history of Quinn Corp. Mostly, it discussed Jerome Quinn's younger days and his invention of quinitite—the strong but lightweight plastic matrix which could be grown like crystals in microgravity. Quinitite actually helped to dissipate static charges, making it ideal for use in computer boards. Computer chips were far less susceptible to being destroyed by someone's touch. Being strong and lightweight made it ideal for the solar sail framework.

As Freeman scanned the website, she saw a photo that made her heart skip a beat. She looked up at the pilot's console. Fortunately, Pilot was off the command and control deck. She debated what action to take next and whether or not to show the photo to Captain Jefferson.

Taking a deep breath and letting it out slowly, she looked around at the stations. The ship had the newest and best computers. The walls around them had kept them alive for nearly eight months in space. Even the ship's ergonomic design was pleasant, she thought as she looked at the functional carpet that covered C-and-C's floor and the design of the desk she used.

She looked back at the command console's screen and a chill went down her spine even as things began to make more sense.

Chapter 15
Through the Belt

A month and a half out from Mars, Pilot announced the *Aristarchus* had entered the asteroid belt. He had Daryl LaRue make a slight course correction based on data Neb O'Connell had taken. "We've had smooth sailing so far," said Pilot. "We have four months in the belt. Let's hope it continues to go well."

"Indeed." Jefferson sat at the command console. Pilot started to leave the command deck, but the captain stopped him. "Say, have you learned anything about that coin we found on Mars?"

"Nothing definitive."

Myra looked up from her work at the biosciences console. "Pilot, would you mind if Lisa and I come up and take a look? Lisa's good at seeing patterns—after all, she helped me see that the whales were speaking in binary code. Maybe we could help."

Pilot pursed his lips and rocked back and forth on his feet. "I'm not sure what you could contribute at this stage."

"Even if we can't contribute, I'd like to take a look at your setup. It sounds fascinating."

He rolled his eyes. "All right, why don't you meet me up there in an hour." With that, he turned and left the deck.

*

An hour later, Myra and Lisa ascended the ladder into the *Ares* launch bay. On the other side of the shuttle-lander, Pilot typed on a laptop computer atop a small folding table. A little servomotor responded to his command and adjusted the laser's position relative to the disk. The women stepped up behind him, looking over his shoulder.

"I'm scanning the surface of the disk at different angles, trying to see if I can pick up any evidence of encoded data," said Pilot. "So far, I haven't had much luck." He pulled up a chart he'd made of his scan results. It looked like a child's drawing of a field of grass. "It's nothing but noise."

Lisa's eyes narrowed. "Can you zoom in on that noise?"

Pilot shrugged, then did as she requested.

Lisa pointed at the peaks and valleys. "If that was noise, wouldn't you expect the peaks and valleys to change height and depth? They look extremely uniform to me."

"But the amplitude is so low," said Pilot. "And there's so much. Why, if that's data we're looking at, the storage capacity of that disk would be millions of times greater than anything we've ever built." At that comment, Pilot blinked a couple of times, then looked from the computer to the disk. "It can't be." He put his hand to his mouth.

Myra looked at Lisa. "Are you saying that the 'noise' is actually the data?"

Lisa nodded. "Looks that way to me, boss."

"Then if I understand right, what Pilot's just said is that there's no way this disk could have been manufactured on Earth." Myra's mouth fell open.

"Let me play with this some more," said Pilot. He looked up at Myra. "Can your translation program compare bits of binary code to other bits of binary code and look for patterns?"

Myra nodded, mute.

"Let me read off as much as I can, then send this to you. Maybe we can match up some more patterns," he said, hopefully.

"I'll take a look," began Myra, "but this all assumes that the people who manufactured this disk speak the same language as the whales have been speaking."

✳

As predicted, the voyage through the asteroid belt proceeded smoothly—at least to start. Neb O'Connell had detected no unexpected objects and asked Angus MacDonald to throw a small party in the ship's galley for Valentine's Day. Angus, happy for an excuse to throw a party, readily agreed. Neb asked several friends from the ship to attend, including Pilot, Captain Jefferson, and Daryl LaRue.

The party started out subdued with people talking quietly among themselves. Soft music issued from the galley speakers. Once most of the off-duty crew had arrived, Neb tapped on a glass with a spoon. "Hello, everyone. Lisa, would you mind coming up here and joining me?"

Looking confused, Lisa stepped up and joined Neb. He handed her a small package. Opening it, she eyed the plain silver ring dubiously. "What's this?" she asked.

"Well, it started life as a length of spare conduit tubing from the shipboard machine shop," said Neb. "Daryl cut off a small section and now it's an engagement ring."

She looked at the ring and then inclined her head, eyeing Neb. "Are you serious?"

"I've never been more serious. Lisa, I would like you to be the keeper of my ring." Neb reached out, took the ring he had given her and carefully slipped it on her finger.

She smiled, wrapped her arms around him, and kissed him. "Yes, I'll keep your ring and I'll marry you, as well."

A cheer rose from the people gathered in the galley. Captain Jefferson stepped forward and clasped Neb's hand as people talked among themselves and made their way toward the snack table.

"Captain, would you agree to marry us in the ship's hub as we approach Saturn?" asked Neb.

The captain opened his mouth to speak, but Lisa cut him off. "Saturn? That's over a year away. Why wait?"

"Why hurry?" countered Neb. "I think the ceremony should be held in the most beautiful place of all and I can't think of anything more beautiful than having Saturn in all its glory right outside the window."

"Well, I'd be happy to oblige." Jefferson cast a sidelong glance at Lisa, "if the young lady agrees."

Lisa narrowed her eyes and looked at Neb. "First people married at Saturn, eh? I've never been one to stand on ceremony, but it sounds like fun." She looked from Neb to Jefferson. "All right, Captain, married at Saturn it is." Then she looked back at Neb, grinned, and whispered in his ear. "But don't think this is the end of the conversation."

Neb smiled nervously and stepped away to retrieve two

glasses of punch.

∗

In the back of the room, Angus MacDonald made his way to Daryl LaRue who leaned against the wall, his arms folded. Angus cleared his throat, but Daryl remained silent and refused to meet Angus's gaze. "I wanted to apologize for calling you a cheater."

Daryl started to walk away, but he stopped. "You put together a good spread."

"Neb and Lisa are good kids," said Angus.

"Hard workers." Daryl grunted. It was high praise. He looked around and was about to say something but bit off the words when he saw the look on the cook's face. "I'm sorry I gave you that black eye."

"Ha!" shouted Angus. "You wouldna' touched me if I hadn't been drinkin'." The two laughed and shook hands. "What I wanted to know was whether you were game for a rematch." The two looked up when they realized a hush had descended on the room and all eyes were on them.

LaRue laughed. "Any time you are."

Angus brought out the cards and the two sat down at a table.

∗

As they dealt the cards, Pilot thought he heard something. He stepped out into the corridor where it was quieter and listened carefully. He realized he felt a vibration more than he heard an actual noise. He stepped over to the intercom. "Pilot to C-and-C, is everything all right up there?"

"Pilot, I think you better get up here to advise," said Freeman. Though still calm and professional, her voice had a note of concern.

"On my way." Pilot took a moment to step into the galley. He whispered something in Captain Jefferson's ear, then stepped over to Neb. "Sorry to end the party early, but I think something's going on we need to check out." Pilot proceeded to C-and-C with Jefferson and O'Connell close behind.

Neb O'Connell went right to the astrosciences console and spoke to Dr. Nagamine who examined data from the ship's sensors. "We seem to have encountered a field of fine particles," reported Neb. "In the astronomy biz, we'd call it 'dust,' but I'd say that the particles are more like pebbles."

Freeman inclined her head. "Why didn't we see this ahead of time?"

Pilot chewed on his lower lip. "The distance sensors aren't designed to detect particles this small. We can only sense them when they impact the hull and sails." He then stepped over to his console and ran a few calculations. "This can't be a very large field or it would have been detected from Earth," he said. "I think the best thing we can do is ride it out."

"Won't these particles rip the sails' aluminum?" asked Jefferson.

Pilot closed his eyes. "Dust fields are an expected hazard and the ship is designed to handle them. The sails are slightly oversized, so a few punctures won't slow our acceleration much. It's just," his gaze drifted to the rounded deck of C-and-C, toward the outer hull, "I didn't expect it to be so loud."

Jefferson put his hand on Pilot's shoulder. "Very well, then. We'll ride it out … and pray."

*

Natalie swallowed hard as she listened to Pilot's voice quaver and watched his hands tremble. The time had come to tell the captain what she knew about Pilot.

The pinging and vibration from the 'dust' particles slowed about a half hour after they began. Neb O'Connell checked the sensors. "Minimal damage from the dust."

"Thanks." Jefferson stepped up to Neb and patted him on the shoulder. "I think you have a party to get back to."

Neb looked down at his hands. "I feel like it's my fault that this happened, that I should have been here."

Jefferson took a deep breath. "It's not your fault, son. Dr. Nagamine was here and the sensors weren't designed to see the particles. Sitting here and sulking isn't going to solve the problem. You have a young lady in the galley waiting for you."

Neb looked up and smiled at the captain. "Thanks, sir." With that, he stood and returned to the party.

The next day, Pilot agreed to take more watches in

C-and-C while the ship continued through the asteroid belt. Natalie thought he seemed edgy. He would place his hand on the walls or on tabletops as though trying to discern something about the behavior of the ship through touch. Even though the external sensors reported no damage, Pilot hovered near the astrosciences station while on watch, his gaze flitting over the readings.

Freeman took the opportunity to ask Jefferson to join her in the ship's gym. She rode a stationary bike while Jefferson walked on a treadmill. "I've figured out who Alonzo Thomas is," she said as she pedaled. "I think you should know in case it has a bearing on the safety of the ship."

Jefferson lifted his eyebrows but kept walking on the treadmill.

"He's Jerome Quinn's twenty-two-year-old son." She thought for a moment. "Actually, he's just going on twenty-three, now."

The captain stopped walking and was nearly pushed off the treadmill as the belt kept rolling. He hopped off. "Are you sure?"

Natalie stopped pedaling and climbed off the bike. She led him over to the computer playing music over the gym speakers. Opening a window, she brought up the file she'd found about the Quinn family. "This is a photo of Jerome Quinn, his wife, and two sons." She zoomed in on the photo. The lanky young man closest to Jerome in height had the same wiry hair, the same angular features, and the same thoughtful eyes as Alonzo Thomas.

Jefferson shook his head. After a moment, he stepped back to the treadmill. He turned up the speed and began a brisk walk.

Natalie folded her arms and watched the captain from her seat at the computer console. "What's your assessment of the situation, Captain?"

"All we've learned is that he's about six years younger than we thought from the files." Holding onto the treadmill's handle with one hand, he pointed to his gray hair with the other. "From my perspective, that's not much difference. He's a young pup no matter how you cut it." He indicated the ship around them. "Pilot may be a young man, but he's proven his abilities."

Natalie cleared the photo from the computer console, stood, and returned to the stationary bike. "Those six years can make a big difference in maturity and in experience, Captain. My God, man, he just got his bachelor's degree a year before we started this flight."

Jefferson nodded. "What would you have me do? Order him to turn the ship around?"

Freeman shook her head as she resumed pedaling. "What good would that do at this stage? But we need to watch him ... maybe guide him a little more."

"He's a strong-willed young man," said Jefferson. "He probably won't take to being 'guided.'"

"But..."

Jefferson turned off the treadmill and held up his hands. "I hear what you're saying and I share your concern. I'll keep my eyes open and do what I can." He stepped off the treadmill and poured some water from a dispenser in the wall. "In some ways, he already did what was necessary. He put you and me in command of this ship. That shows a maturity I've seen lacking in some much older people."

Freeman considered that as she continued pedaling. "Why do you think he's using an alias?"

Jefferson shrugged as he sat on a bench and picked up two dumbbells. "The very existence of this mission concerned the president. What do you think would have happened if the president knew that Quinn's own son led the expedition?"

Freeman stopped pedaling. "He would have looked much harder at the expedition and probed much more thoroughly into its purpose."

Jefferson nodded. "Rather than simply send you aboard, he might have found a way to stop it." He lifted the dumbbells. "Do you regret coming along?"

"No." Freeman stepped off the bike. "I wouldn't trade it for the world."

*

The *Aristarchus* continued through the asteroid belt without incident. However, Pilot still insisted something had changed in the ship's behavior. "I can't quite put my finger on it," he said to Daryl LaRue. "It's like there's a slight wobble or vibration that wasn't there before."

The tech manager shook his head. "I don't feel anything, sir."

"Still, I'd feel better if you did a complete system's check."

"Right away." Daryl ordered the mechanics through the ship to visually inspect the masts, bearings, and motors. Using telescopes mounted in the steerage rooms, they were able to inspect the sails themselves. The crew also went through and checked all of the thruster components to make sure the thrusters weren't somehow leaking fuel, adding to the ship's natural motion.

"Well, the only thing we can see are some punctures in the sails. That shouldn't cause any vibration, though," reported LaRue. "That is if there's any vibration at all. We're not measuring any."

"And we've not slowed down," said Pilot. "That's the only thing I really feared about holes in the sails. Apparently, it's not enough to slow us given the amount of sunlight we're getting out here."

"I'm guessing the vibration is just your imagination, sir."

"You're probably right." Pilot sighed. "I'm probably just nervous."

"Nothing to worry about, sir," said LaRue. "We just need to sit back and drift into Jupiter's orbit."

Chapter 16
Alien Data

Natalie Freeman knocked on Neb O'Connell's door. His mouth dropped open when he answered, but he quickly closed it and smiled nervously, asking her to come in. "Congratulations on your engagement," she said in a conversational tone.

"Thanks. I'm kind of nervous but kind of looking forward to the wedding all at the same time."

"I think that's the way it's supposed to be." Natalie sighed, briefly remembering a couple of her own boyfriends from the past. None had ever been serious about marriage.

Neb sat down in one chair, and held his hand toward the other. "Have you ever been married, Captain Freeman?"

She smiled wistfully and sat back. "They say a captain's married to her ship. I suppose I've felt like that at times, especially with the *Daniel B. Sherman.*"

"What about the *Aristarchus?*"

"It's not quite the same." She reached out, touched the wall, and frowned thoughtfully. Clearing her throat, she faced Neb again. "*Aristarchus* is Jefferson's ship, not mine. In many ways, it's even more Pilot's ship than either of ours. He oversaw construction. It's his baby. I'm just along for the ride."

Neb's brow furrowed. "Is that the only reason you're aboard the ship?"

"Well..." Natalie remembered her childhood, remembered playing with cardboard boxes and wearing coveralls that really weren't very different from the ones she currently wore. "I always wanted to be an astronaut. In some ways, this mission was my one opportunity to fulfill the dream."

"Yeah, I had the same dream. My parents had DVDs of all the great science fiction shows from the twentieth century. I used to watch them all the time and pretend I was aboard a ship exploring strange new worlds." His eyes took on a faraway look.

"And here you are." Though she'd first seen Neb as awkward and a little strange, she wondered if he were, in fact, something of a kindred spirit.

"Say," he said, "can I get you some coffee or tea? Something to drink?"

Natalie held up her hand. "No thanks. Really, I only came by because I had a couple of quick astronomy questions."

Neb flashed a sheepish smile. "Dr. Nagamine might be the better person to talk to. I'm only a telescope operator. He's the full-time astronomer."

"Actually, the questions relate more to your observing experience than to astronomical theory." She paused, thinking how best to phrase her question. "As I understand, you worked at the Very Large Array. They do a lot of solar system work these days, don't they?"

"Some." The corners of Neb's mouth turned down. "We get proposals from a lot of small colleges, which means a lot of thesis work."

She nodded. "That's what I understand. What I was wondering is whether you ever observed anything unusual about the Saturn system, particularly something where Saturn and our Moon might have something in common."

He shook his head. "Nothing like that. I can't think of anything that the Moon and Saturn have in common at radio frequencies, except for the fact that the Moon and Saturn's rings are both fairly radio quiet. Heck, Saturn's moons and our Moon don't even have that much in common." He sat back, brow creased. "However, I did have one really unusual observation of Saturn's moon Titan. I was observing for our boss, Alonzo Thomas, and the moon was flaring in one particular radio frequency. It almost looked like an exploding star."

"What exactly was the frequency?" asked Natalie.

"I don't remember precisely." He stood and retrieved a pad of paper and a pen from the desk drawer. Sitting down again, he wrote a number. "It was something in that range." He handed the paper to Natalie. "The funny thing is Pilot called me to ask about joining this mission only a few days after I made that observation. I've wondered if there was a connection, but Pilot's never talked about it."

She took the paper, folded it up, and put it in her pocket. "You must have impressed the powers that be at Quinn Corp, somehow." She stood and moved toward the door. Just before she left, she turned. "Thanks much. Sometime you, Lisa, and I should get together and talk about those old science fiction TV shows."

"I'd like that," said Neb.

Natalie Freeman gave a curt nod, then walked down the corridor. Ahead of her, Pilot left his quarters and climbed the ladder toward the ship's central hub. Once he was out of sight, she stepped into his quarters and located the report she'd seen before. She opened the report to the table of contents and found an entry labeled, "Detection of chronotons using radio frequencies." Opening the report to the indicated page, she ran her finger down the paper until she came to a number. Holding her finger on the number, she retrieved the paper John O'Connell had given her. The number in the report was right in the middle of the frequency range for the detection of the mysterious chronotons.

She flipped back to the beginning of the report and read the abstract at the top of the first page. It told her scientists had discovered some rather unusual particles on the Moon. Upon study, it was determined the particles could jump into the fourth physical dimension, speculated by some to be the dimension of time. At the end, the abstract speculated that if a sufficient quantity of chronotons were located, they could have many applications including the construction of a time machine, a weapon, and more.

Natalie let out a long, low whistle. Now she knew what Thomas Quinn was after at Saturn and why.

*

During the months traversing the asteroid belt, Myra Lee and Lisa Henry devoted much of their duty time attempting to decrypt the data disk found on Mars. Lisa, working with a computer tech named Jenna Reynolds, wrote a program that compared the binary code from the whale songs to the binary code on the disk. They found a match for every word of the whale message somewhere on the disk.

"I think we should send some of these data segments back to Earth and see if Cristof and Harmer can make anything of them," said Myra. She composed an email message, explaining the discovery of the Martian disk, taking care to emphasize that they were still not certain whether the disk came from an Earth spaceship or was alien in origin. "All the same," she wrote, "we feel there are enough data segments in common between the disk and the language used by the whales that you should have a look." After attaching the data segments to the message, she sent it away.

Meanwhile, Pilot worked on another segment of the disk. He asked Jenna to come up to the *Ares* bay and take a look at some data he'd downloaded onto his laptop computer. She stared at the binary data for some time, then looked up at Pilot. "This almost looks like a binary encoded image to me, or a sequence of images."

"Is there any way to decode the image?" asked Pilot.

Jenna nodded. "Assuming the people who dropped this disk use pixel encoded data like we do, there are only so many ways an image can be coded, presuming there's not some kind of encryption on the disk. Are you plugged into the ship's network up here?"

Pilot nodded.

"Send me that image sequence and I'll see what I can do with it. I've got a few image decoding algorithms. It may do no good, but it might still be fun to try them out on this sequence and see what I come up with."

The next day, Myra received an email back from Joyce Harmer. In the message, Joyce wrote:

"The data segments are fascinating. They do, in fact, appear to be related to the whales' language. We're working through it now. With a little time, we might be able to add more words to the translation program."

✱

Jenna Reynolds called Pilot and Lisa Henry on the intercom

and asked them to meet her in command and control. Fifteen minutes later, they all converged at the biosciences station.

"What's going on?" asked Captain Jefferson from the command console.

"Pilot found a string of images on that disk you recovered on Mars," said Jenna breathlessly. "There's something on it I think you need to see."

Jefferson looked to Neb O'Connell and they stepped up behind the biosciences console. Myra stood up, letting Jenna sit in her place. She typed in some commands and an image appeared on the primary display.

"It's Olympus Mons," declared Jefferson. "Not far from our landing site."

Jenna brought up three more images. All were views around the caldera. Then she brought up a fourth image. It showed a silver, egg-shaped craft sitting on the ground on three thin landing legs. Symbols, similar to those on the disk, adorned the craft.

"That's like no Earth vessel I've ever seen." Jefferson shook his head. Daryl LaRue and Vanda Berko, who had been working at the thruster control station, grew curious about the images and stepped up. "Look familiar to either of you?" They shook their heads.

"You ain't seen nothin' yet," said Reynolds. She pushed the button.

The next frame showed a creature apparently seated inside the spacecraft from the previous image. The creature was vaguely humanoid in appearance. Its head looked a little like a soft, overripe orange. Set into the head were two black, bulbous eyes. A thick purple mustache sat underneath a long, thin nose. No mouth was visible under the mustache. The creature wore a long, flowing black robe. Its hand rested atop the ship's console. Myra counted six fingers in all and noted that the fingers on either side of the hand were jointed as though they were both thumbs. Dr. Garcia stood up at the life sciences console to get a better view. Everyone was silent for the better part of a minute as the realization that they were seeing intelligent extraterrestrials for the first time sank in.

"Is that what the whales were talking to?" asked Pilot,

quietly, almost reverently.

Myra's hand was up to her mouth. "Your guess is as good as mine." Her voice caught in her throat.

"I was able to interpret one other frame," said Jenna. She brought it up on the screen. It showed an animal of some kind with its mouth open, revealing razor sharp fangs. However, the creature itself appeared to be covered in soft, smooth fur. Above its muzzle, it had two small, black button-like eyes. Two small round ears sat atop its head.

"It's like a teddy bear," said Neb, chuckling nervously.

"More like a teddy bear from hell," said Lisa with a wry grin. "Look at those teeth."

"The people who dropped that disk must be explorers," declared Myra. She moved from one foot to another in a motion that would be excited pacing, except everyone on deck crowded in to get a better look. "What order are the pictures in?"

Jenna shrugged. "I'm pretty sure it's chronological, but it's hard to tell whether it's forward or backward."

"Let's assume they dropped the disk after taking that picture of Olympus Mons," said Myra. "That would imply that we just saw the sequence in reverse order. I'd assume that the creature we saw at the end was some animal they encountered on their journey. Presumably before they went to Mars."

"I just hope we don't have to meet it." Dr. Garcia had crowded in with the others. "It's hard to tell how big it is, but even a small creature like that could tear a pretty good hole in someone."

"Well, we've learned one thing for sure," said Pilot. "That disk is definitely alien in origin and it contains data. Whether it will help us as we continue our journey is hard to say, but it's certainly quite an artifact."

Myra spun around and faced Pilot. "We've discovered life," she said. "There's life out here and we might just be able to talk to it!" She turned to Lisa. "We've got to get a message out to Harmer and Cristof right away—getting more words for our translation program's top priority!"

Jenna hopped out of the seat and joined in the excited murmurings behind the biosciences station as Lisa Henry sat.

Captain Jefferson did his best to usher people back to their stations. As he did, he realized more people began to drift into the C-and-C from other parts of the ship, to see the images on the screen. "We've got a ship to run, people." Jefferson tried to force a note of authority into his voice in spite of the excitement. "Quick look and back to work. We'll get the images on the ship-wide network, so you can look at them when you're off duty."

*

Natalie Freeman composed a secure message to President Oscar Van der Wald. She opened her message by announcing that the artifact found on Mars was definitely extraterrestrial and there was a good chance the whales of Earth were speaking the language used by the disk's creators. "*In my estimate,*" she wrote, "*it's possible that we will meet this extraterrestrial life before the mission is over. If so, I will do my best to represent the United States adequately. Please send any special instructions.*"

She then reported she had searched Alonzo Thomas's quarters and found nothing more than a few textbooks and some memos on Quinn Corp letterhead related to the *Aristarchus's* construction but did not give any details as to the purpose of the mission other than Quinn Corp's interest in exploration. She sent the message. As she did, her stomach knotted and churned. She hated to lie in an official report. It went against everything she'd been taught in the military. However, her instincts told her telling the United States government about the possible existence of particles that could be used to manipulate time itself could be the biggest mistake she could possibly make.

She thought about Captain Jefferson's words regarding Pilot's true identity. Aboard the *Aristarchus*, she was in a position to watch him and even influence his actions. She wanted to see what Quinn would actually do with the time particles before she alerted the entire world to their existence. She also suspected the extraterrestrial life they discovered might somehow be connected to the time particles. If true, diplomacy may ultimately prove the most important skill needed on the mission.

Looking at the timestamp on the computer display, she

realized it was only a few days before Christmas. Angus prepared another party. With a sigh, she put aside her keypad,
and realized this was a time to be with friends. She called
C-and-C to see if Lisa and Neb would like to join her for some
good old twentieth century television.

Chapter 17
Drifting Toward Jupiter

As the yearlong transit from Mars to Jupiter neared its end, Neb O'Connell and Lisa Henry entered the central hub to look at the solar system's biggest planet. *Aristarchus* was now close enough and their angle of approach was such that they could just make out the frail, solitary ring encircling the planet. Neb noticed Lisa looked at the solitary ring encircling her finger. "Are you having second thoughts about the wedding?"

She looked up at him and smiled reassuringly. "Not second thoughts really, just a few concerns." She looked out the window at the brown, white, and red planet beyond. "What are our plans after this mission? After all, you live in New Mexico and I live in Alaska. Where do we settle?"

"I assumed I'd work for Quinn Corp after the mission was over." Neb gave a little shrug. "My days at the VLA were numbered." When she looked up at him with a creased brow, he quickly amended his words. "I should say, the VLA's days are numbered. If I returned there, I'd just find myself out of work in about five or ten years."

"So, did Thomas say you would be working at Quinn Corp?"

Neb nodded. "With the experience from this mission, perhaps you could get a job there, too."

"Working for Quinn Corp would probably mean sitting in an office all day." She wrinkled her nose in distaste. "But maybe I could work as an assistant for Dr. Cristof. That would at least put us in the same state."

Neb and Lisa fell silent and both stared out at the planet for a little while longer. The great red spot, a storm that had been brewing for several centuries, was just rotating into view. He thought about his mother who had looked very pale in her last video and expressed her disappointment she couldn't attend her son's wedding in person. "Our careers are not your big worry, are they?" he asked after a few minutes.

"It sounds kind of silly ... especially since I never really wanted a big church wedding and all, and I certainly didn't want to be married in one of those big silly white dresses, but it just occurred to me that I didn't pack a single dress of any kind for this trip."

"I like you as you are." Neb smiled at her. "I think you look great in coveralls."

She looked down and sighed. "Thanks, but I at least want to look pretty and feminine for my wedding."

"I thought you didn't care about silly princess weddings and all that."

She looked up and met his eyes. "It's not that. I just don't want to look like an auto mechanic." She snorted and looked out at Jupiter. "Unfortunately, I have my doubts that Natalie Freeman or Vanda Berko even own dresses and if they do, why would they have brought them along?"

"What about Myra?" asked Neb innocently.

Lisa laughed. "If you haven't noticed I'm a bit bigger around the middle than she is. Even if she did bring a dress, it'd probably kill me to try to squeeze into it."

Neb sighed. "We'll work out something." Then he smiled wickedly. "Hey, I just remembered, Angus MacDonald owns a kilt. He's about your size."

Lisa punched Neb in the arm. "You are *so* strange sometimes." Then she pulled him close, giving him a hug. "I suppose that's why I love you."

*

When Vanda Berko and Angus MacDonald started their pool, taking guesses about the Martian disk's origin, it was met with much amusement and a few people put their guesses in. Once everyone knew alien life really had created the disk, interest in the pool increased. At the end of each meal, people washed their dishes and then stepped over to the chart and placed their guess into the jar.

Angus watched when Daryl LaRue wrote 'Betelgeuse' on a slip of paper. The cook shook his head. "Don't you know that you can't have life at Betelgeuse?"

"Why not?" asked LaRue.

"It's a red supergiant," said the cook. "If there was a planet with life, it would have been swallowed up centuries ago."

LaRue shrugged. "Well … maybe they evolved at a planet near Betelgeuse and then left before the sun expanded."

"Maybe," said Angus, "but you still can't enter Betelgeuse into the pool."

"Why not?" pressed LaRue.

"Because that's my guess!"

✳

On Earth, the president of the United States sat down at his desk with a cup of coffee and several morning newspapers. He sighed as he opened the *New York Times*. Legitimate newspapers were starting to look like tabloids. There were reports of car crashes happening because someone thought they saw an extraterrestrial spaceship or murders occurring because someone believed the aliens had spoken to them. The headline that caught the president's eye was almost as bad. "*Aliens speak to whales*," it announced. Natalie Freeman had been reporting the progress of Myra Lee and her Earthbound colleagues in translating the alien disk they found on Mars. So the news didn't surprise him. In fact, he had security agencies keeping tabs on Cristof and Harmer's work in case it proved to be an issue. The president snorted and nearly turned the page when a thought occurred to him.

He put the paper down and picked up the phone. He pushed the speed dial button for Diana Aguilar's office. "Diana," said Van der Wald, "what kind of fuel do you suppose aliens would use?"

✳

Thomas Alonzo Quinn floated in the *Aristarchus's* hub, preparing to control the ship's entry into Jupiter's orbit. This stage of the flight was crucial and he wanted to see the ship's trajectory with his own eyes. If he got it right, the ship would orbit the gas giant planet ten times, then move into a hyperbolic orbit that would slingshot the sailing ship onward to Saturn at a speed that would get them there in a little under six months. If he got the calculations wrong, their flight would be slowed so much, they would be better off turning around and going home to Earth.

Pilot's tablet displayed information about Jupiter's most unpredictable feature, it's bow shock—the place where the solar wind collided head-on with Jupiter's own intense magnetic field like warm air and cold air colliding over Kansas to create a tornado. The last few months of the journey, the solar wind had been a bit more intense than normal. While not the primary force pushing *Aristarchus*, Pilot realized that the outflow of charged particles from the sun was contributing more to their motion than predicted. He tried to convince himself that was the reason for the vibration he felt yet the techs could not measure. Pilot took several deep breaths as the ship approached the bow shock, telling himself several small, unmanned spacecraft had done the very maneuver he hoped to accomplish, there was no reason he should be afraid.

He began a countdown, "Ten, nine, eight ...." When he got to five, his thumbs drifted over the sail controls, ready to adjust course to compensate for the bow shock, if needed. When he got to three, there was a loud bang. The ship hit the bow shock unexpectedly early.

Lights flickered on and off intermittently. Before hitting the bow shock, Jupiter seemed to stand still. Now, the planet grew noticeably closer. The motion seemed slow because of the distances involved, but a dial on Pilot's tablet confirmed they were careening into the planet. Gently, he eased the sails around, trying to bring the ship into orbit. As he did, the ship rattled and groaned all around him. He was slowing the ship, but not enough. Jupiter's gravitational field, charged particles, and photon pressure from both the Sun and Jupiter vibrated the sails at their resonant frequency.

"The masts are reaching critical stress," called Neb O'Connell from C-and-C. "If you don't back off the sails, the masts are going to snap."

"If I back off the sails, we'll go sailing right into the planet!" said Pilot through gritted teeth. "LaRue, give me some thrust! Help me out."

The ship's thrusters fired, and the acceleration drew Pilot

back, away from the front window. If anything, the ship vibrated even more.

"There's a stress fracture on the number three mast." Neb's voice had risen at least an octive. "We've got to do something quick or the ship's going to fly apart."

Pilot kicked off the back window while studying the tablet's display and suddenly had a thought. He put his thumbs on the sail controls and locked his gaze on the clock in the upper right-hand corner, counting down seconds.

"Prepare to jettison number three sail," called Jefferson from C-and-C. "LaRue, stand by on thruster control. Get Berko to the towing shuttle, now."

"No! You don't have time for all that. It's too late!" said Pilot.

"I'm not going to let this ship fall into the planet," said Jefferson, threateningly.

Without another word, Pilot commanded the sails to turn ninety degrees. As the sails turned, the ship shuddered hard and he almost tumbled into the wall. All of the console's indicators moved into the red. Gripping the tablet so hard, his knuckles turned white, he discerned something just a little hopeful. The planet's motion slowed … just a little. As the sails reached position, the vibrations settled down.

After several achingly slow minutes, the planet drifted to the side. They were no longer plunging toward Jupiter. He counted down on his clock again, then moved the sails forty-five degrees back to normal. The console indicators crawled back into the yellow zones. One or two remained red. The ship had sustained damage. The important question, could it be repaired?

Chapter 18
Damage Control

In command and control, Jonathan Jefferson's emotions warred with one another. He was ecstatic to be alive, yet furious with Pilot for trying such a crazy stunt with the sail controls. Likewise, he wanted to go down to the planet, yet he also worried about the condition of the ship. He looked over at Neb O'Connell, who sat at his console, visibly shaking. "Neb, what's the sail status?" The captain knew he needed to give the technician something productive to think about.

"Number three mast appears to have suffered serious structural damage," said Neb, a little timidly. He checked the readouts on his console. "We may also have some damage to the number eight mast. I'm getting indeterminate readings from one of the sensors."

"Could be the sensor itself is damaged," offered Daryl LaRue.

"Better get me a visual," said Jefferson. "Check the scopes and see how the sail is doing."

"Right away, sir." LaRue turned to his intercom.

Jefferson noticed Dr. Garcia had left the life support station. He called the infirmary. "Doctor, are you there?"

"Yes, sir," came the prompt response. "Along with about five wounded. Nothing serious, just some bumps and bruises and one minor concussion, but she's showing no major symptoms."

"Who?"

"Lisa Henry, sir," said the doctor.

Neb O'Connell stood up. "Can I go down and see her?"

The captain waved him back into his seat. "Later, son. I need you at your post. The doc says she's all right. I'll let you go down as soon as things are a bit less critical."

LaRue looked up from his console. "Sir, the tech has just

reported that there's no visible damage to sail number eight."

Pilot descended the ladder into C-and-C and strode across to the captain. "I've just been running some calculations, I think we can still salvage most of our time at Jupiter if we act fast." Jefferson glared at Pilot who heaved an exasperated sigh. "You ordered Berko to the towing shuttle. Have her launch immediately. I'll send her the coordinates to pull us to."

"What about the stress fracture on the number three mast?" The captain leaned forward.

"If it's not a complete break, it'll make little difference to the ship's operation. We'll have Berko unhook after she's finished towing us into position and evaluate the damage."

"I'll want to have words with you once we're in the clear," growled Jefferson, coldly.

"Understood," said Pilot, hotly. "Now launch the shuttle. You're wasting time."

The captain pursed his lips, but then called Berko and gave the order to launch. Pilot nodded, then stepped over to his console and sent the instructions.

*

Vanda Berko launched the tow shuttle from its bay and accelerated at the slowest rate the tiny craft would allow. She felt the resistance as the tow cable pulled taut behind. Pilot's instructions flashed onto her console. She pulled the joystick back and a little to the right, ever-so-gently pulling the larger craft behind her onto a new course. *Aristarchus* required her sails for fine steering control, but Jupiter's gravity overwhelmed that ability. Pilot needed the ship placed in a higher orbit than they'd managed, otherwise they wouldn't be able to perform the slingshot maneuver that would send them on to Saturn.

Looking out the window, Vanda caught her breath. She passed near the red and yellow moon Io. One of the great volcanoes on the surface erupted, spewing a cloud of sulfur high over the moon where it spread out like a golden fountain and rained back down to the surface. She towed the *Aristarchus* out beyond Io's orbit. Once she arrived at Pilot's target, she disengaged the towrope's magnetic clamps and reeled it in. She pushed the joystick forward, so the shuttle moved out ahead of the giant ship.

"Vanda," came Myra Lee's voice. "The captain says he'd like you to inspect the number three sail to see how bad that stress fracture is. Neb says it's about two miles in from the tip. I'm sending a schematic now."

"Acknowledged." Berko maneuvered the shuttle around in a wide arc, coming up behind the *Aristarchus*. Activating the keel thrusters, she moved three miles out from the hub, so she was at the same level as the damaged mast. She then matched speed and watched as the sails rotated in front of her. The damage soon became apparent. She executed a long spiral, keeping her in one place relative to the sail and evaluated it carefully.

"I see the fracture," she reported. "It doesn't appear to have broken all the way through. I'll take some pictures, so you all can decide the best course of action. The aluminum fabric of the sail is ripped through, but it's still anchored to the struts. We have repair sleeves we can install on the mast. But I'm not even sure that's absolutely necessary. I'd be inclined to leave it alone. If we need, we can repair en route."

"Thanks much," came the captain's voice from the intercom. "Bring the shuttle home."

✳

In C-and-C, LaRue stepped up to Pilot. "I have to admit that maneuver you executed was pretty clever," he said. "I would never have thought of using Jupiter's own magnetosphere as an alternate 'wind' to save the ship."

Pilot looked down at the deck. "I always planned to use the magnetosphere to get us into the orbit we needed. Thing is, we came up on the bow shock sooner than I expected. It caught me by surprise."

The captain stepped up to Pilot. "Let's talk." He looked around to LaRue. "You have the bridge. We'll be right out in the corridor."

As Jefferson turned his back, Pilot rolled his eyes and followed the captain out into the corridor. There, Jefferson turned on Pilot, pushing his finger into the other man's chest. "You may be Thomas Alonzo Quinn, son of the most powerful man on Earth, but you hired me to be captain of this space vessel. The course of action I took would have guaranteed our safety.

The course of action you took could have ripped the sails right off the ship, preventing us from returning home."

Pilot took a deep breath. "Congratulations, Captain Jefferson, you figured out who I really am. How long have you known?"

"That's beside the point," said Jefferson. "What matters is that in countermanding my orders, you put this ship in more danger than necessary."

"Your actions would have forced a return to Earth. My actions put us in a position where we can still salvage this mission." Pilot took two steps down the corridor, away from the captain's accusing finger and stare, then turned around. "Since you know who I am, you probably know that this ship and this mission are my dream. They have been ever since I was nine years old. I can't let you jeopardize my entire reason for living."

The captain gritted his teeth, took one step forward, and punched Quinn, leaving him sprawled out on the deck with a bloody nose. "I don't care who you are. Your dream doesn't give you the right to take matters into your own hands, to kill every man and woman on this vessel because you want to save the mission. You hired me to be the captain, to keep this crew together and because of my expertise in space. I can't do that job if you keep interfering."

Pilot wiped blood from his nose. A single tear escaped his eye. He wiped it angrily away, leaving a bloody smear on his face. "You're right, of course. I'm sorry."

Jefferson held out his hand and helped Pilot to his feet. "LaRue is right. What really matters is that you saved the ship. Just be aware I won't tolerate you putting your dream ahead of the ship's safety again. Understand?"

"I understand." Thomas Alonzo Quinn sighed, then straightened his coveralls. "How did you figure out who I am?"

Jefferson took a moment to collect his thoughts. "I saw your picture on a website."

"What website?" Quinn's brow furrowed.

"It was a biography of your father."

Pilot closed his eyes and shook his head. "I never thought about…" He sighed and looked up at Jefferson. "Does it bother you that I only just finished college?"

"If it did, I would have confronted you about it sooner." The captain ran his fingers through his white hair. "What matters to me is your ability—and you've proven that by building this ship."

"Thank you," said Pilot.

Jefferson put his hands in the pockets of his coveralls and looked to the deck. "If I had taken a plane and did what you did at your age, I would have been booted out of the military. My career would have been over." He looked into Pilot's eyes. "Just because you're Thomas Quinn and you built this ship doesn't mean that you aren't responsible for your actions."

Quinn's eyes narrowed. "Anything else?"

The captain shook his head. "Get cleaned up. Vanda will be landing soon. I'll need you to look at that stress fracture on the mast to decide if we need to take any action. Then we need to prep for the Jupiter mission."

"We're still going down?" asked Pilot, hopefully.

"If the ship doesn't need repair, or we can repair en route to Saturn, I don't see why not. We're here, let's look around."

*

When Jefferson returned to the command deck, he dismissed Neb O'Connell to visit Lisa in the infirmary. Most of the rooms aboard *Aristarchus* were small enough that it was hard to tell that the floors curved. However, the infirmary was a long room with five beds. At one end of the room was a desk and supply cabinet for Dr. Garcia surrounded by a privacy screen. Lisa sat up in one of the beds, propped up on pillows, holding an ice pack to her head. Her shoulders were slumped and her feet were slightly splayed, body language indicating boredom and she wanted to be somewhere else.

"How's it going?" Neb folded down a seat mounted to the wall next to the bed.

"Other than a headache, I'm doing fine," said Lisa. "Doc wants to keep me here for some observation, though."

"What happened?"

Lisa sighed and rolled her eyes. "Do you really want to know?"

"Well, I'm concerned about you."

"I was in the shower when the ship started shaking." Color rose in her cheeks. "I slipped and conked my head against the showerhead." She reached out and took his hand. "I'm okay, really."

"I've been so worried about losing my mom." Neb's voice quavered. "The thought that something could happen to you never crossed my mind before."

She shushed him and placed her other hand on top of his. The doctor stepped out from behind his privacy screen and folded down the seat on Lisa's other side. He pointed a flashlight into her eyes and examined them. "You're looking pretty good."

"They're talking about continuing with the Jupiter flight," said Neb. "Will she be able to go?"

Dr. Garcia pursed his lips, then looked into Lisa's eyes again. "I'd rather you not."

"All I did is slip in the shower," she protested.

"And you gave yourself a concussion. You can go to work in C-and-C on the next duty cycle, but I'd rather you not go into a shuttle to be jostled around."

Lisa looked down at the sheets.

"If you want, I can stay here with you," said Neb.

She looked up at him and smiled bravely. "That's sweet, but you don't have to. You're the one who found the disk on Mars, remember? They might be able to ground one of us, but not both of us. We're a team, now, and that's part of what a team's about. One of us can do what the other can't."

Neb squeezed her hand, silently thanking her.

In C-and-C, Pilot, Berko, LaRue, Jefferson, and Freeman huddled around the thruster control console where photos of the damage to the number three mast were displayed.

"Looks pretty bad to me," said Freeman. "The crack might go all the way through."

"What we have to keep in mind," said Pilot, "is while this *is* a sailing ship, we aren't dealing with the same kinds of stresses. We're basically talking about light pressure pushing us through a vacuum. There's very little actual force on the sail and we don't have air friction. The only real stress on the mast comes from gravity."

"Or from rocks like that dust field we went through," said Natalie.

Pilot inclined his head. "True, but we're through the asteroid belt. It's unlikely we'll run into anything like that again, even when we go back through the belt on the return trip."

"What about the ring plane at Saturn?" LaRue shifted from one foot to the other.

"You do have a point there," conceded Pilot.

"What about the resonance we encountered coming into orbit?" asked Freeman.

"That was the result of numerous effects that were a little larger than expected," said Pilot. "With the measurements I have, we can compensate for the problem when we come back. If we decide the risk is too great, we can bypass Jupiter altogether." He looked hopefully to Jefferson.

Jefferson nodded, satisfied.

Neb O'Connell returned to C-and-C and approached the others. He whistled as he looked at the damaged mast.

"I think we should patch it." Jefferson clasped his hands behind his back, then looked at Berko. "But you said something about repairing en route?"

"Yes." Berko leaned back against the console, facing the others. "We travel about the same speed between planets as we do when we're in orbit. Also, outside of orbit, we don't have a planet's gravitational force to contend with. Though it sounds a little strange, I think we'd actually be better off patching the sail between Jupiter and Saturn."

LaRue and Pilot looked at one another, then nodded.

"That sounds good to me," said Jefferson. "Berko, LaRue, put together a plan of action." Then the captain turned and looked at the schematic over Pilot's console. "Now, I think those of us who've been on duty should get some rest. I'd like to get started for Jupiter in about eight hours."

Neb cleared his throat. "Sir, the doc won't clear Lisa to go on the shuttle."

Jefferson frowned. "I know she's disappointed, but we're not likely to find life on Jupiter. It's a gas giant planet. I don't think we need two biologists to accompany us." He looked to Pilot. "I was going to have you replace Berko this trip. Any recommendations for someone to replace Lisa?"

"Bring Jenna Reynolds," said Pilot, without hesitation.

"The computer tech?" Jefferson raised his eyebrows.

"I hired her away from the National Weather Service. She used to model storm patterns on Earth. I wanted her along for this trip anyway, so she could see Jupiter's weather first hand, work with Dr. Nagamine to help him develop some good models of the wind and cloud patterns."

"Until tomorrow, then," said Jefferson.

Chapter 19
Whales in the Clouds

At breakfast, the morning of the launch to Jupiter, Myra Lee and Neb O'Connell sat forlornly across from each other, eating in silence. Both felt lost without Lisa Henry, who was on duty in command and control, still recovering from her head injury. Dr. Nagamine and Jenna Reynolds held an animated conversation, discussing the measurements required to improve their understanding of Jupiter's atmosphere. Pilot and Captain Jefferson reviewed a chart showing Jupiter's atmospheric pressure as a function of depth.

The captain pointed at the chart. "It doesn't seem like we have to get all that deep before it's more like traveling underwater than in an atmosphere of methane, water vapor, and ammonia."

"Indeed, we used that fact to our advantage when we designed the Jupiter shuttle." Pilot beamed in spite of his swollen nose. "The *Zeus* is equipped with a ram scoop option. You can suck in the atmospheric methane and use it to power the ship, conserving fuel."

Myra looked up at Pilot and the captain. "I've heard there's a solid core at Jupiter's heart. Will we be landing?"

Pilot shook his head. "No. There probably is a solid core, but it's so deep that the atmospheric pressure and gravitational forces would crush the shuttle. For the most part, we'll be flying around in the upper atmosphere."

"Very good." The captain looked up at the others. "Are we ready to go?"

The others nodded. They stood and followed the captain to the *Zeus* shuttle bay. Once there, they suited up, then boarded the shuttle. After completing the preflight checklist, Jefferson requested permission to launch.

"Have a good field trip," said Natalie Freeman from C-and-C.

With that, Jefferson launched the shuttle and started a long, slow drop toward Jupiter's cloud tops. Dr. Nagamine leaned forward in his seat, looking up and down at the sheer vastness of the solar system's largest world. Alternating brown and white bands swirled and churned as they circled the planet. Jenna Reynolds caught sight of a small, white storm dancing its way along one of the belts like a dervish.

"The planet's so bright." Myra turned in her seat. "And yet the sun's so far away and tiny."

"Indeed. Mars was so dead, yet Jupiter is so alive," said Nagamine.

"I thought you said Earth was the solar system's living world." Jefferson turned the shuttle on a southward course, crossing the terminator to the night side. Several lightning flashes arced across the cloud tops.

"Earth is alive because of the plants and animals that swarm across its surface," said Nagamine. "Jupiter is a living, breathing world, alive in its own right and a force to be reckoned with. It's fitting that it should be named for the king of the gods."

A short while later, as the shuttle crossed back into day, it passed between the ring and the planet. It sounded as though the shuttle passed through a rainstorm as tiny sand-like grains pelted it, leaving a fine yellowish haze on the windows. Neb O'Connell gasped. Following his gaze, Myra looked up to see Jupiter's thin, frail ring arcing high overhead, then looked down to see the churning cauldron of Jupiter's atmosphere below.

The captain took the shuttle down over the largest, longest-lasting storm in the entire solar system—the Great Red Spot. The storm had been swirling in Jupiter's atmosphere for over four hundred years and showed no sign of slowing. Jefferson would be foolish to fly the shuttle into the storm, but apparently, he did want to see it up close. Still well above the cloud tops, he slowed the shuttle and drifted over the storm. They were low enough that the red spot seemed to extend forever in all directions. Dr. Nagamine's instruments took photos and movies from which they would get estimated wind speeds. Again, the astronomer craned his neck, as if simply appreciating the sheer size of the red storm swirling slowly below them. "You could drop two Earths into that whirlpool and they'd both be swallowed whole," he said.

Coming to the edge of the Great Red Spot, Jefferson aimed the shuttle northward again and eased slowly downward into the raging white and brown clouds. As the tiny craft skidded into the atmosphere itself, flames once again leapt around the vessel. Seeing the vision outside the window, Jenna—a devout Catholic—made the sign of the cross.

Pilot gripped his own armrests tightly.

The winds began to buffet the tiny craft and the captain had to fight to hold onto the joystick. Before long, the flames dissipated and they approached the top of a white, fluffy cloud-bank that extended as far as the eye could see.

The descent into the atmosphere reminded Myra of air-plane trips she had taken, flying through cloudbanks, either on the way up to a good cruising altitude or heading down to land.

As they entered the cloud, a gray mist surrounded them, as though they had entered a fog bank. The mist condensed on the shuttle's hull, and little rivulets streamed up the windows, carrying the yellow powder that had been deposited earlier, away.

Using the compass, Jefferson continued to steer northward, diving as they went. Soon, the shuttle shot out of the clouds. The captain touched a button on the console and a set of wip-ers emerged from shielded compartments above the windows, clearing them of the water and yellow grime that had accu-mulated. As the windows cleared, a collective gasp rose from the shuttle's occupants. A rich, blue sky like one might see on Earth arced above. A golden halo surrounded the too-tiny sun. Below, brown methane clouds billowed like dirty cotton candy. Jefferson turned the ship, so he flew alongside the light-colored cloudbank they'd just left. The clouds rose like a great, gray wall, towering high overhead. As they continued forward, a thin white cloud swirled like a giant pie plate among the brown clouds below. Lightning flashed, illuminating the edge of the swirling, white clouds.

As they passed over the spinning white storm, a channel appeared, almost like a great riverbed running through the clouds. The captain took the shuttle down along the channel and followed it for several miles until the brown clouds below fell away and the 'river bed' ran on all by itself through seemingly open air. Jefferson took the shuttle a little lower, over another bank of clouds.

Just then, Myra caught sight of something like a ring of bubbles appearing along the cloud tops and then bursting. "What's that over there?" she asked. "Humpback whales on Earth swim in circles blowing air through their blowholes, making bubble 'nets' that help confine plankton. The bubble nets almost look like that from the surface."

Dr. Nagamine and Neb O'Connell looked where she pointed. "It must be some kind of atmospheric disturbance," said the astronomer. "Captain, would you be so kind as to circle around. I would like a closer look."

Jefferson brought the shuttle around, closer to the bubbles. As they approached, something broke through the cloud layer in front of them. The captain pushed the joystick hard to the right, avoiding the great mass that suddenly appeared. Another erupted from the clouds in their path, and Jefferson swerved hard to port, then a third arose and he steered back to starboard. Finally, he shot forward and climbed, then doubled back. In front of the shuttle were about a dozen fleshy objects, mottled brown, white, and gray, matching the clouds around them.

"They're like hot air balloons," said Neb.

"But look at the size of them," said Nagamine. "Those 'hot air balloons' must be miles across."

Pilot gasped. "They're easily as big as the *Aristarchus.*"

"Are they alive?" Jenna's gaze was glued to the fleshy objects drifting on the wind.

Myra tried to stand in spite of the harness that held her in her chair. "Possibly."

"Jupiter's long been known to contain many of the basic building blocks for life," said Nagamine. "It's long been speculated that life could evolve here, floating among the clouds."

"Much like marine life floats in the water," agreed Myra. "Some marine life never even sees the ocean floor, just as these creatures can never go to the depths of the atmosphere."

The shuttle shook for a moment, then settled down. Pilot

craned his head, trying to see around the captain's shoulder. "What's going on? More wind?"

Jefferson shook his head. "We're in something of a jet stream. It's really smooth flying at the moment." Looking down at the control panel, he saw they were deep enough in the atmosphere that he could switch from the fuel tank to the ram scoop. He flipped two switches. Every few minutes, a jolt rocked the shuttle and nearly knocked the joystick from the captain's hand.

"Could it be some kind of resonance?" Pilot wracked his brain, trying to think what could cause the shuttle to vibrate periodically. "This shuttle's designed to slip through high speed winds. I don't like these sudden jolts."

"Could these creatures be vocalizing?" asked Myra. Everyone looked at her. "Certain whales make sudden, loud vocalizations that divers feel. These creatures are thousands of times larger than whales. If their vocalizations are similar, I wouldn't be surprised that we would feel them here in the shuttle. Do we have some kind of audio recorder?"

Pilot nodded and Dr. Nagamine turned it on. A low rumble came through the speakers that would build at irregular intervals into a *whump*. Each time that happened, the shuttle jolted and Jefferson fought to hold onto the controls.

"Is that sound from the creatures?" asked Neb.

Myra smiled and nodded. "I think so. Are we recording?"

"Video and audio," confirmed Nagamine.

Jenna looked at her watch and counted the intervals between the jarring *whump* sounds. "I think we'd better analyze this back at the ship. There's a chance that they're speaking in binary code just like the whales back on Earth. It's a very regular pattern that could be interpreted as a sequence of ones and zeroes."

"Or it could be a hunting sound," said Myra. "The spermaceti whales of Earth make loud clanging sounds to stun their prey. This could be the same thing."

Neb's brow wrinkled. "What would they be hunting? I don't see anything else that looks like an animal."

"The whales on Earth eat microscopic organisms," explained Myra. "These could do the same."

Nagamine checked his sensors. "There's no shortage of organic chemicals out there. It's certainly not impossible that if there are giant life forms like this, there are also microscopic life forms all around us." He looked back at Pilot. "When we get back to the ship, we'll have to clean out the shuttle's ram scoop and see what's there."

The shuttle caught up with the floating creatures and slowed, matching their speed. Myra looked out at them. Their bodies looked very much like hot air balloons, fat and bulbous on top, tapering underneath. It also occurred to her that the creatures looked a little like toys of whales made for children, only there were no fins or tails. "They must just drift around the planet, going where the wind takes them," she said aloud.

"Not such a bad life," mused Captain Jefferson.

Pilot looked at his watch. "I'm sorry to have to end this, but we're going to need to get back to the *Aristarchus*. We need to start preparations to slingshot out of orbit for our last leg to Saturn."

Jefferson nodded and sighed. He took one last look at the city-sized fleshy creatures swimming in the air currents and tipped the shuttle's wing in a wave.

Myra thought she saw several of the creatures roll ever-so-slightly in their direction, as though they also waved. The captain switched back to the main fuel tanks and took the *Zeus* shuttle upward.

Back aboard the *Aristarchus,* Myra went straight from the shuttle to the locker room. Instead of getting changed, she opened her locker and retrieved a Petri dish and a knife from a toolbox. She returned to the bay where she saw Vanda Berko had drafted Dr. Nagamine—also still in his flight suit—to help her attach the shuttle's fuel line.

When they finished, she flagged the astronomer over and asked for help. He reached as far as he could into the ram scoop and scraped off some of the residue into the dish, then handed it to Myra. "Let me know what you find," he said.

Chapter 20
Slingshot

Cleaned up and back in her coveralls, Myra Lee entered command and control, sporting a wry grin and handed Lisa Henry a sealed, transparent box. Inside was a Petri dish full of brownish, black sludge. "A gift … from Jupiter."

Lisa took the sealed container, carefully set it down on the console, stood, and almost tackled her boss with a hug. Then she retrieved the box and peered at the dish within, as though she could discern its secrets with her naked eyes. "I take it there's something alive in here."

"We think there could be." Myra sat down at the console and checked that the data upload from the shuttle was complete. Satisfied, she took a moment to search through the shuttle's logs, then brought up an image of the gigantic, fleshy creatures they'd encountered floating in the planet's atmosphere.

Natalie Freeman, sitting at the command console, looked up at the display and stepped over to the biosciences station. "What in the world are those?"

Lisa's eyes went wide. "They're alive, aren't they?"

"We're pretty sure they are," said Myra. "If they are, they need to feed on something. I think whatever it is must be in that Petri dish. I'd like you to take a look and see if you can figure it out."

"Thanks," said Lisa. "I'll get on it right away."

"Let me get this straight," said Freeman, standing ramrod straight. "You brought something alive from Jupiter aboard the ship?"

"It's just residue from the shuttle's ram scoop," said Myra. "It would have come aboard no matter what we did."

Freeman's brow furrowed. "So, it went through the vacuum of space." She took a deep breath and let it out slowly. "I suppose that means whatever's in there is dead."

"Probably," said Myra. "Although it's not definite. There could have been just enough of Jupiter's atmospheric gas trapped in the sludge to keep a microscopic organism alive. However, it won't last long. I suspect our atmosphere would be poisonous to whatever's in there. They're running the decontamination sequence on the shuttle now, just to make sure it's clean."

"So, if it's likely the organisms are dead, why are you having her test the sludge?" Freeman shook her head, confused.

"We'd still see evidence of the organism," said Lisa. "It might be nothing more than tracks where they moved through the sludge or tiny bubbles showing respiration, but if there were microscopic organisms, we should see some evidence."

"There's something more," interjected Myra. "The giant creatures—presuming they are alive—vocalized much like whales. Jenna Reynolds is converting the audio we recorded into a binary sequence. We'll try our translation program on their language."

Lisa patted Myra on the arm. "I think *that's* a bit too much to ask ... that whale-like creatures on Jupiter should speak the very same language as whales on Earth."

"Well..." said Myra. "The whales on Earth started speaking some hitherto unknown language. If aliens taught it to them, why wouldn't they teach the same language to the 'whales' on Jupiter?"

Lisa held up the box again. "I suspect I'll have more luck finding something alive in here."

"If you *do* find something alive," began Freeman, "let me know, so we can get the bio lab sterilized. I don't want something alien crawling around on this ship."

Lisa laughed. "Natalie, you really *have* watched too many of those twentieth century science fiction shows."

*

Thomas Quinn returned to his quarters to take a shower. Once done, he stepped out, toweled off, and looked at himself in the mirror. He reached a tentative finger toward his nose, then pulled it back with a slight yelp. He scowled, thinking Jefferson had treated him unfairly. After all, he was the one who built the *Aristarchus* while Jefferson sat languishing as an underpaid engineer for the competition. Quinn himself knew the ship's capabilities better than anyone else. Who was that has-been astronaut to tell him what he could and couldn't do with his own ship? Even so, Quinn knew he had taken a rather arrogant tone with the captain, a man he admired and the very man he had hired to see to the ship's safety.

That last thought prickled at Pilot's conscience. Technically, the ship wasn't his at all. It belonged to his father. Pilot thought about his brother playing video games as a child and learning to play financial games at college. Those experiences couldn't compare to what he'd just seen and experienced firsthand in the clouds of Jupiter. He smiled, suddenly feeling justified in pursuing science instead of business. With a sigh, Quinn realized he didn't have time for introspection. He needed to get the ship onward to Saturn. Much as the discoveries they'd made so far on the voyage had advanced science decades or even centuries, Titan was where the big prize lay.

After getting dressed, Pilot climbed the ladder to the *Aristarchus's* central hub. Looking out at Jupiter, he took a few minutes to remember the creatures he'd seen on the planet. He floated in front of the window and closed his eyes. For just a few moments, he allowed himself to imagine he was a miles-wide creature drifting in the winds of Jupiter. The throbbing in his nose brought him back to the task at hand. He set to work calculating the slingshot out of Jupiter's orbit.

*

Jenna Reynolds knocked on Myra Lee's door. The biologist answered, wearing her nightgown. She yawned. "Didn't you get any sleep?"

"I haven't been able to." Jenna shrugged.

Myra invited her in and looked at the time. "I should be getting up, anyway," she said. "What can I do for you?"

"I converted the creatures' songs into binary code." Jenna stepped over to the table and fell into one of the two chairs. Her wide eyes scanned the room, looking at pictures of whales and sailing ships on the walls.

"Very good." Myra stepped over to the small kitchenette

alcove and started some coffee brewing, then joined Jenna at the small round table. She picked up the keyboard and displayed the translation program on the video display unit. "Now, where's the file?" she asked. Jenna told her and she typed it in, trying to stifle a yawn. Looking up, she was glad to see that the coffee had finished brewing. She resumed the program, then stood and retrieved a cup. She offered one to Jenna.

"No thanks," said the computer technician who stood and paced. "I really do need to get off to bed soon. I was just anxious to see if we had a match."

Myra sipped her coffee as she padded back to one of the blue chairs by the table and sat down. Looking up, she smiled. "Bingo. It looks like the creatures on Jupiter also have a line open to the keepers of the rings. They're using many of the same words. I'll send this to Cristof and Harmer. It should help us build up some more words for the database."

Jenna dropped down on the edge of the bed. "So what do you think we're going to find at Saturn? More whales in the clouds?"

"I begin to wonder." Myra took another sip of her coffee. Looking up, she noticed Jenna had fallen backward on the bed and snored softly. Myra lifted the technician's feet onto the bed and pulled a blanket over her, letting her get some well-earned sleep.

*

Lisa Henry whistled to herself as she labeled a number of microscope slides—difficult with the gloved fingers of the biohazard suit she wore—then put a sample of the sludge from the Petri dish on each one. She began to think she would give a lot of money for an electron microscope and she hoped the old fashioned microscope in the ship's biology lab would be sufficient to see any signs of life.

There was a knock at the door. "If you're suited, come in," she called cheerily.

Neb O'Connell entered. "How are you doing this morning?"

"The boss brought me a present from your trip to Jupiter." She held up the Petri dish.

"She brought you slime?" Neb blinked several times, then dropped into a chair.

"Well … yes." Lisa smiled. She mounted one of the slides in the microscope and took a look, adjusting the magnification. With a shake of her head, she set the slide aside and mounted a new one.

"I came to ask if you wanted to get some breakfast," said Neb. "It just wasn't the same making the trip to Jupiter without you."

"Yeah, Myra showed me pictures of the creatures you saw." Lisa sounded distracted. She stood up, blinked, and then looked again. "Say, come over here a moment and tell me what you see in the microscope."

Neb stepped over and bonked the faceplate of his suit into the eyepiece. Lisa showed him how to look into the microscope while wearing the suit. He tried again. Standing, he shrugged. "I dunno, it looks like a speck of sand or something cut a groove in the gunk."

"Exactly," said Lisa. "I think we found our microscopic organisms. The creatures you saw on the planet *were* alive. They feed on the thing you just saw in the microscope."

"Good for the creatures on the planet," said Neb. "I need something a little bigger to feed on. Are you coming?"

Lisa held her hand to her faceplate, blew a kiss, and then touched Neb's faceplate. "Let's go eat," she said.

Pilot clambered down into C-and-C from the central hub, went to his console, and brought up the flight plan. He then went to the thruster control console and talked to Daryl LaRue, then double-checked his calculations with Kurata Nagamine, sitting at the external sensors console. Looking up, he saw Captain Jefferson sitting at the central console. "We're ready to execute the maneuvers to take us out of orbit, Captain," he reported.

"Very good," said Jefferson. "I'd like to take a look at your calculations for myself."

"I assure you…." Pilot looked down at his feet for a moment, then looked back up. "Yes, of course, sir." He stepped over and typed a command on the captain's console bringing up the information.

Jefferson scanned the numbers and nodded his approval. "Carry on, Mr. Thomas."

Pilot stepped over to his console, entered several commands, then pointed at Daryl, who in turn fired the thrusters, adjusting the ship's course. Once again, the solar sailing ship fell toward Jupiter, but this time on a carefully controlled trajectory. The ship would not hit the planet, but be thrown around it. Pilot brought up a chart that showed the ship's speed. The ship had orbited Jupiter at a speed of two kilometers per second. As the ship fell toward the planet, it rapidly accelerated until it whipped around the other side of Jupiter at thirteen kilometers per second. "Whoo hoo," said Pilot, his hand in the air. "We're on our way! Next stop is Saturn!"

*

After the successful slingshot maneuver, Pilot was happy to take a watch in C-and-C. The captain took the opportunity to find Natalie Freeman. She sat in the ship's galley holding an animated discussion with Angus MacDonald about the value of red peppers in cooking.

The cook shook a meat cleaver menacingly. "Och! What good is food you canna eat?"

"You should talk." Natalie folded her arms. "You're the one who makes us eat haggis on Burns Night."

MacDonald caught sight of Jefferson standing in the doorway. "Well, I do admit it's a lot better with scotch, but he willna let us have any."

Jefferson held out his hands. "Don't blame me," said the captain. "She agreed with those rules." Then he looked at Natalie. "Would you mind coming with me for a moment, Captain Freeman?"

"Sure thing." She stood and followed the captain to the ship's observation lounge.

Jefferson closed the door. Through the porthole in the floor, Jupiter already appeared smaller than when they'd been in orbit. "Sorry to pull you away from your off time, but I need to know something. Have you figured out what Thomas Quinn is looking for at Saturn? I presume this isn't just some joyride."

Freeman shrugged. "I have no idea, Captain. Sorry."

The captain gritted his teeth and sat down. "The President of the United States put you on this ship to find out what Pilot was up to. I can't imagine that we've been away from Earth for a year and a half and you still have no idea."

Freeman put her hands on her knees. "Why are you suddenly so concerned?"

Jefferson held his hand out toward the porthole. "Because of what he did at Jupiter. He nearly destroyed the ship trying to save the mission. I don't buy that he did that because he's young and reckless. He's too smart for that. I think he expects to find something further on that's worth dying for—or worse yet, something he thinks is worth all of us dying for."

Natalie Freeman looked down. Jupiter disappeared from the porthole as the ship's spin continued. "Don't you think you may be overreacting? Quinn designed this ship. He knows what it can and can't do ... better than you."

The captain sat back as though she'd hit him. "You're the last person aboard this ship I'd expect to defend Thomas Quinn."

"Why's that? Just because I was sent aboard this ship to find out what he's doing? That doesn't make me his enemy. I'm simply doing my best to make sure the interests of the United States are being served."

"You *do* know something," said Jefferson, matter-of-factly. He shook his head. "I know better than to press a trained military officer for details, but I just want to know this, are we getting in over our heads?"

Freeman stared at the porthole for several minutes, watching Jupiter come back into view. "I don't know," she finally admitted. Jefferson started to say something, but she held up her finger, stopping him. "All I ask is that you trust me. Quinn's my responsibility, not yours. I'll ask for your help if I need it."

"Fine. But the ship's my responsibility."

"I will say this," said Freeman. "I've observed Quinn long enough to know he's in this for the intellectual prize. He may not care much about your life or mine. To be honest, I don't even think he cares about Quinn Corp. He does care about his own life, though. He will do everything in his power to make sure he gets his prize. That means he'll keep this ship safe. If he dies, he loses."

"I hope you're right." Jefferson ran his fingers through gray hair. "I'm getting too old for this."

Chapter 21
Repairs En Route

The *Aristarchus* sailed on to Saturn at a speed determined less by the diminishing sunlight and more by the gravitational boost gained from the slingshot around Jupiter. Two weeks along, and Jupiter had already shrunk to the size of a ping-pong ball in the rear windows of the ship's central hub. Captain Jefferson called a meeting of the senior officers to discuss the repairs of sail number three. Pilot outlined two possible courses of action: "First option is that we just climb out to the stress fracture. The masts are thin and lightweight, but strong. We have safety lines on collars designed to go around the masts. The advantages of doing that are we conserve fuel in the tow shuttle, and we can visually inspect the sail as we go, making sure there aren't any other stress fractures or major tears in the sail fabric we're not detecting."

Daryl LaRue chewed on his lip and Vanda Berko shook her head. "Pilot," she said, "you're talking about a three-mile climb along a rotating sail. If anyone looks out at the stars, they're going to get dizzy and disoriented. This ship spins pretty fast and it's going to be very noticeable the further you go out on the mast. In fact, the gravity perception will increase out there. You'll feel like you're about to be flung out into space."

"Not to mention that those masts, while strong, are low mass. They'll sway under the weight of a team of people." Daryl put his hands in the pockets of his coveralls. "It could even be enough to turn the sail and change our course. I don't really like that option."

"Me either." Pilot nodded. "That brings us to option two, which is a little trickier, but probably better all around. We take the tow shuttle out and match the *Aristarchus's* spin. Four people spacewalk out on safety lines and do the repair. The disadvantage is that it'll require some tricky maneuvering. If anything goes wrong and the shuttle hits a sail, we'll be worse off than we are now. We'll need to work fast, since the fuel supply on the shuttle isn't indefinite. The advantage is, done right, we could be finished with the job in about an hour."

"There is a third option," said Daryl. "We could simply leave the mast alone as we talked about before. There's not that much pressure on the sail. It will probably survive the rest of the voyage even if we take no action."

Captain Jefferson shook his head. "I'd feel better if we at least tried to repair the mast." He moved around the command console, running his fingers along the edge. From the opposite side, he looked up. "If there are any signs of problems, though, we'll abort and leave well enough alone. How's that?"

"Sounds fine to me," said Pilot. With that, he named off the members of the repair crew, which included Berko, LaRue, and two mechanics. "I'll fly the shuttle. Let's get our gear together this afternoon and we'll fly out first thing tomorrow morning."

While the technicians assembled their gear, Myra Lee read her email from Earth. Among the messages was one from Cristof and Harmer with a program and a video file attached. She played the video file and was delighted to see Stirling Cristof's face.

"Hey, Myra," he said. "Between the data from that Martian disk and the songs from those creatures on Jupiter, we think we have a rudimentary translation program for you. It will take binary encoded sequences and translate them into a printed message on your monitor. In turn, you can type in a message and it should turn it into a binary encoded audio message that the ring keepers should be able to interpret."

When the message finished, Myra installed the program and tried it out. She typed in "Hello there." A few seconds later, a set of tones issued from the speakers.

Captain Jefferson stepped up to her console. "The language of our Saturn people?"

"Presuming there are Saturn people." Myra shrugged.

"You still aren't convinced?" Jefferson lifted his eyebrows. "What about the Martian data disk?"

Myra shrugged. "The data disk is exciting, but all it proves is that the ring keepers exist. Nothing that we've been able to pull off the disk says that they're from Saturn."

Jefferson nodded, understanding. "You and your team have done an excellent job." With that, he turned and stepped back to his console.

Myra hit the record button on her console. "Thank you, Stir." She sent the email on its long flight back to Earth.

*

The following morning, Pilot and the repair team boarded the tow shuttle. After receiving clearance, Pilot lifted the shuttle from the bay and took it out ahead of the *Aristarchus*, then doubled back behind the ship. As Vanda had done when she evaluated the damage, Pilot took the shuttle to the correct distance out from the hub, then waited for the damaged sail to approach. As it did, he fired the thrusters, causing the shuttle to spin with the sail. It took Pilot some practice to get the hang of the maneuver. He tended to overcorrect and undercorrect a bit, causing the shuttle to wobble with respect to the sail. However, after about fifteen minutes, he got the hang of it and the shuttle and the sail rotated together.

"Time to get to work," said Daryl. He and the rest of the team put on their helmets and checked their suits. He gave the thumbs up and Pilot began the slow process of closing off the air tanks and depressurizing the shuttle. When the shuttle's interior reached vacuum, Daryl attached his safety line and opened the door. He pushed himself out of the shuttle, toward the sail. Once there, he grabbed on to the mast, feeling it wobble as he did. The crack sat right above his hand and the sail's aluminum fabric was torn and jagged. With no gravity or air pressure it proved eerily still, not flapping at all.

Vanda Berko left the shuttle behind him and grabbed his hand to stop from flying through into the sail. Daryl swung around and allowed Vanda to grab onto the mast. They each clipped on safety lines. At that point, she handed him a repair sleeve. He placed it on the mast and she pulled out a heat gun. The application of heat would allow the crystal-like quinitite to grow together, forming an unbreakable bond.

Once the mast was repaired, the two mechanics, Chung and Rodriguez, left the shuttle. Chung went to one side of the sail and grabbed on to the quinitite frame and held out a roll of fine, woven aluminum. She clipped it to the frame while Rodriguez took the other end and unfurled it to the other side of the sail. Just as he clipped one corner of the patch onto the frame, they all felt a tugging on the safety lines.

Daryl looked around. Once again, Pilot had trouble keeping control of the shuttle. "Hey, what's going on?"

"The ship's acting like it's starved for fuel, even though the gauge shows an adequate supply." Pilot sounded distressed. "You all better get back aboard, we need to abort the mission."

"But we only have the sail patch clipped in three places and it's not bonded in the middle," protested Vanda.

"Abort, now!" ordered Pilot.

With that, the technicians pushed away from the mast and frame in unison and clambered back into the shuttle. As soon as the door was closed, Pilot rolled the shuttle and took it back toward the central hub without taking time to re-pressurize the cabin. As they approached the hub, the shuttle sputtered again.

"Something's seriously wrong," said Pilot.

Vanda pointed out the window. "We're losing speed with respect to the *Aristarchus*."

"That's it folks, abandon ship," called Pilot. He unbuckled his harness while Daryl once again opened the shuttle door. This time without attaching safety lines, the team of five took turns pushing off the shuttle and launching themselves toward the *Aristarchus*. Daryl caught on first, finding one of the external handholds. Vanda followed, grabbing Daryl's hand. Chung and Rodriguez followed in turn. Finally, Pilot pushed off. He missed Chung's proffered hand, and his hands scrabbled on the smooth, silver hull of the *Aristarchus* trying to find some kind of handhold as he continued to slide toward the ship's bow. At last, he managed to grab hold of one of the sail masts. From there, he was able to grab a handhold. He looked up and watched the tow shuttle drift away behind them. With a sigh, he climbed the handholds, following the others toward the airlock.

*

Once inside the ship and out of their suits, Pilot sat in the locker room, in his underwear trembling.

"What happened out there?" asked Daryl, pulling on his coveralls.

Pilot shook his head. "The gauge showed fuel, but we weren't getting any thrust. It's as though the fuel had somehow been converted to some kind of inert matter."

"The *Aristarchus* uses the same kind of fuel. We'd better check the supply," said Daryl, somberly.

Feeling numb, Pilot nodded. Daryl tapped Rodriguez on the shoulder and the two left to check the ship's fuel.

Half an hour later, Pilot trudged into C-and-C, bearing bad news. Shoulders slumped, he fell into the chair at the pilot's console. When the shuttle had been lost, Jefferson called Freeman to control. She stepped over to Pilot, and knelt down next to him. "How bad is it?" she asked.

Pilot shook his head. "I don't understand how it happened. Somehow all the fuel aboard the ship and the shuttles is being neutralized. It's as though something is eating it up and converting it into something else."

Myra, sitting at the communications console, gasped. "Oh, my God," she whispered.

Freeman, Pilot, and Jefferson all turned to look at her.

Myra turned away from their stares and brought up an image of the whale-like creatures from Jupiter. "These creatures need to eat," she said, slowly. "I hypothesized that they ate microscopic creatures in the atmosphere, much like whales on Earth eat plankton." She changed the display, so it showed a picture of something that looked like a grain of sand. "Lisa found these microscopic creatures from material inside the *Zeus* shuttle's ram scoop."

Jefferson rubbed his chin. "The atmosphere of Jupiter contains large amounts of methane and ammonia, chemicals not unlike the fuel this ship uses."

"So much so," said Pilot, "that we could run the shuttle on Jupiter's atmospheric gasses."

"The creatures got into the shuttle's engine and found their way into the fuel tank." Jefferson sat down at the command console.

"Then Vanda Berko and Kurata Nagamine attached the fuel line to the shuttle," said Myra.

"Giving the creatures access to *Aristarchus's* fuel supply," finished Pilot. He looked down to the deck. "Only thing is the system's designed to prevent this. There would have been positive pressure on the fuel line. Fuel isn't sucked in from the shuttle."

"Jupiter's atmosphere is a violent, turbulent place," said Myra. "The creatures would be used to it."

"You mean they swam upstream?" asked Pilot in disbelief.

"Like salmon swimming back to their home stream to spawn." Freeman stood and adjusted her coveralls. "What does this mean for the mission?"

"It means there's no chance of slowing down for a Saturnian orbit," said Pilot, dejected. "The best we can do is slingshot around Saturn and head for home."

Jefferson's stomach lurched. All at once, the warning voices about a ship rushed into flight by an inexperienced team sounded in his thoughts. For the first time since the voyage began, he wanted to be back in his cubicle. He would see the ship safely home where he would be content to stay.

The mood throughout the *Aristarchus* grew subdued as word spread among the crew that there was no hope of flying in Saturn's clouds or landing on Saturn's largest moon, Titan. Jefferson and Freeman worked to raise the crew's spirits, though. They assembled the crew in the galley, had Angus MacDonald and the volunteer cooks prepare a buffet of party foods, then showed the videos from the Mars and Jupiter expeditions.

Captain Jefferson, his medals pinned onto a clean pair of coveralls and one of his Air Force service cravats around his neck, stood up in front of the crew once the movies were finished. "We have accomplished more in the last year and a half than any space mission in the history of humankind. We have no reason to feel we have failed or even fell short of our mission's objectives. There is even more to come. We *will* see Saturn and its moons up close and with our own eyes. No human in history has ever accomplished that. We will succeed in our mission. No matter what happens, you will be heroes when we get back to Earth … and we *will* get back to Earth because I expect you all to give me the best you've got."

He sat down and Natalie Freeman, attired in her full-dress Navy whites—a sword belted around her waist—stood in front of the crew. Solemnly she removed her hat. "When I was growing up, three of my greatest heroes were Jim Lovell, Fred Haise, and Jack Swigert, the crew of Apollo 13. They were to be the third crew to land on the Moon. However, an accident aboard their ship prevented them from landing. It took everything they had to return safely to Earth. Those three men did not panic, they simply did their jobs and they *did* see the Moon, even if they couldn't land on it, and they *did* return to Earth safely. Thing is, their ship was in far worse shape than ours is. We're just out of gas and the nearest filling station is two billion miles away."

Genuine laughter rippled through the audience. Pilot sat back in his chair and rubbed his chin. Freeman continued, "But, due to Alonzo Thomas's brilliant design and execution, this space vessel is in much better shape than the Apollo 13. We'll be able to sail home in comfort. We'll still be able to get better orbital measurements and photographs of Saturn and Titan than any other craft in history. We have already made history. Let's make some more."

A cheer rose from the crew. "Let's see the movies again," called Angus MacDonald from the back of the room.

Jefferson and Freeman smiled at one another and started the show again. Freeman looked over at Pilot, but noticed he wasn't watching the movies. Instead, he seemed deep in thought. She shrugged it off.

After the movies were over, the crew stood and mingled, eating the food and talking excitedly. Neb O'Connell and Lisa Henry—each holding plates brimming with Freeman's chicken wings, Dr. Garcia's flautas, and Angus's short bread—stepped up to Freeman and Jefferson.

"We've been talking it over," said Lisa. "We'd still like to get married on the approach to Saturn."

"We just wanted to check whether that would cause any problems with the timing on the slingshot around the planet.

We certainly don't want to prevent the ship from getting home," said Neb.

Freeman waved Pilot over and explained the situation to him. Pilot thought for a moment. "No," he said. "Shouldn't be a problem at all." Pilot then led Captain Jefferson aside. "Captain, I wanted to take a moment and apologize for what I said at Jupiter. You're absolutely right. The safety of the ship comes before the mission."

Jefferson looked down at the deck, then back up at Pilot. He held out his hand. "I'm sorry I hit you. I realize now that you know this ship better than anyone aboard. I should have realized that you will do everything in your power to keep us safe." Jefferson and Pilot shook hands. "If I'd still been in the service, they would have court-martialed me for striking a fellow officer," said the captain, solemnly.

"Forget it. I was being cocky and deserved it." Pilot rubbed his hand on his nose. "But next time, please just tell me."

*

Two weeks later, Jefferson relieved Freeman in C-and-C. As she left, she passed Pilot loitering in the corridor. "Captain Freeman, I was wondering if we might have a word."

"Sure," she said. "I was on my way to my quarters for the night, but we can talk for a bit. I'll make you a cup of coffee."

Pilot smiled. "Thanks, but I'll be calling it a night shortly." He was silent for a moment as they strolled through the corridors. "I was thinking about what you said at the party the other day about the nearest filling station being two billion miles away. The thing is, there *is* another filling station and it's less than a billion miles away at this point."

They stepped inside Natalie's quarters. Pilot went over to the computer interface and brought up some schematics. "What are you talking about?" asked Natalie.

"Saturn's atmosphere is largely the same as Jupiter's. Instead of going into a slingshot orbit, we could turn the sails such that we go into a long elliptical orbit, actually taking the ship into Saturn's upper atmosphere. We could scoop up enough of the atmosphere to use as fuel for several orbits of Saturn followed by an easy return to Earth."

Natalie sat down on the opposite side of the table and studied Pilot's display. "It sounds awfully risky. If you miscalculate at all, we'll go right into the planet. Perhaps you should take this to Captain Jefferson, not to me."

Pilot took a deep breath as he set the keyboard aside. "Not only did I build this ship, I designed it. I know what she's capable of."

"I accept that." Natalie pursed her lips. "Fact of the matter is this is still a risky proposition. Why take the risk when we can get home safely without doing it?"

Pilot stood up so fast, it caused Natalie to blink. "Captain Freeman, there's no need for pretense any more. You know who I am. You've been in my cabin. You've read the report I prepared for my father. You know all about the chronotons."

"How do you know that?" Natalie narrowed her eyes.

Pilot leaned over, hands on his hips, and looked into her eyes. "My alias was not built on the spur of the moment. I've been using it for years to look up information in the company files and conduct research on the side for my father. I was successful because I learned to watch people. I learned to watch them when they were close to discovering the real me. You may be a good captain of an aircraft carrier and a good diplomat, but you're a lousy spy. Didn't you think I would have security cameras set up in my cabin?"

Natalie stood and went over to the coffee maker and scooped coffee into a filter. "I figured that was a possibility, just as I assumed you had communications bugged. Why haven't you confronted me before now?"

Pilot pushed his hands into the pockets of his coveralls. "I've been hiding behind Alonzo Thomas for a long time now. I'm not used to confrontation and you haven't told anyone … except Jefferson." He chewed on his lower lip. "I've been thinking you may be someone I can trust."

"Even though I've been sneaking into your quarters?"

"How's that different from me sneaking around Quinn Corp as Alonzo Thomas?"

She started the coffee, then turned around. "All right, I know you want the chronotons, but Captain Jefferson isn't going to let you risk the ship to get them. Not now."

"I know." Pilot sat down. "But you know how important the chronotons are. Not just for me, but for Earth's entire future. I want you to help me talk to the captain, to try to convince him that we should at least try the refueling maneuver. I've already ordered LaRue and Berko to begin dumping and sanitizing the fuel tanks. Adapting them further would be minimal effort."

"Cleaning the tanks is certainly a good idea," said Natalie. "I'll feel better knowing that the little organisms are off the ship. Who knows what other trouble they might cause."

"Exactly."

"How do we know there aren't microbes like we encountered at Jupiter in Saturn's atmosphere?"

Pilot shrugged. "We won't be going as deep. It's colder. The odds of similar microbes existing on two gas giant worlds in the same system seems astronomical." He took a step toward her. "Will you help me?"

The coffee finished. Natalie poured two cups and brought one to Pilot. She sat down and sipped hers. "The problem is even I think it's not worth the risk to go after the chronotons." She looked down into her coffee, avoiding Pilot's gaze. "What I think we should do is get this ship safely to Earth. From there, we can put together a proposal for another mission to Titan. I'll even help you put it together. We can come back out."

"Do you really think the chronotons belong in the hands of the Federal Government?" He picked up his cup of coffee and took a sip in spite of his earlier objection.

"If they exist, they belong to the whole world." Natalie slowly looked up into his eyes. "They don't belong to the United States and they certainly don't belong to Quinn Corp." She set the cup down. "Whether you call yourself Alonzo Thomas or Thomas Quinn, you're one of the best scientists there is or ever will be. Surely a discovery of this magnitude should be used by all scientists and not just by you."

"But will they know what to do with it?" he asked, glumly.

"Who are you to judge?"

Pilot took another sip of the coffee, then put the cup on the table. "Perhaps you're right." He stood and moved toward the door, then turned. "Captain Freeman, will you help me start the proposal on the trip back to Earth?"

"Sure thing, Mr. Quinn."

He smiled, then turned and left the cabin.

As the journey to Saturn continued, Natalie kept a close eye on the ship's progress, making sure that they continued on the slingshot course and didn't start turning toward the planet. As Saturn grew large in the ship's windows, she started breathing easier. The closer they got to the planet, the harder it would be for Pilot to change course. She talked to him several more times, and became more convinced he really did want to write a NASA proposal with her on the return trip rather than attempt anything foolish.

*

The remaining months of the voyage to Saturn continued smoothly. The crew fell into a routine, much as they had during the year between Mars and Jupiter. Myra continued working on her translation program with Lisa's help. Even though Myra was skeptical, she hoped they'd be able to find out who was communicating with the whales of Earth and the floating creatures of Jupiter as they sped past Saturn. Myra and Lisa told Natalie about their work.

"Excellent," said the executive officer. "Pilot and I are going to propose a new mission to Saturn. If we find there's intelligent life out here, that will only improve our chances of getting a new NASA mission out this way."

In her off duty time, Lisa worked on wedding arrangements with Neb. Lisa was not surprised when she spoke to Vanda in the galley and found out that she didn't have any dresses aboard. "However, there's the aluminum sail fabric," she said. "We have a large supply. It would have to be folded over a few times to make it strong enough for a dress, but I'm sure there's enough extra."

"There's only one problem. I'm not a seamstress," said Lisa.

"Neither am I," admitted Vanda. "I've always been better with power tools than sewing machines."

Angus, leaning over the counter, interrupted. "Sorry to eavesdrop, but I not only cook, I'm pretty handy with a needle and thread."

"Can you sew up an entire dress?" asked Lisa.

"It won't be the most elegant wedding gown," said the cook, "but it'll look lovely nevertheless. I promise."

Lisa held up her hands and tried to refuse. "I couldn't ask you..."

"It would be my pleasure," said the cook.

Lisa then asked Pilot about the logistics of holding the wedding in the ship's hub. "We don't want to be in your way if you need to work up there during the wedding," she explained.

Pilot looked at her darkly for a few minutes, then brightened. "No problem, I can do what I need from C-and-C. The only problem I see is the lack of gravity up there. I don't want you bringing anything that can float around and get into the equipment."

"We'll leave the hub just like we found it," agreed Lisa.

*

At last, the day of the wedding arrived. "John, I wish you could be here on Earth for your wedding," said Debra O'Connell. Neb and Lisa sat hand-in-hand in his quarters watching the video message. "The weather here has turned lovely and the flowers are blooming." Neb smiled, less because of the news of the pleasant weather, but at the hint of rosy color that had returned to his mother's cheeks and the twinkle in her eye. "It's hard to believe you're getting married. Why I remember your senior prom and you took your cousin Vanessa."

Lisa looked at Neb and giggled. "Did you really take your cousin to the prom?"

Neb put his face in his hands and turned bright red. Preparations for the wedding saved Neb from further embarrassment. He borrowed trousers and a nice shirt from Pilot's closet. Dr. Nagamine agreed to serve as Neb's best man and Myra Lee was Lisa's maid of honor. Again, Captain Jefferson donned his medals and cravat. Captain Freeman remained on duty in C-and-C. Captain Jefferson agreed to take over after the ceremony, so she could attend the reception in the galley. Natalie donned her dress uniform for the occasion.

Jefferson made his way to the central hub to await the wedding party. Neb was already there, pushing himself off the rotating walls, floating back and forth. The captain busied himself making sure the cameras were all set to record the ceremony while Kurata Nagamine stood in front of the forward window, looking out at Saturn. The rings—sparkling like delicate, frosted crystal in the sunlight—were turned such that the tops could be seen. "When Galileo first saw the rings of Saturn, he didn't see that they encircled the planet. He just saw them as knobs on each side and called them 'ears.' It seems such an unflattering description," said the astronomer.

Soon after, Myra poked her head through the opening into the hub. "Okay, Lisa's ready."

Jefferson grabbed one of the wall consoles and started the music. Neb and Nagamine floated in the center of the room as Myra entered. Lisa, wearing the aluminum skirt and blouse Angus sewed for her, followed. The skirt proved sufficiently stiff that even in the hub's null gravity, it didn't float up and around her legs, yet it was also cloth-like so it drifted and swayed, almost as though she were dancing, even when still.

Myra pulled her forward and Nagamine pushed Neb forward, so the two drifted side by side in front of Jonathan Jefferson.

"It has always been the happy privilege of ship captains to be able to perform wedding ceremonies. We are gathered here," the captain paused and pointed out to Saturn beyond, "in this most beautiful of places in the solar system to witness the union of Lisa Marie Henry and John Mark O'Connell." He faced Lisa. "Lisa, will you have this man to be your wedded husband, to live together after God's ordinance in the Holy estate of matrimony? Will you love him and comfort him, honor and keep him in sickness and in health, and forsaking all others, keep you only unto him as long as you both shall live."

"I do," said Lisa, with a broad grin.

The captain turned to John and repeated the question. "I do," answered John, looking into Lisa's eyes.

"The ring please," said Jefferson. Like the engagement ring, Daryl LaRue had cut the wedding rings from conduit tubing.

Dr. Nagamine handed the first ring to Neb, who put it on Lisa's finger and said, "With this ring, I thee wed, and this gold, I thee give and with my body, I thee worship, and with all my worldly goods, I thee endow."

Myra wiped a tear away with a tissue as the captain handed the other ring to Lisa. She repeated the words and put the ring on Neb's finger.

"I now pronounce you husband and wife," said the captain. He leaned in to Neb. "You may kiss the bride."

Neb O'Connell and Lisa Henry embraced and exchanged a deep, passionate kiss. Myra smiled. Nagamine turned and looked out the window again. "Something's wrong," he said. "Saturn's shifted position ever so slightly."

Jefferson turned, caught the wall, then pulled himself to the console. "Son of a bitch! They're changing course!" Jefferson reached over and tried to activate the intercom, but found the system had been shut down. He reached over and blew into a speaking tube. "Captain Freeman, why are we changing course?" There was no response. "Captain Jefferson to C-and-C, what's going on?"

"Captain Jefferson, this is Captain Freeman." Her voice came from one of the other tubes. "I've been removed from C-and-C. Pilot has barred the door. Can you take control from the hub?"

Jefferson scanned the console. Red lights indicated all systems were locked out. He tried to override the controls with his command password. He wasn't surprised when he found access was denied. "He's routed all controls down there and locked me out of the system. I'll be down in a minute."

Without another word, Jefferson pushed himself off the console and went to the ladder, climbing down two decks. Neb, Lisa, Myra, and Nagamine followed close behind. Reaching the corridor one deck below, they ran until they came to the ladder that descended into C-and-C. The hatch was closed and the handle wouldn't spin. Jefferson pounded on the hatch, but received no response.

The wedding party ran back to the ladder that descended from the hub and climbed down one more deck, then ran to the door that led to C-and-C. Natalie Freeman straightened to attention as they approached.

"Quinn," called Jefferson through the door. "This is mutiny! I'll see you hang if I get in there!" He turned to Freeman who wore a deep frown. "Round up everyone you can and any tools you think might help. We're going in."

"Yes, sir!" said Freeman. She saluted and took off down the hall.

Chapter 22
The Undecipherables

Captain Jefferson paced back and forth outside the door to command and control. It took about half an hour for Natalie Freeman to arrive with fourteen others. Neb and Lisa, still dressed in their fine clothes, had remained by his side along with Myra and Nagamine. He smiled a bit to see that both Dr. Garcia and Angus MacDonald were in the group of new arrivals. "He has Berko, LaRue, Chung, and Rodriguez with him, sir," said Natalie.

Jefferson stepped forward and addressed the remaining crewmembers. "Alonzo Thomas has committed mutiny and is endangering this ship. We must break into C-and-C and take the ship from him. I know many of you consider the people on the other side of that door friends. But we can't let them circumvent the chain of command. We will confine them to quarters and deal with them later once we've put the ship back onto a safe course."

"When cooler heads will prevail," interjected Freeman. She directed two of the mechanics forward with tool kits. They began dismantling the door hinges. All eyes were on them. Freeman passed a pistol to Jefferson. "I hope you won't need this."

Jefferson placed the pistol in his pocket. "I didn't think we had any guns aboard."

She pointed to the dress sword still belted at her waist. "This wasn't the only service weapon I brought along. I didn't know what I was going to find aboard this ship."

"Good thinking," said Jefferson. "We don't want to fire unless we have to. We could do more damage than Pilot has." He thought about asking how Pilot and his crew managed to get Natalie off the deck, especially when she was armed, but she looked embarrassed and time was short, so he decided not to press the matter.

The mechanics finished unbolting the hinges and worked on the door with crowbars. After a moment, they pulled it from the frame. Jefferson and Freeman rushed forward into C-and-C, followed by the other crewmembers. Angus plowed into Daryl pushing him into the wall. Natalie stepped over to Vanda and grabbed her by the wrist. Rodriguez and Chung both put their hands in the air, surrendering to the others. Jefferson drew the pistol and pointed it at Pilot. "Back away from the pilot's console," he said.

"Captain, this is a critical maneuver I'm performing. If you don't let me do it, we'll crash into the planet and we will all die," said Pilot.

"You've committed mutiny, mister," he said. "I don't care who you are or what you're doing. You must surrender control of the ship to me."

"I can't." Pilot did not take his hands off the console or his gaze from the displays.

Jefferson stepped forward, pushing the gun to Pilot's temple and disengaging the safety.

"If you fire in here, you could destroy a console wrecking everyone's chances," said Pilot calmly.

"I'm willing to bet your skull will slow the bullet down," said Jefferson through gritted teeth.

Pilot let go of the controls and backed away, his hands in the air. "Captain, you must let me finish laying in the course. It's too late to change back to the slingshot."

Jefferson looked over to Freeman. "Get these people out of my sight," he growled. "Confine them to quarters."

"Aye aye," said Freeman.

Berko, LaRue, Rodriguez, and Chung lined up at the doorway. Thomas Quinn, eyes bright with tears, took a deep breath, then turned and lined up with them. Natalie, Angus, and two of the mechanics escorted them to their quarters.

Jefferson glanced around at the others still in C-and-C. "I need people to man their stations." He caught the eye of the control system technician, Barry Bonden. "Bonden, of those left, I believe you know the sailing controls better than anyone."

Bonden swallowed hard. "I think so, sir."

The captain pointed to the console. "Take control, see if

you can get us back onto the slingshot course." He then saw
Jenna Reynolds. "Ms. Reynolds, see if you can assist Bonden.
He may need some help with calculations."

"Right away," she said.

O'Connell and Nagamine both hovered over the astrosciences station. "We're accelerating into Saturn," said Nagamine.
"If we don't alter course, we're going to go straight into the
planet."

The captain turned to Bonden and Reynolds, who were in
deep discussion. Reynolds brought up several plots above the
pilot's console.

Freeman returned. "Pilot and the others are confined to
quarters," she reported then dropped her voice to a near-whis-
per. "I hate to say it, but it might have been better to let Pilot
finish the maneuvers. I don't know what chance we have now."

Reynolds approached Jefferson and Freeman. "It would
appear that we have lost our opportunity for a slingshot course.
We've also lost our opportunity to do what Pilot was attempting."

"What choices do we have?" asked the captain.

"If we swing as wide as we can, we'll miss the planet—just
barely. We'll graze the outer atmosphere, but we won't be able
to swing into orbit. It'll put us onto a course that will take us out
of the solar system."

"So," said Freeman, "our choice is a quick death into the
planet, or a lingering death between planets."

Jefferson shook his head. "No, if we survive, there's a
chance for a rescue." He looked into Reynolds' eyes. "Put us on
the wide course. We'll fight as long as we can."

She nodded and returned to the pilot's station. Jefferson
surveyed the deck. Lisa sat at the biosciences station. Myra
stood next to her, her hand around her shoulder. At the astronomy station, Neb stood next to Dr. Nagamine with his hands
behind his back. They were about to skim Saturn's upper atmosphere and it would be a rough ride. "We're overmanned," he
said to Natalie. "I think we should take Lisa and Neb off duty.
Let them go to their quarters. They'll be better off there."

Freeman nodded quickly. "I agree." She stepped over to
the external sensors and spoke quietly to Neb. He went over to

Lisa. Together they left C-and-C.

The captain walked around the deck. Myra took the vacated seat at communications as he approached. "How are you
doing?" he asked.

"Pretty well, considering," said Myra. "Why did Pilot do it?
Why did he mutiny?"

"He didn't want to go home without stopping at Titan,"
said Freeman, stepping up next to Jefferson. "He was planning
to go in close to the planet and scoop up some of the atmosphere for fuel."

"It's so pointless," said Myra. "This mission was such a success. He could have come back."

Bonden looked up from the pilot's station. "We're coming
up on the closest approach to Saturn. I'd recommend we get
people as safe as we can."

Jefferson had a thousand questions for Natalie. He simply
turned to her and said, "Go strap in."

She snapped a salute, turned, and left the deck.

Jefferson nodded to Myra, then stepped to the command
console. He sounded the collision warning. Around the deck,
people buckled themselves into their chairs. The ship began to
shake violently.

"The sails!" called Nagamine. "We're close enough to the
planet that we're getting atmospheric resistance. The sails are
slowing us down and dragging us in."

"Jettison the sails," ordered Jefferson.

"Sir," said Bonden. "If we do that, we'll lose steering control, we'll continue to spiral into the planet."

"Belay that, then," called Jefferson. He studied the readouts on his console trying to decide what to do.

"We've developed several stress fractures in the masts,"
said Nagamine. "They're breaking apart. Outer hull is starting
to heat as we're being pulled into the atmosphere."

Just then, the ship jolted. Only the captain's seat harness
kept him from flying into the forward wall. Then his stomach
fluttered, as though the ground had fallen away. The ship no
longer rotated and the simulated gravity ceased.

"My God," said Nagamine. "All motion has stopped. We
were moving over fifty kilometers per second and we just

stopped." He checked the sensors, then looked up at the captain. "There's some kind of object behind us. If I'm not mistaken, we're caught in a magnetic beam of some kind. It's pulling us back, away from the planet."

"We're being rescued." Jefferson allowed a note of hope into his voice. "But by whom?"

A series of tones issued from the communication's station. Myra inclined her head, as though trying to figure out what she was hearing. Then, with a start, she turned and activated the translation program. "I think we're being signaled."

A message appeared on the screen above Myra's console:

"We are the [undecipherables]. We have your [uncertain: possibly conveyance or wood] in our [no word available]. Once you are safe, we will [uncertain: possibly embark] and attempt to help."

"What in the world?" asked the captain. "What's the message mean?"

Myra chewed on her knuckle as she considered just that. "Well, much of our vocabulary comes from whales. They wouldn't share a lot of concepts with us, but I think it says, 'We have your ship in our … was it a magnetic beam? Once you're safe, we will board and attempt to help."

"Undecipherables?" asked Jefferson. "Who are they? Are they from Earth?"

"I don't think so," said Myra. "I think they may be the so-called keepers of the rings. They use the same language. I'll run another pass on the name, but it doesn't seem to make any sense. It keeps coming up as a bunch of consonants all strung together. Something like RDDGN. Sometimes the program tries to toss in a 'Y' or an 'IA,' but it doesn't help."

Jefferson turned his attention back to the pilot's console. Bonden brought up a schematic showing the *Aristarchus*, Saturn, and the alien ship. With considerable relief, Jefferson saw that the alien ship pulled *Aristarchus* away from Saturn. Natalie Freeman drifted through the open door back into C-and-C.

"What's happening?" she asked. "I heard the collision warning, then suddenly we lost all gravity."

Jefferson pointed first to the communications station, then

to the pilot's station. "Apparently, we're being rescued."

"Who by?" Natalie's brow furrowed.

More of the chirps and twitters issued from the communications station. "Captain," Myra's voice trembled, whether from awe or fear, Jefferson couldn't tell. "We're being contacted again."

A new message flashed on the communications screen:

"This is the [undecipherable] [uncertain: possibly leader].
You are now in a stable [uncertain: possibly circle or ellipse].
Please open one of your [uncertain: possibly chamber, mouth
or blowhole]. We will board and attempt to assist."

Myra bobbed up and down in her chair. If not for the seat restraint, she would have launched herself. "I can't believe it. It's working! The translation program is really working!"

"Working?" asked Jefferson. "I'm having a hard time making heads or tails out of it."

Myra shook her head and then pointed at the screen. "It says the undecipherable leader—I'm guessing the captain—is calling. He says we're in a stable orbit and he wants us to open something." She thought for a moment. "He wants us to open our airlock, so they can board and assist."

Instinctively, Natalie reached down and grabbed her sword hilt. "I've been taken by surprise once today. I'm not sure I like the idea of letting them board until we know more."

"What other options do we have?" asked Jefferson. "We can talk to them over the radio or we can talk to them face to face."

"They are intelligent," said Myra. "They rescued us."

"They could be pirates," cautioned Natalie. "Perhaps they rescued us just so they can salvage the ship."

Jefferson nodded, conceding the possibility. "You're the diplomat, Captain Freeman. What do your instincts tell you?"

Natalie Freeman's hand tightened and loosened on the sword. Finally, she let go. "I vote that we let them board. My instincts tell me Myra's right. Even if I'm wrong, we're in no position to fight them."

Jefferson touched the button opening the tow shuttle's

bay. He looked over to the communications station. "Dr. Lee, would you like to come along and welcome our guests?"

She nodded, then turned to the console, retrieving a computer tablet from its slot, and then undid her harness. The captain also undid his harness. He looked back at the life support station and the sensors. "Dr. Nagamine, you're in command here. Dr. Garcia, I think you should accompany us."

Dr. Garcia undid his harness and pushed himself off, following the captain, Freeman, and Myra into the corridor. The four drifted to the ladder and climbed up to the shuttle bay hatch. The captain reached out and turned on the intercom. "Are they aboard yet?"

"A ship just entered the shuttle bay and turned off its thrusters," reported Nagamine from C-and-C.

"Close the door and re-pressurize the shuttle bay," ordered the captain. Freeman watched the display next to them. Once the bay pressurized, she opened the door and they drifted up through the hatch.

In the shuttle bay, a silver, egg-shaped craft sat on the deck, perched on three thin legs, presumably using magnets to hold position. It occurred to Jefferson it was identical to the photo from the disk they'd found on Mars. The door opened and a seven-foot tall creature in a silver flight suit drifted out. Like the creature from the Martian disk photos, it had orange skin and black eyes. Over its mouth was a purple mustache-like growth. The mustache wiggled of its own accord as though each 'hair' was alive. In its large hands, it held a device similar to Myra's tablet computer. It typed some commands into the computer and a series of beeps emerged.

A set of words typed out on Myra's computer:

"I am [undecipherable] [uncertain: possibly leader]. Greetings."

"Can you tell it I'm Captain Jefferson of the *Aristarchus*. Welcome him—I guess it's a him—aboard."

"I'll do my best." Myra typed the phrase, "*Our leader welcomes you*" on the computer and a series of tones sounded from her own palm-computer. More tones issued from the alien's computer.

The phrase *"Please speak to one another"* appeared on Myra's tablet.

"What's he mean?" asked Freeman. "We just need to stand around talking to one another?"

"I guess so," said Myra. The alien typed something on his computer as they spoke. "I wonder if he has some kind of translation program on that computer."

"It's possible," said Jefferson. "Do you suppose he's one of the keepers of the rings?"

"No," came a voice from the alien's computer, startling the humans. "I am not keeper of rings. I am Rd'dyggian. Thank you for speaking. It has helped me to calibrate my translation program."

Jefferson looked up at the alien. "Red Dychian?" he asked, trying to get his mouth around the word. "We are humans, from Earth, the third planet of the sun."

"We know." The alien captain spoke softly to his computer and it translated for him. "Earth is protectorate world of the Confederation. We acted to protect."

"Confederation?" asked the captain. "What confederation?"

"The Confederation of Homeworlds," explained the alien. "My name is Alepex. How may I serve you?"

"I don't even know where to begin," said Jefferson. His hand trembled. He wasn't sure whether it was from excitement, fear, or just adrenaline.

"Thank you for saving our ship." Freeman pushed herself forward. "Is it possible for you to help us with repairs?"

"It is possible," said Alepex. "Or we can return you to Earth. Whatever is best for you."

Another creature appeared in the doorway of the alien craft. It leaned down and spoke to Alepex. Jefferson and Freeman looked at Myra who had backed away slightly, putting a little distance between herself and the newcomers. She shrugged. "I have no idea what they're saying. They're not speaking in the binary language."

"They say they're not the keepers of the rings," said Freeman.

"That must mean the binary language actually belongs to someone else."

Myra nodded. "That makes sense. Perhaps the binary language is some kind of generic language used by a number of
species in this confederation Alepex is talking about."

Alepex looked up at the humans. "We have been sum-
moned to the world you call Titan by the keepers. They request
a delegation from your ship accompany us."

Jefferson looked at Freeman. "Of the two of us, you're the
diplomat. Take Myra and Dr. Garcia and go down to Titan."

Freeman shook her head. "You're the captain. You should
go down."

Jefferson smiled. "Thanks, but I'm the captain of the ship.
My place is here. You go down with them. Take a camera and
send back lots of pictures."

She grinned at that. "Very well." Then she looked up at
Alepex. "Captain, do we need to bring survival gear?"

"No," said the alien captain. "Our atmosphere and yours
are similar enough. Come now, we must not keep the keepers
waiting."

Myra hesitated a moment, then pushed herself off the back
wall, holding up her tablet computer. "I'll get some pictures for
you."

Freeman, Myra, and Dr. Garcia followed the alien captain
into the shuttle. Jefferson watched the door close behind them.
With some regret, he turned and climbed down the ladder,
sealing the hatch behind him. He turned on the intercom. "Dr.
Nagamine, depressurize the shuttle bay and open the door.
Our guests are departing."

Chapter 23
The Keepers of the Rings

Aboard the alien shuttle, Natalie, Myra, and Garcia found chairs much like those aboard the human shuttles. However, as they sat down, the chairs' fabric seemed to morph around their bodies, holding them to the seats. Dr. Garcia let out a yelp of surprise. Natalie reached over and put her hand on his shoulder, reassuring him. There were only two aliens aboard the shuttle—Captain Alepex and his lieutenant. Through the windows of the shuttle, they saw Jefferson leave the bay. After a few minutes, the shuttle bay opened. The aliens worked the controls and the shuttle departed.

Once outside the ship, they saw just how bad the damage to *Aristarchus* actually was. It no longer looked like a pristine metal flower. If it looked like a child's pinwheel at all, it was one that had been out in a hurricane and was now ready for the trash. The sails were broken, bent, and torqued, all at different angles. The central sphere was burned and pitted. Natalie Freeman caught her breath. She knew it would be bad, but for the first time, realization dawned on her just how close they had come to dying.

The shuttle turned away from the planet and made its way toward Saturn's largest moon, Titan. At a distance, the reddish yellow world looked like Mars. As they came nearer, it became apparent the world was vastly different. Its color came from clouds, not from barren ground. The shuttle smoothly entered the atmosphere and dove below the clouds. The terrain made Natalie think of a mix of West Virginia and Arizona. She saw smooth, rolling hills with lakes here and there. However, no vegetation dotted the hillsides, they were as barren as the hills of Mars.

Myra leaned over toward Natalie. "You'd think that as far from the sun as we are, there wouldn't be liquid water out here."

"I don't think that's liquid water," said Natalie. "I've been reading up on Titan. Those are lakes of liquid methane."

Myra swallowed hard. "I take it you wouldn't recommend stepping outside without a jacket, then."

The shuttle approached a rise. Beyond the hilltop, silver domes stretched across the plains to the horizon. Countless vehicles moved between the domes. Natalie tried to count the number of shuttles lifting from the domes into space over the course of a minute. She lost count somewhere after twenty.

"This is a busy place," said Natalie, astonished.

"It should be," said Alepex. "It is the capital of the known galaxy."

Natalie's jaw dropped, Myra gasped, and Dr. Garcia shook his head. "That's impossible," he said. "If there had been intelligent life on Titan, we would have known about it. We may be the first humans to have come this far, but we've had probes out here for over a century."

"You are but primitives," said Alepex. "It is easy for ones such as the keepers of the rings to hide themselves from you, just as you might hide yourselves from animals in the forests of your planet."

The shuttle approached one of the domes. The dome's surface irised open and the shuttle dropped inside and landed on a platform. Alepex opened the shuttle's door and stepped outside. The chairs released Natalie, Myra, and the doctor. They stood and followed the Rd'dyggians.

"Gah," said Natalie as she stepped up to the door. "What is that smell?"

"Sulfur, if I'm not mistaken." Myra wrinkled her nose.

"And ammonia," said Dr. Garcia. He looked up at Alepex. "Are you sure this atmosphere is breathable?"

"Similar nitrogen oxygen content as your world," said the seven-foot tall creature. "However, we adjusted the atmosphere of our shuttle to match your world. Here in our dome, the atmosphere is much closer to that of our world."

"Doesn't sound like a pleasant place to visit," said Garcia. "At least to us humans."

"It is lovely," said Alepex. "Many more colors than you have on your world. We even have a ring around the world much like the planet you call Saturn."

With that, Alepex led the humans through a set of twisting, turning, silver corridors. Natalie was reminded of the Pentagon on Earth and mentally kept track of their route. Of course, she reminded herself, she was now at Alepex's mercy. Even if they returned to the *Aristarchus*, it would be impossible for them to return to Earth without help.

Alepex showed the humans to a window that looked out on the surface of Titan. Deep, reddish light illuminated a mechanical contrivance. Natalie lifted her eyebrows as she recognized the object. "That's the Huygens probe!" Fiber optic lines ran to the cameras and sensors on the primitive craft that had landed on Titan in 2005.

"Yes, it is a probe from your world," said Alepex. "It was intercepted and fed images of the primitive parts of Titan. As I explained earlier, it is easy for ones such as the keepers to hide themselves from ones such as you." He led them further down the corridor and into a room.

Myra stopped cold and Natalie sidestepped to avoid running into her. She looked up and saw what caused Myra to stop so suddenly. A silent creature that looked like a five-foot tall Teddy Bear stood in the room's center. It turned and faced the group. "Welcome, Alepex," said the creature in greeting. As it spoke, it revealed frightening, serrated teeth. Myra and Garcia each took a step backward.

As the creature spoke, it flickered slightly. "It's a hologram," said Myra as wonder apparently overcame fear.

"This is Rodasa of Titan," said Alepex. "She is the protector of your world. What you might call a game warden."

"Indeed." Rodasa turned to Myra. "Dr. Lee is correct that the image you see is a hologram. However, rest assured that I am very much real. You see, I am a native of this world and breathe its air. Your atmosphere is toxic to me." She turned toward Alepex. "Alepex of Rd'dyggia, you know the fines for interfering with creatures from protectorate worlds."

"I am aware, my lady." Alepex gave a slight bow at the waist. "However, I could not stand by and watch these creatures perish."

"They are primitives," said Rodasa. "Their ship failed

because they began fighting among themselves. They are not ready to know about us yet."

"They are much like the Rd'dyggians," said Alepex. "They have nearly the same technology as we did when you contacted us."

"Yes," said Rodasa. "They are warriors and imperialists just as you Rd'dyggians. I can understand why you'd have an affinity for them." She snorted. "You were not ready for contact with us. They are even more primitive ... even less ready for contact."

Natalie stepped forward and imitated Alepex's bow. "Ma'am, I respectfully submit, we've already made contact. We live in the same solar system. We'd like to pursue relations between our worlds. Perhaps we can discuss trade or—"

Rodasa raised a clawed paw. "You have nothing we want," she said. "You should have died in Saturn's atmosphere. You should not be here."

Myra raised her hands to her chest, her eyes going wide. "You're not going to kill us, are you?"

Rodasa turned to face Myra. The black button-like eyes seemed as though they could bore a hole through the biologist. "Unlike you, we are not primitives." She then faced Alepex. "We will allow Alepex to return you to your world." Then she turned to face Natalie. "Now that you know about us, we are certain you will return in due course. Let us hope that in that time, you can become a bit less primitive."

"Thank you." Natalie made a diplomatic bow and then took a deep breath. Though she, like Jefferson, was angry at Pilot for his actions, taking over the *Aristarchus*, she knew she could not come all the way to Titan without asking a question. "There is one among our people who sought particles we call chronotons. Your world is surrounded by the particles."

"Yes," said Rodasa, slowly. The air next to her shimmered for a moment and the three humans gasped as Pilot materialized next to her. He stood, wide eyed looking from side to side. "Thomas Quinn, the architect of this voyage," announced Rodasa.

Dr. Garcia reached out to touch Pilot, only to discover he was as insubstantial as the Titan—a hologram. "This is amazing," said Pilot, looking at Garcia. "I was in my quarters and they dissolved around me and now it's as though I'm standing right here, with you." He took a step forward and crashed into something. Natalie thought she saw the brief outline of a chair.

"I suggest you stand in one place," said Rodasa. "What you are seeing is holography. You are still in your quarters aboard *Aristarchus*."

"What is this place?"

"This is the Rd'dyggian dome on Titan." Rodasa looked into Quinn's eyes and snarled. "Thomas Quinn, you have endangered your fellow humans on a greedy, foolish quest."

Pilot shook his head quickly and wrung his hands. "Not greed. I never sought to make a profit from the chronotons. Unlike my father, I was curious about them. I wanted to study them."

"Chronotons, as you call them, are part of nature," said Rodasa. "I believe you observed them on your own moon, where you already had facilities."

Pilot nodded and licked his lips. "But there were so few and they were transitory. I wanted more, so I could study them, learn about their properties."

Rodasa's massive head bobbed up and down. "And what is greed if not that? Your father's perhaps less greedy than you. When has he ever sought something without concern for his fellows?"

"His only concern is money!" snapped Pilot. "He only wanted what I could create and discover for him. I sought the chronotons to advance humankind."

"You sought the chronotons because they gave you an excuse to build the ship you wanted," said Rodasa firmly. "You are a mere cub who undertook this adventure to seek glory in the eyes of your father."

Pilot hung his head. "I am no cub." A note of bitterness was in his voice.

"From our perspective, your whole species are cubs," said Rodasa. "Do not despair, though. All cubs grow up. Humans will, as well. There are more chronotons on your moon than you know. Capture a few and you will unlock more secrets.

You will find soon enough that you will be able create them yourself. You do not need to collect them from our orbit."

"When you say 'you,' do you mean me personally or others like me?" Pilot's brow furrowed as his image shimmered and vanished, the question unanswered.

Rodasa turned back to Alepex. "We will contact you about fines. Now you may take the humans back to their world."

"Wait!" called Myra. "There's one thing I have to know." The Titan swung its massive head around toward her and she recoiled. "If humans are too primitive to establish a relationship with the Titans, why are you talking to the whales of Earth?"

"The whales of Earth are more advanced than you," said Rodasa. Just as Myra was about to question further, she continued, "They do not build tools, but they compose poems and songs beyond compare. Their stories are among the most sought-after in the galaxy. It is from them that we know the ways of humans."

Myra's mouth fell open. "You know about us from … the whales?"

"How can you expect to be citizens of the galaxy when you can't even speak to all of the people of your own planet?" Rodasa heaved a great bellowing harrumph. "You have much damage to repair in your relationship with the whales. I can think of no one better equipped to start that work. That too is part of growing up." She looked at Alepex and inclined her head.

He bowed low in response and the hologram of Rodasa vanished. "It is time to go," said the Rd'dyggian captain.

Back aboard the *Aristarchus,* Myra, Natalie, and Dr. Garcia floated out of the Rd'dyggian shuttle followed by Alepex. Jonathan Jefferson and Neb O'Connell entered the shuttle bay. "We will tow you back to Earth," explained Alepex. "Our ship can travel much faster than yours, but our analysis shows your ship won't handle the stresses of our cruising speed. Still, we should have you back on Earth within the month."

Jefferson nodded. "Thank you, Captain Alepex."

Alepex looked at Natalie and spoke through his translation

tablet. "Rodasa is right about one thing. Our two species are very much alike. We look forward to getting to know yours better."

"When we're a bit less primitive," scoffed Dr. Garcia.

"Primitive, yes, but advancing quickly," amended Alepex. "The keepers of the rings think they know everything. However, I have a feeling you humans may have something to teach the keepers before it's over." He turned toward his shuttle, then paused. "I look forward to the day when humans and Rd'dyggians will be friends."

"I think we already are." Natalie Freeman smiled.

Epilogue
Looking to the Future

A few days later, as the Rd'dyggian ship towed the *Aristarchus* back to Earth, Natalie Freeman monitored ship activity from the command console. There was little to do, but sit back and enjoy the ride. Even so, Myra Lee worked hard at her station. Lisa Henry drifted through the hatch and pulled herself to the worktable next to the communications station and grabbed on.

"How's the honeymoon going?" asked Myra.

"Stressful to start. Interesting and kind of fun now. The lack of gravity is a little bit of a bonus." Lisa's cheeks colored a little. Natalie smiled to herself, trying not to give away that she listened in.

"I can't tell you how happy I am for you." Myra took Lisa's hand. "Have you given any thought to what you're going to do when we get back to Earth?"

"Neb and I talked a little before we got to Saturn." She shrugged. "We haven't had much of a chance to think about it since then. Things have been so busy."

"I've been chatting back and forth with Cristof and Harmer. We've been talking about the Titans and what they said about the whales." Myra looked around at the monitors lining the walls, then down at the communications board. "We humans have been sending radio and television signals into space for close to two centuries now. When we were down on Titan, we saw just the briefest glimpse of the communications technology they possess. There's not one scrap of doubt in my mind the Titans have received every signal we've sent into space. However, they choose to listen to the whales. I think it's time we learned what the whales have to say. We're going to start a foundation and try to establish a real dialogue. We'll need all the help we can get and we'd love to have you and Neb work for us."

"You can count on me for sure, boss," said Lisa with a smile, "and I'm pretty sure I can talk Neb into joining us."

Before Myra could say anything, a light flashed on the communications console. She reached over and answered the incoming signal. A moment later, she turned around and faced Natalie. "Captain Freeman, it's the President of the United States."

"Alert Captain Jefferson," ordered Freeman. "Have him come up here. Put the president on the command monitor as soon as the entire message is in."

Jonathan Jefferson drifted into C-and-C just as Oscar Van der Wald's face appeared on the monitor in front of Natalie. Jefferson pushed off the wall and grabbed onto the edge of the command console. "Crew of the *Aristarchus,* I gather communication is not real time yet, but will be sooner than I dreamed possible. It's hard to describe the scene here on Earth. There's jubilation mixed with fear. Some can't wait for the Red-dy-chee-ans," he stumbled over the word, "others are fearful. I gather you have news feeds, so I'm sure you've seen the protests, the riots, and the parades, too. I've never seen anything like it.

"We're preparing a reception for the Red-dy-chee-ans at the United Nations in New York. In your report, you said that Captain Alepex wanted to keep contact brief. We will do that. However, we do want to thank him and his crew for saving the *Aristarchus* and show him human hospitality. Also, we feel the best way to prevent a worldwide uprising is to have this meeting be as multilateral as possible with as many heads of state present. We have requested that they keep their addresses as brief as possible."

"Alepex is just gonna love that," said Jefferson. On the trip back to Earth, he and the Rd'dyggian captain had become acquainted. Natalie saw they were kindred spirits in many ways. Alepex had seen many years in space and looked forward to a quiet retirement on his home planet. Jefferson's gaze drifted around the C-and-C. She wondered what he thought, but suspected, like her, he'd been pleased to make the voyage. Perhaps he thought it was time to settle down. What would a man like Jefferson do in retirement?

Natalie Freeman finally interrupted his reverie. "I'll leave you to send the official response." She unbuckled her harness and drifted away from the console.

"Huh, what?" Jefferson looked around, as though yanked back to the present. He pulled himself into the chair and asked Myra to replay the message. "I'm getting too old for this," he muttered to himself.

Natalie Freeman drifted into her quarters and strapped herself into a chair. As she suspected, the president's message carried a sub-carrier transmission. She played it. At the end of the message, her jaw dropped open. She played it again and shook her head. "He can't do this."

She sent her response. An hour later, the president sent a reply. "Your orders stand, Captain Freeman."

Natalie Freeman stood and walked to Pilot's quarters. She knocked on the door and thought she heard a muffled "come in" from within. She opened the door and entered. Thomas Quinn floated in a lotus position a few inches above his bed, a deep frown etched on his face. "I'm sorry," he said, sadly. "I shouldn't have put the ship in danger."

"I'm glad to hear you're sorry." Natalie drifted into the room. "I wish we would have stuck to the original plan. We could have been back out here in only a couple of years. You need to learn patience."

"I know." Pilot's voice was barely above a whisper. He turned and looked at Natalie. "How much trouble am I in?"

"If Jonathan Jefferson had his way, you'd be skinned alive," she said. "However, the president and I have a different view. Your father's the owner of this ship, therefore you're entitled to some slack as far as maritime—and space—law is concerned."

"Okay," said Pilot, slowly. "So, what does that mean?"

"The president tells me your father denied all knowledge that you were really Alonzo Thomas. I don't believe that."

"My father told me I should sign up with the military for a time." Pilot shook his head. "He said it would build discipline. I'm sure he knew people would be listening in. I also know he'd love more insights into what the military wants and needs."

Natalie snorted. "Your father may have ulterior motives, but he is right. You need discipline. And the president told me I'm the one to give you that discipline." She rubbed the bridge of her nose. "You are to come and work for NASA. Rodasa said you're closer than you know to working out what the chronotons can do for humans. You will be working for me when you figure it out."

"My father agreed to that?" asked Pilot.

"It would seem your father gave a very substantial campaign contribution to the president to make that happen. I gather Quinn Corp will, in exchange, get certain patent and trading rights. They're already referring to the chronotons as Quinnium."

"You don't seem too happy about that," said Quinn. He looked away. "I can't say as I blame you after what I did."

"Mr. Quinn, after you work for me for a few months, you may wish I threw you in jail, but I agree with the president about one thing. It would be a waste to lock you up."

"What about the others?" asked Pilot. "What about Berko, LaRue, Rodriguez, and Chung? What happens to them?"

"The Rd'dyggians needed technical help when they grappled onto the ship. I convinced the captain to rescind his order to confine them to quarters. They've been back to work for the last two days. They can either work for us, or I suspect your father will keep them on if they choose not to."

"Good." Pilot looked down at his hands. "They're good people. They only wanted to help me see the mission succeed."

"They're not the only ones." Natalie reached out and touched Pilot's shoulder. "Your mission was fine, whether it was to build a solar sail for its own sake or to seek out the chronotons. The problem was that you put the mission above everyone, including your friends."

Pilot nodded, understanding.

"I'll keep a watch on you from now on," continued Natalie. "You see, I expect you to figure out the chronotons and I expect you to build me a bigger and better ship for the return to Titan. I don't accept what our 'game keeper' called us. We humans are not primitive, and I'm going to work you day and night until you help me prove that, Mister. The stars are our destiny. Are you with me?"

Thomas Quinn reached out and shook Natalie Freeman's hand. "We will sail the solar sea again, I promise."

Acknowledgements

Much like the journey recounted in this novel, the story of its writing is something of an adventure. I conceived the idea for this novel in 1983 and started writing it then. A few years later, after I had grown as a writer, I found the first humble chapters, and embarrassed by them, threw them away. I tried writing the novel again around 1994 and again, I wasn't satisfied with where it went. Finally in 2004, Jacqueline Druga-Johnston, then editor of LBF Books, challenged me to try the National Novel Writing Month. I decided it was time to finally write this novel and complete it. The novel you hold in your hands is the result. So, first and foremost, thank you, Jake!

Many thanks also go to my first readers who gave me valuable feedback and helped to improve the novel: Janni Lee Simner, Laura Givens, Kumie Wise, Myranda and Verity Summers. Giovanna Lagana edited the novel's first edition and taught me much about the craft along the way.

The novel tells the story of how humans became involved with the world of my Space Pirates' Legacy novels. Several brave souls have signed aboard my Patreon page to help me reenvsion the stories and novels in this world. I am grateful to the support of Anthony R. Cardno, John D. Payne, Robert E. Vardeman and all the others whose monthy contributions subsidize this work. If you want to sign aboard, check out my page at http://www.patreon.com/davidleesummers

Finally, I would like to send thanks to my physics and astronomy professors: Paul Heckert, Mike Zeilik, Jean Eilek, Stirling Colgate and Steve Shore. You gave me the tools to lend plausibility to the journey recounted in this novel.

About the Author

David Lee Summers is the author of eleven novels and numerous short stories and poems. His most recent novels are the global steampunk adventure, *Owl Riders*, and a horror novel set at an astronomical observatory, *The Astronomer's Crypt*. His short stories have appeared in such magazines and anthologies as *Cemetery Dance*, *Realms of Fantasy*, and *Straight Outta Tombstone*. He's one of the editors of *Maximum Velocity: The Best of the Full-Throttle Space Tales* from WordFire Press. He's been nominated for the Science Fiction Poetry Association's Rhysling and Dwarf Stars Awards. When he's not writing, David is paving the way for ships like the *Aristarchus*, by operating telescopes at Kitt Peak National Observatory in Arizona. Learn more about David and his writing at www.davidleesummers.com